NICE PEOPLE

Clare Curzon

Chivers Press • Thorndike Press
Bath, Avon, England • Thorndike, Maine USA

This Large Print edition is published by Chivers Press, England, and by Thorndike Press, USA.

Published in 1995 in the U.K. by arrangement with Little Brown & Company (UK) Ltd.

Published in 1995 in the U.S. by arrangement with St. Martin's Press, Inc.

U.K. Hardcover ISBN 0–7451–3063–1 (Chivers Large Print)
U.K. Softcover ISBN 0–7451–3074–7 (Camden Large Print)
U.S. Softcover ISBN 0–7862–0361–7 (General Series Edition)

The text of this Large Print edition is unabridged.
Other aspects of the book may vary from the original edition.

Set in 16 pt. New Times Roman.

Printed in Great Britain on acid-free paper.

British Library Cataloguing in Publication Data available

Library of Congress Cataloging-in-Publication Data

Curzon, Clare.
  Nice people / Clare Curzon.
  p. cm.
  ISBN 0–7862–0361–7 (lg. print : lsc)
  1. Large type books.   I. Title.
[PR6053.U79N53 1995]
823'.914—dc20
94–39579

Errors, like straws, upon the surface flow;
He who would search for pearls must dive
below.

Dryden

NICE PEOPLE

CHAPTER ONE

Monday, 24 August. 08.43 hours

'FORDS GREEN?' ANGUS MOTT QUERIED, slumped on a corner of Mike Yeadings' desk. He leaned closer to the phone to catch why his chief's mobile brows had formed a single black bar above narrowed eyes.

The Superintendent grunted, 'Right. I'll get back to you with allocations,' and replaced the receiver. He looked up sombrely at his young Detective-Inspector. 'Fords Green,' he confirmed.

'Something serious, like a strayed cat?'

'Fords Green is suddenly into the big time. With a body. Male, youngish, apparently the victim of a vicious attack. And divisional CID is thin on the ground, DI Hadden overdue for sick leave.'

'Which leaves Detective-Sergeant Turley as next in line.'

'Not impressive. We'll go right over. You can shelve the Adams inquiry pro tem. Warn Z to be ready to leave with the Incident Caravan.'

'Do you want Beaumont along?'

Yeadings considered. 'Not for a start. I'll see how Turley shapes up before we introduce an outsider of the same rank. I'd like you to work with the locals, not against them.'

1

He patted his pockets, checked he had keys, pen, notebook and tobacco-free pipe: all essentials of his trade, the last item vital to clamp his teeth on when exasperation surfaced, and equally the shadowy recall of a comforting habit, heroically suppressed over eighteen months of fluctuating will-power.

While Angus departed to make the necessary arrangements, Yeadings placed two internal phone calls before returning to his Fords Green contact with a list of requirements and the names of his team.

'We call her Z,' he finalized, after the obligatory spelling-out of WDC Rosemary Zyczynski's name.

Behind the respectful tones of the uniformed Inspector, his keen ear picked up switchboard asides. 'Mott and some Polish bird.' Then, 'Bet she's a hard-faced bitch in aluminium drawers.'

Well, they'd learn. Hard-faced, Z was anything but, though tough in the centre. A good nose for the job, and perfectly capable of dealing with male chauvinist slobs.

Mott reappeared in the doorway. 'Rush hour should be easing up a bit. What a way to start the week.'

'I'll travel with you, fill you in on the way,' Yeadings told him. He lifted his overnight bag from the shelf where it waited ready-packed. 'There's quite a good pub in the outskirts, as I recall. The Robin Hood.'

'The Green Man, sir.'

'Lateral thinking,' Yeadings excused himself, a smile tugging at one corner of his baroque mouth.

Mott glanced sideways at him, grinning back with complicity as he recognized the rising adrenalin, the hounds' eagerness for the hunt. After the tedium of pettifogging crime, a body was their bonus. It took a manhunt to remind you that this was a real man's job. Not that Fords Green was likely to turn up much of a teaser. Coma-ville itself. 'So what have they got?' he demanded.

'An unidentified male, dumped in the forecourt of a roaders' pull-in just off the motorway, so it may have far-flung implications. A police surgeon has confirmed death, with no speculation on time or manner. Strictly professional limits, that, because he was warned that our pathologist will view the corpse *in situ*. Divisional Scenes of Crime team's already present, champing at the bit until he's completed his examination. With luck we can be there before he's through.'

'It could be a traffic accident cover-up.'

'The words "apparently vicious attack" were used. Presumably coming from a police observation. I'm hoping the first to view our body was an experienced man who'd know one from t'other.'

* * *

3

Inside the protective canvas screens they found Dr Littlejohn kneeling alongside an overgrown hawthorn hedge from under which protruded the ankle of a dark-trousered leg ending in a naked foot. A civilian Scenes of Crime photographer stood by with his equipment at the ready.

'Have you got all the site shots you need before I go in?' the pathologist asked him.

'Yessir. Ready for the body close-ups.'

'Well, have someone heave the hedge back a bit before I'm torn to shreds.'

Littlejohn progressed a few inches on his knees while, from the far side, two constables tackled the thorny wall with a pair of garden forks.

'*Ow!*' The pathologist retreated smartly, swearing and wiping a trickle of blood from his pale, domed forehead. Conscious of an enlarged audience, he squatted and looked round at the two newcomers who stood to one side, hands in pockets.

'Ah, Yeadings, Mott. Howdo.' He gestured in the body's direction. 'Officially declared dead by the local man, I understand. Either he's in Casualty now, being bandaged like a mummy, or he assumed all from the ankle's rigidity.'

'Neatly tucked under,' Yeadings agreed, nodding towards the small extent of corpse readily available.

'And I'm giving no further opinion myself

4

until he's been pulled out,' Littlejohn declared. 'Rigor's well under way, so he'll stay the way he is. No chance that he stiffened that much alive, however starchy his customary diet.'

Yeadings approached the hedge from the side and bent closer. 'Get a small saw,' he commanded one of the perspiring constables. The man looked despairingly around.

'Try the restaurant, man, if that's where the gardening tools came from.'

He watched as the constable trudged off, fork still in hand, then pointed down. 'There are several thick main stems at the base here. A section can be removed for examination separately.'

He turned back to Mott. 'Stay and see they don't get impaled on the thorns, Angus. We don't seem to have the pride of the force here today. I'll arrange at sub-division to have the caravan sent on here.'

'Better get the tapes extended to cover half the forecourt. As the lane outside's too narrow for parking, the restaurant must put up with lost custom. Radio in for someone from Traffic to supervise. Where the hell's local CID?'

'Here, sir.' A freckle-faced youngster with bright copper curls was coming in under the tapes. 'DC Lew Duke, sir. We're a bit—'

'Thin on the ground, yes.' Yeadings sighed. 'What's happened to DS Turley?'

'Off duty, sir. We weren't able to contact him at home.'

5

Wearily Yeadings waved off the excuses and started to move away. 'See you at the morgue?' Littlejohn threw after him, in purely social tones.

'You couldn't keep me away,' and the Superintendent departed, catching the ring of keys Mott threw to him as he made for the car.

The pathologist straightened, brushed grit off the knees of his trousers and sniffed the air. 'Smells as though they might make passable coffee over there. Give me a shout when the body comes free, eh?' and he shambled off stiffly towards the restaurant.

Angus Mott, left in charge, exchanged pessimistic glances with the scientific examiners waiting over by their cars. He recalled now the only other murder case he had worked on with the Boss in this area. It had been about five years back, a gruesome job, with a psychopathic killer whose identity was concealed by a genteel and benign exterior. It had taken prolonged dogged spadework and the Boss's intuitive skill to work through the labyrinth. [*Masks and Faces*]

The case of a lifetime. By the law of averages, he supposed gloomily, this one must be a doddle, either an accident or a commonplace domestic.

He moved closer and bent to examine the figure in singlet and dark trousers, loosely curled like a foetus and just visible through the mesh of hawthorn twigs. There was no

6

congealed blood visible on the ground, but all the hair at the back of the head was matted and blackened. The face was hidden, giving no clue to further injury.

The man's black trousers appeared to be of a fine wool worsted: not what you'd expect to find on one of the barefoot brethren. And the foot itself, inner ankle uppermost, showed no sign of neglect under the dusting of grit blown on from the forecourt.

The combination was unexpected, even slightly exotic. Had the dead man been an eccentric? Or did his killer—or whoever else had hidden him under the hedge—have some special reason for removing his footwear? Need them himself? Believe they might present a clue? Even, fantastically, be a sock-and-shoe fetishist?

The more Mott considered the body—as yet with little material to go by—the more he felt this was no outsider haphazardly dumped from the motorway, but the result of local machinations. The disposal of the body and its mismatched clothing invited fanciful conjectures. Was the case likely to prove to be another weirdo?

Maybe Fords Green wasn't the tranquil little backwater he'd rather contemptuously written it off as. Like an apparently healthy body hosting insidious disease, this cosy rural community could for a second time have nurtured a devious killer.

7

If so, beyond the scientific examination of physical evidence, there would need to be a deal of delving into recent local scandals, a good look behind the fair face of everyday respectability.

CHAPTER TWO

Thursday, 20 August

OWEN STAFFORD LOPED ROUND THE corner and there ahead, under the trees, a stocky figure waited in the centre path. As he wheeled around to run he knew it was a mistake but, rattled already, he'd seen Nemesis in the man's stance and panicked. Then, as Owen doubled back round the bend, there came another of them sprinting to meet him. Caught between the two, he turned right and plunged into the undergrowth.

No tracks here. He was ducking under low branches, tearing against brambles, stumbling on hidden roots, zigzagging roughly towards the main road; it seemed for ever.

He was a jogger, no sprinter, bookish, never one for assault courses, but he seemed to be losing them. He halted an instant to listen and above the rasping of his own breath could detect no crashing through the dry undergrowth behind. Just a distant male voice

8

shouting.

And then, as he burst out on to the stretch of rough-mown grass bordering the road, he saw there'd been three, not two. From the cruising patrol car, the driver leant out, signalling him to give up.

He bent, winded, head to knees, hearing the blood's rush drown even the soughing of his lungs. Let them come for him if they must. He wouldn't budge a step to help.

Now that they had him cornered they took their time. Wasn't that their way? With their ponderous pillar-of-society sobriety, bloody right about everything, playing them-and-us for all it was worth, with 'them' being everyone not in their protected clique where you could get away with murder.

'Right, lad.' The patrol man had reached him first. 'On your knees. Hands on the ground, ahead and wide apart.'

He was circling behind, then bending to run his hands over, searching for a weapon.

'What the hell—is this—about?' panted the boy. They couldn't have anything on him. Nobody knew. This was a nightmare, a trick of his own guilty mind.

'We ask the questions. Suppose you tell me just what you've been up to?'

Then louder—not waiting for his answer—to someone approaching, swearing, from the rear, 'He's my body, Pete. Take over while I call in that we've got him.'

9

'Look,' pleaded the boy, straightening, 'you've made an awful mistake. Whatever you think you've pinched me for, you're utterly wrong, and the right guy's getting away.'

'Think so? We don't. Get in the car, lad. We'll have a little chat while we wait for Sergeant Turley.'

Back on his feet, he felt his right wrist pincered by the second man's big hand. Twisted up behind his shoulder, it forced him to his toes and he was propelled towards the kerb. His head was rammed down below the car roof's level and a knee came up to crumple him inside. He fell on the twisted arm, his face buried in the vinyl seating. For a shaming second he felt tears come hot to his eyes.

The one called Pete went round and now heaved himself in alongside, barely missing the boy's head. In the front the driver was talking into a hand-held mike. A crackle of static distorted the reply.

'Right,' said the driver, turning in his seat and producing a notebook from his tunic pocket, 'let's have your name then.'

He could have given a false one, even a comic one, only they didn't look the sort to fool around with. He sat up slowly, ran a shaky hand through his hair. 'Stafford,' he said. 'Owen Stafford. I live in Fords Green, up the main road about a mile.'

Whether it was his educated voice, his willingness to cooperate, or the local

10

implications of what he claimed, the questioner paused to adopt a quieter tone. 'Full address, then.'

Stafford was pulling a notebook of his own from the pocket of his jeans. Two could play at this game.

'You can put that away,' threatened the policeman sitting next to him.

'Why? You've taken my name. Now I'll have yours.' A slow, red anger was rising in him, fighting for a place alongside his fear. Just bravado, and they'd know it, but surely he had rights of some kind.

'It's only reasonable,' the boy said, mortified that it sounded like pleading.

'You can see our numbers,' said the driver. 'No call for our names. Now, suppose you tell us everything you've been doing over the past hour.'

The boy stared back, desperate to make some kind of stand. The pulse in his throat and temples was so strong they must surely see it. 'You said there was a sergeant coming. I'll wait till he's here.'

'Want time to think up a good story?' asked the one called Pete. 'I shouldn't bother. He'll have the right one out of you—in two shakes.' He gave a knowing grin, as if there was special significance in the last three words.

'Belt up,' suggested the driver. 'This is him now.'

An unmarked car approached head-on and

11

drew up a few yards short on the opposite side of the road. From it stepped a stocky man in sports shirt and beige drill slacks, who stood rolling up his sleeves with apparent unconcern before crossing the traffic flow towards them.

He reached the pavement and bent briefly to look in the rear window. 'Out,' he ordered.

Standing beside him, the boy was aware he came barely up to the man's shoulder. He had a square head capped with short-cropped dark hair which started to curl on his flat, wide forehead. His dark eyes were rather prominent and spaced far apart under fat lids. It was the heavy head of a Hereford bull, set on powerful shoulders, thick torso and short, straddling legs.

In return the boy felt the Sergeant assessing him, slowly logging height, weight, age, dress, colouring, personal description. The man flicked a glance at the two in uniform. His eyes, when they came back to rest on Owen's, were unfathomable, opaquely dark.

'Owen Stafford,' the driver offered, and gave his address.

There was a brief narrowing of the sergeant's eyes. A little pulse showed at one temple, like a nervous tic. 'Stafford.' He made it sound significant, as if it was familiar, a name they had on their 'wanted' list. 'Got a car?' he demanded flatly.

'Me? No.'

A long, hard stare. 'Your father got one?'

12

'Two.' An attempt at disdain.

'Licence numbers.'

The boy frowned, then grasped what he was after. He reeled off two registrations.

'Check,' said the plain-clothes man to the driver, who spoke again into the mike.

They waited. Pete climbed out to talk aside with the Detective. Out in the air, the boy leaned against the car's side, breathing less tightly. When confirmation came, they'd know he wasn't whoever they were after.

'What's happened?' he dared to ask. 'You're out looking for someone, aren't you?'

Nobody enlightened him. He hadn't really expected they would. Only, surely he had a right to be told what he was suspected of?

The radioed answer came through, checked on the central police computer. Both cars were the registered property of Paul Randall of Bentham Lodge, Fords Green.

'Randall,' accused the Sergeant weightily. 'You said your name was Stafford.'

'Randall's my stepfather.'

The man stayed totally deadpan, weight evenly balanced on splayed legs, waiting.

'Look, you asked if my Dad had a car, and he has two, like I said. But then I realized it was my address you wanted to check on, so I gave the numbers of the two cars kept there. One's my mother's Fiesta, but it'll be included on her husband's insurance. So that too will be registered as his. Hell, the address *is* the one I

13

gave you!'

'Anybody,' said the Detective-Sergeant slowly, 'can read the name off a gatepost as he's going by. And note the numbers of cars in the drive. Step across the road, lad. We'll have a quiet little talk together, just you and I.'

Owen made another attempt at standing his ground as he was pushed to the kerb's edge. 'Look, I've no idea what all this is about. What's happened, for God's sake?'

'No call to swear,' said the sergeant softly.

'I just don't believe this!' But already the boy was being propelled across the road, public to the eyes of passing motorists. Then, contemptuously freed of manhandling, he submitted to entering the front passenger seat of the small blue Ford. Sweating, but no longer protesting. Ready to vomit.

'Let's talk about everything you've been up to today,' the man invited, coldly menacing. His forearms, one relaxed on the steering wheel, the other extended to display muscle along the back of Owen's seat, were matted with dark hairs. The swarthy, flat cheeks turned towards the boy were close-shaved and shiny, giving off an artificial perfume that failed to cover the male, stale scent of his thickset body.

If I knew what I'm supposed to have done, the boy told himself fiercely, I'd know what to say. I've got to make it sound normal, just another day like any other. Like I got up, had

14

breakfast, went out to see a friend...

The man took him through it, and through it, and through it. Each time there were new questions requiring more detail. If he had lied it would have tripped him. As it was, both were aware that the story was too thin; there was too much time to be covered by a scarcity of events.

'So what are you keeping back?' the man asked at length. 'Suppose we go home and ask your people?'

That was impossible. He couldn't speak, just shook his head dumbly.

'Seventeen and a half,' said the sergeant musingly to the windscreen. 'Awkward sort of age. School-leaver. Not properly into the adult world yet. But wanting to be. So he stays on an extra two years for sixth form study, gets his head full of high-flown academic notions. No experience of life, though. Uh.'

He paused suggestively, then offered, 'For the moment—unemployed. So what next?'

'University,' Owen said doggedly.

Staring ahead, he felt rather than saw the man turn to look at him. The lie seemed to swell between the two of them, monstrously. 'That so?'

'Eventually.' A wretched admission. 'When I get my grades up.'

'Ah!' It was the sound of a punctured balloon, but embodied satisfaction. 'Just got your results through, and you've blown it, eh?'

'They're—not up to the standard required.'

15

Hell, why had it to be this unfeeling slob he first gave the news to? The humiliation was total, when what he needed was someone who could understand the world he lived in.

But empathy wasn't on offer today. He'd walked out to Ned's house to wallow in it with him, and the house was locked up, everyone away. Because, of course, Ned's results too had come through, but his would be something to celebrate. They'd have packed up, his mother and sisters along with him, and they'd be off making some kind of mild family whoopee.

Maybe—yes, *surely*—Ned would've tried to ring through first and pass on the good news, expecting something of the sort in return. But by then Owen had fled the field, damned and abandoned, gone and buried himself in Bardells Wood, stuffed up his ears and considered—well, just for one black instant madly *imagined*—ending it all. He could never admit to anyone the pit he'd been in then. Already it seemed a lifetime of shame away. There was nothing like a touch of down-to-earth aggro to set things back in perspective.

Monotonously, more to himself than to the listener, he found himself again going over the outline of his movements, still holding back the shaming truth of his moment of despair, but releasing more physical detail now that the context was known; how he'd trailed out along the Barrowmead road to see Ned, who'd taken science subjects and was certain of a place at

16

Imperial College.

His own subjects were History, English, French. He'd needed an A and two Bs. He'd got two Bs and a C. He could ring around and try for a vacancy somewhere, except that he wouldn't want the sort of university that'd accept a guy with just those grades.

'Knocks you out, don't it?' said the Detective, with a sour grin. His eyes half disappeared under the fat lids. He seemed to be talking into space. 'All the wheels've come off, and you think, aw shit, what the hell! I'll show the world what I think of it. Skulking in the wood.

'And then along comes this girl—pretty girl, lots of blonde hair, sexy. And you say to yourself, why not? No good for some things, try how I get on with this.

'Only you haven't the experience and you guess she'll not be much impressed. Still the idea's got hold of you by now and you have to do something. So you get behind a tree and when she goes past you've got something pretty to show her. Yup, that's how it was, all right.'

The boy was reeling. 'No! No, there wasn't any girl. I never saw anyone, I swear. You've got the wrong guy. I told you where I was. I walked out to Ned's and when I couldn't find anyone there I turned back. I was on my way home when those two coppers cornered me.'

The Sergeant grunted. 'That was me waiting

17

up ahead. The minute you spotted me you scarpered. People with a clear conscience don't run. Sort of people do that have something to hide.' His voice took on the purr of a large cat.

'And I reckon your movements just match up with the incident's time as reported,' he pursued, the opaque dark eyes expressionless. 'Fifteen minutes to get out to your friend's place, after you'd scared the chick away, and a bit less to get back to where you were when sighted.'

'For God's sake, it wasn't me!'

'If you want to play dirty,' said the man, ploughing on unimpressed, 'you better go elsewhere and choose different company. Not scaring decent kids. Good thing we've got wise to you before you go more screwy that way. Maybe get you some treatment. You listening?'

The boy sat transfixed, rabbit-scared, staring at the man who went on mouthing his nauseating insinuations. The inside of the car seemed full to bursting with small, buzzing sounds, and the outside August light danced with fragmented points of colour. He sat scoring his wet palms with his nails, unable to comprehend.

When the man's voice ceased he managed shakily to find his own. 'Are you arresting me, then?'

There was a short silence while the man scowled ahead over the steering wheel. 'Not this time.' Begrudgingly.

'Can I go, then?' It seemed unbelievable that the man would allow it.

'Remember we're keeping an eye on you now. Never more than a moment or two away. The minute there's any more trouble—' His fist hit the dashboard, making the whole thing judder.

It seemed pointless to insist again that they'd pulled in the wrong one. Stiffly Owen fumbled for the door handle, to slide out into the free air.

'Tell *them*,' and the Sergeant stabbed a finger towards the patrol car parked opposite, 'that they can get on their way.'

So—acting as the man's creature now—he had to stumble out, wait for the double stream of traffic to pass, and then go across to deliver his message. And the two uniformed men weren't bothered, sucking mints, grinning casually at him through the open window as though he was a harmless old acquaintance.

'Knock off?' asked the driver hopefully, and flashed a look at his watch.

'He says I can go too,' the boy mumbled.

'Sure. Pete told him you weren't the right one.' He spoke impatiently, with a touch of something like embarrassment.

Owen stared at him.

The Patrol Officer shrugged. 'Too short. Wrong shoes.' He sighed. 'Still, you were all we'd got.'

They drove off, leaving him staring across at the stocky man in the blue Ford. Who raised his closed fingers a bare inch from the steering-wheel in sardonic salute and followed suit.

He knew, Owen realized. They'd told him. All along he'd known, and he was just giving me bad shit for the hell of it. Filling in time, after they'd lost their man. Justifying being out on a job. He had never intended taking me in, never wrote a single thing down, dragged me through all that crap for nothing, bloody nothing but his own twisted amusement!

The blue Ford indicated right, pulled slowly away from the kerb and joined the traffic flow. As it passed, for the first time Owen caught a spark of some emotion in the man's slatey eyes sliding sideways to take him in. Satisfaction, and a foul kind of mockery.

Sergeant Turley, they'd called him. At least he knew the bastard's name.

CHAPTER THREE

EASING THE DAMP NECKBAND OF his shirt with a stubby finger, DS Turley climbed out, stared round the station yard, wound up his window, then carefully locked the blue Ford. Seeming unaware of three uniformed men who broke off a close conversation to watch him go by, he made for the station's rear door, pressed in the required digits and passed into the comparative cool of the interior.

Norris and Bailey wouldn't be back before the end of their patrol but they would have radioed in a negative on the flasher. No call for himself to report yet, but best let CID office know he was in before dropping down for a bevvy.

He stuck his head through the doorway, recognized Lew Duke's red curls bent over paperwork and grunted, 'Nothing on the Bardells Wood thing. Cold trail. He'll have scarpered when the girl took off. Her nearest public phone was a two-minute run, so there never was much of a chance. Tell the DI if he looks in, will you?'

'Tell him yourself,' said the youngster. 'He wants to see you.'

But Frank Hadden had already sighted him through the upper glazing of his office partition and jerked his head in a summons. Turley grunted and went through to join him.

The DI sank back into his chair, the leather cushion wheezing. He looked awful, drained of colour and his facial skin sagging from the grey eye sockets as if there was no flesh left between. An old man on the way out, Turley reckoned, observing him silently. The poor sod had something a damn sight more serious than piles.

'You missed him,' the DI accused.

Turley gave the obvious excuses. 'He wasn't

21

our old rapist, though. You heard what the girl said.'

'A youngster airing his wick, yes.' Hadden closed his eyes a moment. 'Let's hope it stays at that. Don't want a second one turning up on our patch.' It rankled badly that they had three serious sex offences on the books over five months, last occasion six weeks back. A serial rapist who just might have left the district but otherwise could strike again at any moment.

'Not a copy-cat,' said Turley confidently. 'No mask, no knife, broad daylight. Just a kid.'

'Yes, she was able to give quite a clear description.'

'Which covers eight out of ten of those in their 20s or under round here.'

'How about the lad you questioned?'

Turley permitted himself a tight grin. 'School-leaver, shitting himself over his exam results. Not in the same league, Guv.'

'Did he see anything?'

'No one and nothing. There's not a lot of people cut through that way on foot.'

'Heard nothing? Didn't the girl say she screamed?'

'He could have gone through by the time it happened. Came back later when the flasher'd scarpered. Anyway, it's quite a wild area, just one pathway through the middle where we saw the kid, though there are tracks through the bracken.'

'We'll issue a general warning. Don't want

to risk a repetition. The Super wants more patrolling.'

'This one'll wait for us to lose interest before he tries it on again. Anyway it's no secret we haven't the manpower to maintain a proper watch.'

The DI glared at him, frustrated. 'Does it ever occur to you that everything you say is negative?'

Turley almost smiled back. With one fist he gave a confident swipe at the door jamb. 'Can't say it has done. Well, I'm going for a cuppa now. That positive enough?'

He wouldn't have baited the old bugger like that a couple of months back, he reflected as he sloped off. But things had changed. Hadden had gone downhill, and instead of it opening a chance for his own promotion, Turley had scuppered it with that punch-up in the cells. When Hadden finally got his cards, a stranger would be introduced from another division. Even with a temp brought in, it had already been made clear that Turley wouldn't be moving upwards. He'd been lucky to stay a DS. If the house-breaking little weasel he'd leant on had been the litigious sort, the incident couldn't so easily have been brushed under the carpet.

Not that all was sweetness and light towards him now from the upper echelons. They behaved like a lot of old women. Rules of procedure had changed since they'd bashed

23

their way up from the beat. Now they pretended it was all lace serviettes and best china. And the result of this prevalent namby-pamby was that out on the streets there was a new viciousness and a growing belief that if you showed enough muscle you could get away with murder.

In the canteen a few heads were raised as he came in, but nobody hailed him.

''Allo, love,' said Mrs Cotton through the hatch, 'what's yer pleasure then?' She mouthed such meaningless pleasantries to everyone when there was time to speak between servings.

'Tea, milk, no sugar,' he said curtly. Familiar old cow! He couldn't see why they didn't have men to staff the catering here.

*   *   *

Owen Stafford had almost made it into the house before he vomited, but the act of getting his key into the front door lock was such relief that his rebel stomach caught up with him. So, before he could lie down and let the overall shaking subside, he had to stumble off to find disinfectant and slosh a pail of water over the front steps.

He despised himself for this physical proof of fear. What the Sergeant had said was right: he'd little experience. Of police procedure, none. If he'd given the Old Bill a thought at all, it was to write them off as a drippy crowd who

24

ran kids' cycling tests and lined the route when notables went by. In the local rag they featured as smugly photographed receivers of awards for this and that, or as thickies getting injured during demos. Between the lines you gathered they'd give thump for thump when provoked, but that was during inner-city conflict. There was no word around locally that they deliberately made trouble—as seemed Turley's delight, dragging a guy's private disasters out and twisting his balls just to see him squirm, then inventing a dirty story casting him as a sexual pervert.

But by God, if Turley was looking for trouble and Owen ever got half a chance, then trouble he could have. He'd just have to give it him, however long it took, to work off this acid boiling of the blood.

He tasted bile, living the whole incident over again: the panic of the chase and cornering; the humiliation of huddling in the patrol car while a report was made; the shame of being marched across the road under guard, with passing motorists seeing—maybe neighbours, people who knew his folks; enduring the cold insults of the man's ox-like eyes. But most shaming was his own contemptible state of shock. He'd never before in his privileged young life smelt the sweat of fear coming off his own body.

He threw off his clothes, and under the pummelling shower beat with his fists on the streaming wall, shouting into the drumming water, his mouth filling but unable to wash away the bitter taste of vomit. He towelled off wearily, found clean clothes, went downstairs to leave a note on the kitchen table.

She'd find it with the exam results on her return. Let her worry a little. But she wouldn't. She'd know he'd only gone to look up his father. So he wouldn't bother writing it.

The kitchen clock showed it was lunchtime. Would have been, if he'd felt up to eating. But there were long hours to get through before his father would return to his flat, and Owen had no key to it. He opened the fridge, took out four cans of cola, wrapped enough food for a later meal and put it in his canvas satchel with his toothbrush, fresh underwear and two paperbacks. As an afterthought he lifted three £10 notes from the emergency store in the shoe-box on the floor of his mother's wardrobe. For the first time he didn't trouble to put in an IOU.

*   *   *

On such an airless, sultry day, cottage pie with baked beans might have seemed heavy for some tastes, but Don Turley regarded the salad alternative as a diet fit only for rabbits. He needed meat, he needed the energy of carbohydrates. Above all he required to feel his belt sit reassuringly firm on a well-hung belly. Not that he was flabby, being a convinced games man. Squash and swimming kept the stocky body muscled. Since Marcia had left him, this midday canteen lunch was his main meal. He made do most evenings with a couple of wholemeal corned beef sandwiches and real ale.

He glanced now at the plate of pilchards, lettuce leaves, coleslaw and tomatoes just set down opposite and recognized that he had Duty-Sergeant Downs' company. They exchanged the customary grunted greetings and ploughed into their food.

As Turley pushed away his empty plate and began to tackle the custard-draped mound of apple pie, Downs rose, inquiring, 'Coffee, then?'

'Black, two sugars,' Turley told him and nodded.

Downs came back with the two cups and seated himself at ease. 'No luck with the Bardells Wood flasher, then?'

'Nuh. The one we saw was just a silly kid. Took to his heels at first when he saw us.'

'That's what my lads reported. Said they picked him up and passed him to you. So what had he to say for himself?'

Turley had good recall. He gave an edited part of the conversation almost verbatim, but Downs wasn't picking up any details.

'Why put pressure on when he clearly wasn't the one?'

'Who says it was clear?'

27

'Wrong height, wrong shoes, no jacket, Norris says. He also says he told you as much at the start.'

Turley laid his spoon and fork across the plate. 'You checking on me?'

'Just curious, since there hasn't been a CID report put in. I have a negative one from Norris and Bailey, but nothing on your questioning.'

'I told Hadden about it. He's satisfied.'

Downs was unimpressed, unperturbed. He went on calmly. 'Witnesses get the height wrong most times, so you can never be sure. The shoes, though. The girl said blue-and-white trainers. Your lad was wearing brown leather-soled sandals. I'm surprised you wasted your time on him.'

Turley glowered, stirring his coffee as if to wear away the bottom of the cup. 'Can't be too careful,' he said with a touch of menace.

'Anyway, let's have it in writing, since it's been booked. Right?'

Long, lean and soldierly in his uniform, Downs rose, hovered a moment, then departed.

Turley looked after him with cold contempt, crunching in one large hand the foil from his Choconut biscuit. When he left the building half an hour later, he took his miniature camera, drove back to Bardells Wood, identified the seat where the girl had been sitting and examined the ground closely.

There was no disputing that recent

impressions in the grit surface came from a woman's high heels. And at the edge of the trees just opposite, smudged outlines showed of something softer, probably a rubber or synthetic sole with an embossed trade mark like a large comma. Turley knelt to look closer. He saw then that the logo was a fish enclosed in a circle. A dolphin.

He drew a small steel measure from his pocket, opened it alongside the one good impression and took a photograph. If Downs wanted to rough-ride him, he was ready. Turley had this principle: some gink gets bloody officious, so give him what he wants, and then some more. Keep him busy.

*   *   *

Owen left it till 6.30 p.m. to call on his father, but still there was no one at home. He'd gained admission to the building by announcing over the entry-phone a delivery of flowers for the vague old doll on the top floor. He'd stayed out of sight while she came out and peered expectantly down the stairwell. Now he sat on the floor tiles outside the apartment which had a white card with 'G. Stafford' handwritten in Indian ink, and he ate some of the food he'd brought with him, made hungry now as much by the mental emptiness of the long hours spent stretched out in the water meadows as by the hollowness of his inside.

At a little past 7.15 p.m. he heard a car door slam in the street, the outer door swing open and sigh back on its compressed-air closure. The tread of the steps coming upstairs was firm, unhurried, but still a little alarming.

He should have rehearsed what he had to say. How he put it over could make a difference to the rest of his life.

Throughout the long afternoon—making it impossible to concentrate for long on reading—his chaotic mind couldn't get past the incidents of that morning, the detailed humiliation. He kept going back with increasing anger to one specific moment: his galling mistake in making it sound as if Paul Randall was his father. But when the Detective had asked what cars his father had, he'd known Dad's Range Rover and the new BMW were irrelevant because Dad didn't live with them any more. Mentioning the cars at home had been meant as a sort of shorthand for checking the address. No way had he meant to claim a relationship with Randall. It had been totally unintentional, but a betrayal just the same.

'Hi Dad,' he called in warning as the man's head came round the curve of the stairway.

Stafford halted, then came on more slowly. 'Owen? Hallo there.'

No demand to know what brought him; Dad would have known the date's significance.

Owen felt foolish as well as guilty, because if the exam results had been good he'd have put

30

on a glum face deliberately to kid him. So what was left him for now?

His eyes darted a desperate appeal. The man stepped over his outstretched limbs. 'How's everyone, then?'

'I've flunked it,' he confessed.

Stafford nodded tightly, busy with his keys. 'Any point in asking for a check on the marking?'

'No. I guess now they got it right. I wasn't sure. Always before I've known just about how it would come out. This time—dammit, those two papers on the last day, I can't even remember what I wrote.'

'Come on in. Get it off your chest.'

'Thanks. I haven't told—anyone yet.' That was hardly a lie. The boorish Sergeant didn't count.

Stafford went through to the kitchen, dropping off his briefcase on the way. Owen followed, swinging his canvas satchel on to the settee beside him, hopefully to prompt an invitation to stay.

'Beer?' the man called back, his head in the fridge.

'Sure, thanks. I got two Bs and a C. And the C's History, which I wanted to specialize in.'

'And they'd asked for an A. But you've still got reasonable grades. There are other universities.'

'Not the same, though. And anyway they'd expect me to read English or French. God, I

31

don't want to waste time studying Anglo-Saxon or Langue D'Oc. Literature's OK, but it's second-hand. Modern History's creative somehow. I mean, look what's been happening these last five years in Eastern Europe, in the Middle East, in the Balkans, in Africa. The whole world's a crucible. I wanted to—to, I dunno.'

Stafford sank into a chair, misted beer in his hand. He knew what the boy was after. Your subject was a part of yourself projected outside, a dimension of living which made sense of your place in the scheme of things. Owen was a historian, just as he himself was an architect. Inevitable, unalterable.

'So what's the answer?' he invited.

Elbows on wide-planted knees, Owen was scowling at a square of carpet between his feet. He beat a fist into the other palm before answering. 'I wondered—another year? I don't think I could get a grip on it in time for a re-sit this autumn.'

'Would they keep you on at school? Or were you thinking of a crammer?'

'No. Do it on my own. Take the responsibility. It's the only way I could be sure of getting it all together again. Only—Dad, I don't suppose I could come here?'

His father made a throaty noise. 'It's a dog kennel, son. All right for me on my own, but not a proper background for study. And I don't want to commit myself yet to getting

32

something more spacious. Better stay as you are. You've your own study back home, plenty of room for your books and equipment.'

Owen hammered again with his fist, mouth puckered to stop the hot words rushing out. And *them* there! All the time their rows and screaming and slapping each other around. A sort of monstrous game with an even more horrendous coupling at the end which pulled him in because he couldn't escape awareness of it, couldn't help knowing each movement, each provocative, overheard sensuous sound, so that he seemed to be forced into collusion. God, Dad couldn't be so dumb! He wasn't stupid. He must know what it would be like. A bloody two-person whorehouse.

'Dad, I have to get away.'

Maybe he did understand a little. He sat there saying nothing, his long thumbs quietly crushing the empty can. Then he sighed, rose, went to stand in the window space, his back turned to the boy.

'I'd rather hoped—well, you'd be there if your mother needed you.'

'She doesn't, she never would.' But the words only sounded inside Owen's head as he clamped his teeth shut and waited and waited for the man to relent.

'Well, I'll have to see what can be done.' He sounded flat, almost as if his son had rejected, rather than opted for, him. 'Give me a couple of weeks. I'll look around, see if we can find you some alternative.'

Alternative to staying with them, or to joining his father?

'So what about tonight?' he blurted out. 'I could shove a couple of armchairs together.'

'Afraid not,' and it came immediately after the demand, sounding like 'quite out of the question'.

Owen saw the reason for it when he went to the bathroom for a leak. There were pale, silky underclothes left to dry on the towel rail. Certainly nothing Dad would wear. He didn't know why the thought of a woman here should shatter him, but it did.

'Look, I have to go out soon,' Stafford said, 'but you're welcome to help yourself to what food there is, stay on till about ten, but you'd better head back home then. I shan't be coming back alone.'

At least he hadn't made excuses or attempted to cover up. 'Right,' Owen told him, folded himself into a chair, reached for a magazine and effaced himself while his father went off for a shower.

Stafford went out just after 8.00 p.m. Owen made himself an egg and bacon sandwich with coffee, washed up, cleared away and sat in front of the television until 9.50 p.m. Then he collected his satchel from the settee. Wherever he headed, it wouldn't be back to confront his mother and stepfather.

Out in the street the air was silky cool. He

34

remembered the local building site his father had drawn up the plans for. A pet food factory out on the Barrowmead Road. Last time he'd gone by, almost a week ago, the firm's caravan had still been there.

He knew where Dad kept its keys, but, dammit, he was locked out of the flat now and couldn't lay his hand on them. Maybe the caravan had a loose window he could work on. If it came to the worst he would roll up in some sacking and make a nest underneath for the night. It would do. Anything rather than go home.

CHAPTER FOUR

FORDS GREEN, A JUMBLE OF gold-grey stone and mellowed brick, nestles cosily in its green Chiltern valley. Its two churches, one chapel, three pubs, motley shops and dwellings, dating from the seventeenth century, form a traditional nucleus which regards the more recent 'executive' development beyond Bardells Wood and the Elbourne's hump-backed bridge as alien commutery. The newcomers are achievers, the locals serenely unprogressive. The mean attitude of the community is one of smug self-satisfaction.

While differences are clearly apparent, strict segregation is not practised. Elderly natives gratefully retire from agricultural slums to modern sheltered housing across the stream, and incomers swoop on tumbledown thatched cottages in which to display their corn dollies and reproduction furniture, demanding Brie, Montrachet and Armani from the bow-fronted village shops.

Only the hill-climbing northside terraces of inconvenient Victoriana remain inviolate from commuter invasion. There the lesser tradesmen and horny-handed artisans remain solidly in force. In the two local schools the children of all parties mix without mutual wonderment until vicarious ambition or marital break-up causes certain parents to dispatch their young throughout the length and breadth of the UK.

The second-floor apartment which Guy Stafford rented was in a modern block on the south-facing slope, once farmland but with its pasture so gradually whittled away as to have escaped protection. His earlier home, now surrendered to his ex-wife, was a handsome six-bedroomed creation of the seventies, higher on the east-west ridge, commanding views over fold after fold of meadow and woodlands that screened the distant snakings of the upper Thames.

The house was not of Stafford's own design but, long before being able to afford it, his admiration for its airy elegance had helped fire his ambition to enter—eventually to control—

36

the architectural firm of Canter and Avery.

Shaken by the break-up of his marriage, and desensitized to his own physical surroundings, he had surrendered his prize. He had grimly turned his back on his losses and geared himself ever more obsessively to his work's demands. In these past eighteen months creativity had become a hard-drug habit cocooning him from outer realities.

He had told himself that the flat was only a temporary measure, but already he was into his second year there, regarding it as a place to camp. Owen's suggestion of coming to share it made him freshly aware of its deficiencies. He admitted it was the antithesis of his ideal for family living.

Until now it had sufficed because not only was he cut off from family, but also he barely regarded himself as fully a person; something rather worse than an amputee, with his social core gone. There remained merely a professional drive, a habit of continuance, a few basic physical requirements which precluded dependence or real intimacy. All communication with his ex-wife was conducted through his solicitor. He had even learned to regard his only son as someone quite separate towards whom he had purely practical responsibilities, sharing occasional, not always comfortable, verbal contact.

Owen's entrance under the same roof would threaten this emotional inertia and, from common decency, certain habits would have to be shed, props which he was not sure he was willing to lose yet. Among them were the two village girls who from time to time alternated in his bed. There were mutually beneficial services involved which would require readjustment.

On the other hand the boy was clearly disaffected, or he wouldn't have made a hash of the principal academic subject he was keen on. Trouble at home could be the very devil. He could understand that: he'd had some himself. Better to have no home, simply shelter. He'd need to find rooms for the boy where he could enjoy a measure of freedom in safe surroundings. It was essential that Owen's work pattern at least should be re-established or he could go right off the rails.

Turning this in his mind, Guy Stafford set out to keep his appointment, unlocking the new green BMW which, equally short of a permanent home, spent its nights at the kerbside. By the time he returned at 10.30 p.m. he expected the boy to have cleared off, back to Gillian and her new husband. He would contact her solicitor tomorrow, arranging a meeting to discuss his future.

*   *   *

Unaware of even such rudimentary plans to meet his needs, Owen set out in the failing light to trudge three miles to the new factory site. It meant rejoining the route he'd first taken that morning but, after crossing the hump-backed bridge, he kept to the curving main road instead of using the short cut through Bardells Wood on the near side of The Green. It was from distaste as much as the need not to confront the police again. He knew now that they'd believed his story, but he had to avoid gibes about a return to the scene of the crime. He needed no reminding of the foul Detective-Sergeant who'd made an abject fool of him.

He avoided too the uphill terrace of small Victorian houses above The Green, where Ned lived with his widowed mother and two sisters, taking instead the parallel street to the rear of their sloping garden. He could see lights behind two of the curtained windows upstairs and a dimmer glow from the landing which he knew stayed on all night to comfort the nervous younger girl. Tomorrow he would have to call and congratulate Ned, and confess his own failure.

*   *   *

At the end of his trudge he found the site hut locked, but his father's trailer was still in place at the far side although, with the work's progress, Guy must be looking in only briefly nowadays to check. Owen circled the caravan, tugging at each of the windows in turn. No chance of forcing them. The hasps were of brass screwed into solid mahogany. But the ventilator over the galley window was unsecured. If he could find a length of the right kind of wire or binding tape lying about it shouldn't be impossible to get in.

In the dark he stumbled about the uneven earthworks, bumped into stacks of brick and stones, finally almost tripped on the very thing he was searching for, prised off a load of Thermalite. It was a tricky job threading the rigid tape through and tickling the looped end round the hasp of the casement over the sink, but he made it. His first achievement of the day. If all else failed career-wise, he consoled himself wryly, he could perhaps set up as a break-in artist.

And then he was inside, spreading his weight on his hands as he slid over the plastic sink and eased himself to the floor. Even at this isolated spot he didn't dare switch on any lights. The main road was too close. Anyone out walking might get curious and come poking around.

In the half-dark he recognized the familiar shape of his father's drawing desk with tilted boards and angled lamp, the heavy duty clothes hanging from a row of pegs beside the door, a shelf with four hard hats for the use of visitors to the site. The trailer's interior reassured him, asserting comfortable male qualities, recalling his father's practical detachment. Here was nothing personal, nothing cloying, a total lack of the judgmental.

Next best to having his father's company, this place would do.

He padded about, looking, not touching, decided against the double bed retracted into one long wall, opting instead for the unyielding cushions of the window seat at the rear end. A sultry night, he'd have no need of covers.

On the off-chance, he went back to the galley area and looked in the fridge. It opened with a sticky kissing sound. Its tiny bulb seemed to throw a searchlight through the murk of the uncurtained caravan.

He was surprised to find eatables still on the shelves inside: rye biscuits, cheese, margarine, fruit juice. He poured himself a glass of milk, sniffed it, checked that it said Long Life on the carton, and took it back to the window seat. The slightly concave moon had moved on, leaving only the stars in a huge sky, and if you stared long enough you could believe you felt the firmament above slowly turning, with yourself the pivotal point below.

Opposite, beyond the angular, dinosaur silhouettes of earth-moving plant were the early stages of a building, two-dimensional in this light, with slightly darker oblongs where the sky showed through, pricked with points of light. Unreal, like an outdoor film set. His father's concept on paper had looked solid in comparison. It was as if the builders had cheated on him, erecting canvas flats buttressed at the rear with skeletal timbers.

41

His tired eyes reached again for the sky, and the star scene slowly wheeled, became kaleidoscopic, distant worlds floating towards him, enlarging, forming hexagons, ovals, converting to grouped faces half-glimpsed but inimical, accusatory, then converging to a single flat, sweat-shining visage. The Detective-Sergeant, Turley. The interrogator.

Owen Stafford slept.

*   *   *

Stiff but instantly aware of his surroundings, he awoke as the sun began to spread a watery, oyster light. He had no idea how early the site might come to life but he planned to be away by six. He washed in cold water at the little sink, shaving with his father's battery razor, ran a comb through his hair, sandwiched some cheese between two rye biscuits and stood at the window to eat. In the fridge the level of orange juice looked low, so as an afterthought he filled the kettle and put it on the gas ring for a mug of instant coffee. This he drank black and scalding, tidied up, closed—but did not secure—the window by which he had entered, slid the handy length of plastic tape into his canvas satchel and left by the door, clicking it locked behind him.

He had a whole day to fill, at least twelve hours before he dared come back to seek asylum. He swung his worldly possessions on

42

one shoulder and strode across the rutted earth towards the main road.

* * *

Gillian Randall awoke heavy-headed and stickily hot. During the night Paul had thrown back their cover of a single sheet, and in her threshings it had become wound about her legs. Now the long curve of his back was exposed and she could count the *Pleiade* of dark brown moles across his ribs. Not with tender passion as she'd done in their early days, but with something like resentment, because to her these flaws now symbolized worse defects concealed from public sight, which he no longer considered worth suppressing in front of her.

Nor did he trouble to apologize for any grating little habits once held in check throughout the period of pursuit. 'You don't put cheese in the trap once it's sprung,' he'd casually admitted when she complained of his wholehearted belching, farting, discarding in his wake any object used once and no longer required. That was manly, apparently. It was she who was at fault, being narrow, harping, spinsterly.

And that appreciation of her he'd pronounced immediately after one of their destructive love-making marathons.

Well, that much remained. She had married

43

him on a sexual high and they could still hit the peaks—all the more, she ruefully admitted, for the unspeakable troughs in between. And manly he might be, but she was no longer a lady, at moments a newly emergent fishwife, a bawling, scratching, blaspheming bitch.

She drew the broken nail of her index finger sharply down his back and watched the fine mark whiten on his skin, then grow suffused with blood. He stirred heavily, groaned, reached for the thrown-off sheet. Gillian withdrew her legs, stood on the tufted carpet already warmed by sunshine. 'Nearly nine,' she guessed hazily.

'God, it can't be!' Half-asleep still, he was scrabbling on the night table for his watch. 'You silly cow, it's not even eight yet!'

He rolled on his back, drew up his knees, thwacked the warm space she'd just left. 'Come back!'

She mumbled something about coffee, bending to pick up her slippers under the bed, collecting the folded nightdress from the bathroom stool on her way, in case she ran into Owen in the kitchen.

They had come back late last night, pretty well tanked up, even by Paul's standards, and hadn't paused for a snack before falling together into bed. So she'd missed the official-looking letter she now found open on the kitchen counter. Addressed to Owen, she saw. Then the printed heading got through to her.

44

These were the results he'd been waiting for. And she hadn't remembered they were due!

She filled the percolator, switched on, and went back to smooth out the single page. He'd got two Bs and a C. That was good, wasn't it? A pity the C was History, though, because that was the subject he'd meant to specialize in. C in French wouldn't have been so bad, although he'd be needing a foreign language for one of the history options. An English C then, except that you had to prove you could express yourself in your own language to get anywhere at all. No, maybe if he had to get a C, History was best.

She tried to clear the muzziness from her head, bent to splash water over her face and tasted bile in her throat. There followed a slight dizziness and she held on tight to the edge of the sink, all concentration on her finger ends until it passed. As the percolator started to bubble she sat shakily down. It was probably just due to the stuff they'd had last night. Third time this week. Overdoing it a bit.

So long as she wasn't pregnant. That she couldn't stand, and Paul would be livid, really hurtful. It couldn't happen to her, not with Owen nearly eighteen. All her friends would giggle about her behind her back, the nicer ones saying how pleased they were, really feeling pity.

She could hear no sounds from either of the bedrooms in use. Owen was usually up and off

45

for a jog about now. Maybe she'd missed him. If not, there was enough in the percolator for him too. She'd take his mug of coffee in and say how pleased she was his results had come.

She found the bed made up as she'd left it yesterday, with a pile of clean T-shirts and underclothes laid out on the duvet. It seemed he'd not been back overnight. Well, maybe he'd gone to talk his future over with his father. There'd be final arrangements to make about money, because, due to parental income, he wouldn't qualify for state help. And that was no concern of hers, thank God. The way her own money drained away was worry enough.

There was just a touch of sadness, though, that Owen hadn't left a note for her before taking himself off. Manly, she supposed again bitterly. There should be a stage for male offspring at which growth stopped, well after potty training but well before shaving. The thought of a fully adult Owen to cope with was more than a little daunting.

*　　　*　　　*

Guy Stafford was out on the M4 motorway by 8.00 a.m., at which hour the incoming city traffic began to clog. Travelling in the opposite direction, he was repeatedly overtaking heavy commercial trucks heading for the West Country. Making for Salisbury, he intended turning off before Marlborough for breakfast and a car-wash. Today's meeting could lead to a big contract with some exciting challenges. And profit; he'd need to put even more aside for Owen now that he was out of school and trying to stand on his own two feet.

He could do worse than find out whether any apartments in his block were coming free soon. There was old Mrs Mortimer's above him. She had mentioned recently that she might consider sheltered housing. If she was serious about it he could offer to forward her name to the private scheme over at Maidenhead where he'd put in the plan for an extension. Organizing that would take time, however, and with reasonable luck Owen would get himself sorted out and into university long before Mrs Mortimer was ready to leave.

He'd never been entirely happy about the boy staying on with Gillian, but if it came to a dispute, judges usually preferred mothers to have custody, at least of younger children. So he hadn't challenged her assumptions on this, partly because Owen's presence had seemed to guarantee some degree of security for her. And the house was big enough to ensure the boy's privacy.

Guy had felt that the arrangement offered him a dilute form of responsibility without involvement. However total the family break-up, long-established habits of caring didn't disappear overnight, nor did the pain of loss.

Whenever the junior partner from Barratt, Hogg and Christie notified him that Gillian had reported some difficulty, he had to remind himself of the existence of Paul Randall, her present husband. At first it had needed a conscious effort to take the one step backwards that his new non-relationship demanded, but by now it was firming into established behaviour.

He told himself that he had no feelings about the interloper one way or the other. But when he had found—and removed—a snapshot of a broadly smiling Randall which Owen had left speared to the dartboard after a half-term visit to the flat, he had felt a warm current of sympathy flow towards the boy.

It seemed there was no acceptance of the man as substitute father. So if the situation with Randall had worsened, as Owen's reactions implied, he really should try to secure the lad somewhere else to live.

*   *   *

In the handsome house on the ridge, Paul Randall stood shaving. 'Buggrit,' he muttered between clenched teeth as the blunt blade skidded and left a crescent of blood brightly welling on his chin. By now the stupid woman should have got it into her head which disposables to buy. This must have come from a cheapo lot. Bloody bargain-hunter! And bloody was quite literal this time.

Clutching the towel he went in search of her to demonstrate just what she'd done. She was still in the kitchen mooning over that letter with Owen's results. She looked up at his entry and down again as if he was none of her concern.

He seized her arm. 'Look at that! Where the hell did you get that last lot of razors?'

She looked through him, vaguely troubled. 'You know, I don't think Owen's got the grades he was after.'

'Sod his grades! D'you realize what you've done? I've got an important interview today. It could lead to anything. And now I'm bleeding like a stuck pig, just because you can't remember to get me the right razors. They're going to think I've got the shakes, can't even shave myself. Time you got your head out of the clouds, started to think of somebody other than yourself.'

She looked at him as if he'd struck her, dazed and then with the ever-quickening anger overtaking. 'Time *I* did? Stuck pig is right. Let them see you as you are. You don't listen to a thing I say, do you? I think Owen's flunked his exams. And he wasn't in at all last night. He'll have gone to see Guy, and God knows what arrangements they'll make between the two of them.'

'Why not? He's the boy's father, isn't he?'

'*Why not?* Just think for once, will you? If he

49

can't get into university he'll be unemployed! He hasn't made any plans in case he fails. Suppose Guy decides he wasn't working hard enough, suppose he insists Owen goes to live with him, so he can keep an eye on what he's doing.'

But her husband was halfway back upstairs, banging on the handrail at each step, mouthing obscenities about her late-aroused maternal instincts. 'So let him go!' he roared from the landing. 'How d'you think I feel having that little creep around spying on us all the while?'

Gillian followed after, screaming up at him from the hall, 'How would you like to have his allowance cut off? You know I only got the house and a lump sum for myself. What do you think we've been living on, you moron? Hadn't you better get your skates on and go get yourself a proper job, show you're something more than a heavy stud?'

The prospect hit him between the eyes. 'Stafford would do that—hold back the boy's allowance if he shacked up with him? Yes, I guess he would. Oh, you dumb cow, what else are you going to screw up? Can't you get anything right, for Chrissake?'

His slamming of his bathroom door shook all the windows along the landing.

'Swine!' Gillian ground out, crumpling the paper to a hard ball and hurling it into a corner of the hall. 'Unspeakable, loathsome cretin!'

But his words went on eating corrosively

into her. She *had* screwed it up, not checking that Owen was really keeping at his schoolwork—just as she'd screwed up her first marriage, and was screwing up this one. Like it seemed she'd screwed up her whole life, and there seemed no way to get it straightened out again.

But Paul didn't have to keep rubbing it in. What was happening? Where had all the good things gone?

'Owen,' she moaned into her hands. 'Guy!' No, she didn't mean that. Guy was gone. She didn't want him back.

All the light had gone out of the morning. 'Oh, I wish I was dead!'

But she knew she didn't mean all of herself. Only the part that still so desperately needed Paul Randall.

CHAPTER FIVE

Friday, 21 August

OWEN STAFFORD HAD PUT A good mile between himself and the building site before he felt sure that no one seeing him would make the connection. Not that there was any particular call for secrecy, but he disliked being talked about. There would be enough tongue-wagging among the local scrutineers of exam

51

results without added relish over his sleeping semi-rough.

Distance from the incident and a good night's rest had persuaded him that he hadn't much to worry about over yesterday's brush with the police, although the humiliation of Turley's unwarranted questioning still rankled. Any gossip going round about him seen in police company could be laughed off. He had only to think up a more funky story than the real one and, joke-wise, that's what everyone would prefer to pass on.

It was far too early to go visiting, and he had to work himself into social mode first. To get all functions go, he'd feed himself breakfast at the Spanish transport pull-in before the lead road to the motorway.

On the strength of marriage to a local girl, Paco Martinez had started the place three years back with upmarket aspirations and a bank loan, plus his accumulated tips as long-term wine waiter at the Heathrow Holiday Inn. Originally his *bodega-restaurant* had sported potted palms, a flamenco trio on Saturdays, a considerable wine list and a name—*Los Dos Periquitos*—derived from the squawking presence of two gaudy birds swinging on a perch among sub-tropical foliage.

Its siting had first been the cause of the restaurant's decline and later of its recovery. Early lukewarm interest had cooled among locals, who preferred to seek high life in

London or a motorway dash to gourmet country establishments farther west.

A malicious client ejected for drunken brawling had reported that the parrakeets had been smuggled in from Lanzarote. They had to go, banned under an order restricting the import of livestock. Paco still suffered pangs over the injustice of his heavy fine. But, resilient and ingenious, within two days of the birds' departure he had renamed the place, with the substitution of only five letters on the splendid hanging sign. The amount by which he economized on this, he had lost several times over in the purchase of two enormous, weirdly patterned ceramic cylinders, in the hope that *Los Dos Paragueros* would become a household name locally. But even *The Two Umbrella-Stands* didn't guarantee a discriminating clientèle. Gradually proximity to the motorway was effecting a more crucial change.

In place of the earlier sprinkling of smart diners, there came flocks of travellers and heavy-goods drivers for a cuppa and a fry-up in a smoke-choked environment which fast saw the palm trees on their way. The ceramic monstrosities remained, never to reach their intended use but regularly cleared of accumulated fag ends and crumpled packaging, spoiled football pool entries, tired home-made sandwiches, occasional plates of rejected food, even once a large carrier bag of disposable, overworked nappies. Small wonder that to its new regulars the place was soon known as The Caff.

But it was never empty, drew all manner of men, few women, made a name as somewhere cheerful, warm and earthy to take refuge, and because Peggy Martinez and her sister were good at producing nourishing spicy meals at a reasonable price, actually made money too. Paco Martinez, a born survivor, had evolved into an almost-contented almost-average Thames Valley tradesman.

The Caff had long been a rallying place for sixth-formers of the Crane School who, indifferent consumers, were tolerated as long as there were unoccupied tables. Owen made for its long, white-stuccoed shelter now, secure in the knowledge that in holiday time none of his mates would be there so early. He slung his canvas bag on the empty chair next to him and squinted through steam at the tariff board hung high behind the stainless steel of hissing drinks dispensers.

'Eating?' asked the solitary waitress on duty, deserting a group in donkey jackets who had pushed away their plates and reached the anecdotal stage.

She was a bouncy blonde just about his own height, with kohl-rimmed eyes and high-painted eyebrows which made her seem constantly surprised. But he knew brash cheerfulness was her customary approach.

'People do,' he crooned back.

She gave a cheerful chirrup. 'What I meant was, are you hungry?'

'Ravenous.' He wasn't, but it seemed the right line to take.

'Leave it to me.' She wiped the table over rapidly with a damp checked cloth and leaned close. 'You're from the Crane, aren't you? Owen, is it? Seen you in here before.'

Her left breast barely skimmed his shoulder. He felt her warm breath on his cheek. She smelled faintly biscuity with a hint of rose-scented soap. He grinned. 'Stafford,' he said, then wondered why he should have given so much away. It wasn't sophisticated, decidedly uncool. 'All that's behind me,' he boasted shyly.

'Left, have you? Got a good job stacked up waiting?'

'Sort of. It's at the hush-hush stage.'

She laid a finger alongside her nose like a cockney barrow-boy, total gamine, and he found himself laughing. She was saucy and she was fun. She was just what he needed to perk up his self-esteem. When she came back he'd ask her for a date. She must be eight, even ten, years his senior, and she'd probably turn him down flat, but it was worth a try. With the shoe-box tenners he could stand her a back seat at the Playhouse and maybe a couple of drinks afterwards.

She unloaded a large plate of mixed grill

with two slices of fried bread, a rack of toast, with butter and three miniature pots of jam. She upturned his cup and poured coffee from her flask. 'More of all that when you're ready,' she promised, and bounced off to welcome an influx of drivers.

He spun his breakfast out, until the place was thick with smoke and the mixed aroma of bacon, kippers, toast and coffee. The tables had filled up and Paco too was in there serving, a starched white apron round his portly little middle. He came across to slap down a chit by Owen's plate. 'One traveller's special,' he monotoned, met his eyes doubtfully and checked the slip again. 'Schoolboy, it says here. You want cut-price?'

'That's right.' Why not? Sometimes it was more important to save money than save face. And Delia was away behind the noisy cappuccino machine, out of hearing.

He paid up. No chance to speak again with her. He guessed that she'd knock off when the afternoon shift came on at three. If he was out this way he'd hang about and hope to pick her up then.

He'd used up over two hours there. A dawdle back towards Fords Green and he should reach Ned's at a reasonable nine o'clock. The family would have cleared breakfast away, and not yet have set off anywhere. He swung his bag over one shoulder and went out into the fresher morning air.

56

Already he didn't feel so bad.

Correction, he insisted: I feel pretty good.

The worst had happened. Yesterday he'd hit rock bottom. The only way now was up.

*   *   *

Ned opened the door to him, a cool raising of the sandy eyebrows all that indicated the big grin inside. 'Hi, feller, walk this way.' He turned and minced down the passage with an exaggerated hip-wiggle.

Owen declined literal acceptance and shambled in behind. 'Morning, Mrs Banks. Hallo Susie, Renata.'

It had to be baking day. All the paraphernalia was spread over the kitchen's pinewood table. Ned's mother wore a flowered overall his own wouldn't be seen dead in. 'Hullo, dear,' she said and, as ever, offered a soft cheek for his kiss. 'You're a bit early for the uglies, but we'll have the first batch out in ten minutes.'

'I've flunked my "A"-Levels,' he told them, making it come out casual.

The woman's plump arm hovered a moment over the flour bin but she didn't look up. 'I don't believe it. You set yourself too high a standard, and you didn't quite meet it. Isn't that right?' Now she did look at him, directly, not all schoolmistress but a Mum as well. Maybe it made a difference working with the

57

under 7s; no teacher he had would offer unsolicited excuses for people of his age.

'What did you get?' Ned inquired.

Owen told him.

'A lot depends,' Mrs Banks said, 'on how the others did who're wanting the same place as you. If results are a little down right across the board you could still be in, Owen. Have you been in touch to find out?'

'No.'

She pointed a floury knife at him before cutting the edge of her pastry. 'You know where the phone is. Do it now. This is no time to play laid back.'

'Want me along?' asked Ned, hovering.

'Why not?' At least they could get the miserable business of comparisons over before he had to meet the two girls' wide-eyed silence again.

The university woman on the other end of the line sounded clued-up and pleasant. Yes, he hadn't performed quite as expected, but it was early days yet to say if it meant exclusion. Some prospective students were abroad and hadn't yet contacted her with their intentions. Fifty-fifty chance? No, she couldn't promise anything like that. More like twenty-eighty. But ring again tomorrow, in case.

'It's a no-no,' Owen told Ned gloomily, 'only she's too nice to admit it.'

'Rubbish.'

'Anyway, a lot of guys prefer to take a year

58

off between school and university. If I can move in with Dad I'll be able to dig in better with my work. It could mean I take a fourth subject, go for it next time with a string of As.'

Ned groaned. 'Manic-depressive, that's you. Why can't you just be schizophrenic like the rest of us?'

'Because schizos like you have to be bloody bright. Four As, that right?'

'Three As and a B.'

'Tsk, you should have done better.'

Ned punched his shoulder, grinning down from his superior height, and with that it was all over. Owen felt the guilt lift off. Maybe Ned's joke wasn't so far from the truth after all: recently he had been swinging between gloom and relief for very little reason. God, he wasn't going to go monkey-brained like Mother, was he?

They went back to join the others, and Owen reported on the phone conversation.

'Never overlook any opportunity,' Mrs Banks instructed self-mockingly. Then, more sombrely, 'It's not a hand-out world, whatever the adverts say. You've got to get in there and drag out what you want.'

'That how you got to be Prime Minister, Ma?' Ned suggested. '*Carpe* bluggy *diem*?'

'With such good command of Latin, you might select a less questionable adjective,' she said firmly.

Owen sank into a squeaky cane chair,

59

observing that during the banter little Renata was wiping an exploratory pinky round the inside rim of a newly opened pot of mincemeat, and that the next-door cat had turned up again for its dietary supplement. Sensible beast. This was, after all, the place to be.

'Well, I'll be off,' Susie announced, rising from the window-sill and shaking out her skirt. She picked up a basket crammed with library books.

'Now I'm edificated, I don't need no more book-larnin',' Ned claimed.

'Did you put mine in?' their mother asked, lifting a tray of hot pasties from the oven, then blowing upwards to cool her flushed face.

'Two, that right? One on the meaning of surnames and a collection of children's poems. I haven't finished all of mine yet. There's one I want to read again.'

'Sloshy romance,' Ned mocked.

His sister gave him a cool glance. 'It's a classic, and a whole heap better than your sex manual. I do think you might have the decency to return that yourself.'

During these exchanges Owen was disturbed by the realization that, library-bound, Susie would normally go by the short cut through Bardells Wood. If the flasher was still hanging around today, it might not be the most pleasant encounter. Much though he'd rather stay on and enjoy the Banks' company, there was really no choice. He'd have to go with her.

'I'll come along,' he offered, rising.

There was a chorus of protest. 'Sit down, both of you,' the woman insisted. 'There's no great hurry over the books. If you don't want a hot pasty, Sue, I'm certain Owen does. Just give them a minute to cool before I lift them. Pop the kettle on, Ned, there's a dear, and we'll take a coffee break.'

Susie stood there a moment, dangling her basket. Briefly she balanced unneeded calories against losing the chance of Owen's company, and her intended slimline future took a rain check. She sighed: once the pasties were off the baking tray and held under her nose, she'd be incapable of refusing. Perhaps tomorrow was soon enough to start the apple and lettuce routine.

Well aware of her elder daughter's vying temptations, Mrs Banks smiled as she rinsed her floury hands under the cold tap. This interest of Owen's in Susie was a new thing. She'd thought until now that he found the girl's modest form of hero-worship embarrassing. But he was growing up. With Ned away at university from October, it was good to know there could be another young man looking in from time to time.

But the keen-eyed Ned wasn't letting Owen's offer pass unremarked. 'Since when this interest in my maiden sister, man? Declare yourself.'

Owen, caught in the crossfire between the

two sets of watchful eyes, clamped his mouth shut in embarrassment, then felt obliged to admit his true motive. Despite the badinage, something not unlike resentment had shown fleetingly in Ned's expression.

'There's been a flasher reported in Bardells Wood. He might still be about. I wasn't going to mention it, but yesterday the police were milling around asking questions. I ran into them on my way back after I called here.'

'You'd think they'd send a loudspeaker van round to warn people,' said Mrs Banks. 'I expect we'll get the full story in the local paper next Thursday.'

'Did you speak to the fuzz?' This was Ned, curious.

'Sure. They stopped me, wanted to know who I'd seen, where I'd been.'

'An actual suspect. Fame at last! What wise old bird said it was better to be wanted for murder than not wanted at all?'

'Miss out on university, and qualify for a prison cell instead? Big deal!' Owen felt reckless now, as though yesterday's disagreeable incident had happened to someone quite different, some comedy character, never himself.

'But you can't go to prison!' wailed Renata, rushing to bury her face in his lap, cuddly cloth desperately clutched in one hand.

He'd boobed again, misjudged his audience: his and Ned's brand of humour wasn't something the nervous youngster was up in. He pulled her on to his knees. She was warm and sticky, unsurprisingly smelling of fresh mincemeat. 'I'm not going to prison,' he promised. 'I have a full-time job pushing your swing. Should we go and do some now?'

With female perversity she twisted round, peered up at him with unshed tears still bright on her lashes, and said, 'No, I want one of Mummy's lemon-curd tarts. We can have a swing later.'

CHAPTER SIX

IT WAS ALMOST 11.00 A.M. WHEN Owen eventually left with Susie. Renata hadn't been content with a session on her swing but insisted on six 'glissandos' as well.

On the shallow covered terrace at the house's rear stood a concert-sized grand piano: abandoned, legless and lidless and tipped on its straight side. The strung frame was still complete, though horribly untuned. Renata was small enough to climb up, push off, and take the polished curved side at speed on the seat of her dungarees, trailing her fingers through the ghostly-sounding strings and landing in the arms of anyone up to taking the force of her passage.

This performance was forbidden without a

catcher, since a yard after the piano's end the terrace stopped suddenly in a flight of eight stone steps down to the hillside garden. Owen, as visitor and most long-suffering, was Renata's favourite to fill the secondary role. It always surprised him that the small girl, a prey to all kinds of anxieties, was physically quite fearless. Still distraught over her father's death last Christmas Eve, she seemed not to connect the piano with his work as assistant manager of a music shop in Aylesbury. For her mother the link must certainly be painful, and as she watched from the kitchen doorway, Owen thought her frown due as much to grief as to apprehension. But as long as Renata saw the derelict piano as a plaything, he knew it would remain.

'That's enough for now,' Mrs Banks decided as Renata tried to wheedle a bonus on the offer. 'Owen will be quite worn out. Which could put him off coming to visit.'

He had thought Ned might go with them down to the shops, but he had suddenly decided to wash the car, a second-hand Metro which Mrs Banks had bought out of the insurance payment on Arthur's life. She was ruefully aware that if they'd launched out and had a car earlier he might never have been killed returning home by motorbike on a night of freezing fog, the victim of a hit-and-run driver.

*   *   *

Once clear of the house, Susie seemed to blossom. After the kitchen's heat, and, once past the spicy Chinese takeaway at the terrace's lower end, the air was gently fresh, smelling of gorse, freshly cut grass and sun-warmed hedgerows. She pulled the ribbon off her hair and shook it loose on her shoulders, where it lay tangled like smooth little brindled snakes.

Owen left her to start the conversation. She had a clear, high-pitched voice and spoke in short, jerky rushes, frequently pausing to frame the next phrase. At home she seldom aired her opinions, preferring to follow the banter between her mother and brother, but occasionally calling Ned to order over some extravagant claim. Fascinated by words, she was telling him now about an Edwardian poet she had just discovered, and of one poem in particular, *A Runnable Stag.*

'There's no such word,' he challenged.

'Not in a dictionary perhaps—but there is in life. When huntsmen run a stag down—it's runnable. One that doesn't—offer them good sport—isn't heroic at all.'

'Don't you think hunting's vicious?'

'For us, yes. But then there are—all sorts of people. They don't have to—be like us. If there weren't staghounds—there wouldn't be this poem—and it's wonderful—in its own way. He runs until his heart feels fit to burst—and the

65

hunt's just upon him. Then he takes to the water and swims in deeper and deeper—until his strength gives out. But he's beaten the hunters. I've got a copy at home. I'll lend it you if you like.'

They walked on, each immersed in private thoughts. It struck Owen as ironic that if he told her how yesterday he'd been run down himself, the prey of police bullies, she would be horrified. Runnable? He'd been a bit of that, but it hadn't been heroic.

There was no evidence today of any police presence in or near Bardells Wood, but as they went through they were never long out of sight of other people. Three local lads perching on the white-painted stretch of fence at the entrance gawped at Susie, sniggered between chewings, and followed their progress down the central path with just-audible, loutish conjecture. Farther in, a wizened pensioner called to heel a circling golden retriever which approached from the bracken, waving its silky plumed tail, to sniff their proffered hands.

As they reached the final straight, instead of DS Turley's stocky figure waiting in mid-path there was an old lady in a washed-out blue cotton dress shaking bread crusts from a paper bag. They slowed and finally stopped until the last crumbs were gone and the gathering of small birds broke up. Certainly no under-cover policewoman, but someone a flasher might well have got some mileage from as a shocked

66

observer.

If news of yesterday's incident had circulated in Fords Green it seemed not to have affected everyday life. But small-town tongues could be busy wagging over the sight of his own pulling-in by the fuzz, Owen reckoned.

At the branch library he amused himself in the reference section while Susie chose new books and had them stamped. By then he had made up his mind. 'Come back with me for a sandwich?'

As he had known, the house was empty and the fridge well stocked. Yesterday would have been his mother's weekly visit to the Amersham Tesco; today she was putting in eight hours as an agency nurse.

Before her first marriage she had worked full-time in the local hospital's casualty unit. That was how she'd first met Owen's father, when he'd brought in a dazed motorist who'd crashed into a tree. Then, according to Dad, she'd been impressively long on practicality, short on scenes. It had taken Guy three months to bring off their engagement, seven more before the wedding, and then Owen had promptly made his intended presence known.

So, full-time mother, and mistress of a large, comfortable home, Gillian had given up outside work. Now, after raising a son to his teens, playing the field with several of her husband's friends and finally settling for divorce and marriage to the outsider Paul

Randall, she had returned to nursing a short period back, at first in a Health Service hospital, then switching to the hitherto scorned private sector, where nurses were reputedly spoilt darlings, and money and free hours came more easily.

And money, Owen guessed, was an increasingly important factor in their life now, like her alternating moods of depression and frenzied socializing. Nursing paid a few bills, filled the empty hours for her, for a while kept her hand off the bottle and perhaps her mind off the current corner she had painted herself into.

He barely recognized her these days as the caring mother he had known in the secure years, but he consoled himself that children seldom understood their parents, and lately there had grown such a great gulf between them that real communication was impossible. He tried not to consider where blame lay for the present alienation. Too many people were involved beyond Gillian herself. He acknowledged that it could not be entirely his mother's fault, nor his frequently absent and work-loaded father's, nor even the outsider Randall's. In blacker moments he questioned what part he himself had played in the way the world was falling apart. But wasn't it inevitable—more healthy even—that in your teens you shrugged off the smothering and learned to walk away?

'OK,' said Susie, walking alongside and hugging her basket of books.

It startled him. 'OK to what?'

'You asked me back for some lunch—just before you fell into—a catatonic trance.'

'Sorry. Deep thoughts.'

Unhappy ones, she decided, but said nothing. They walked on together, up the other side of the valley towards the handsome house on the ridge.

On arrival they put together a picnic for the garden. She had made no comment about his flunked exams, not even when, binning cheese wrappings, she came on the screwed up paper that recorded his results. She stroked it out flat and left it on top of the dishwasher where he could deal with it as he felt fit. He noticed, folded it twice and slid it into a pocket. It occurred to him briefly that it was his mother who must have crumpled the paper. Was that in sudden anger at his failure, or from casual offhandedness? He couldn't even be sure of that.

They loaded a tray from the fridge and went out on the terrace to eat. From under the striped awning the garden shimmered with midday heat, giving off a dry pot-pourri scent, bumble bees clumsily lumbering into roses, two stout clumps of purple buddleia covered with a secondary blossom of fluttering orange butterfly wings.

Susie sighed drowsily. 'I'd love a real garden

69

like this,' and Owen recalled the Banks' small patch of antirrhinums and calendulas that broke the downhill area of rough grass with its unlovely deposits of dilapidated tricycle, rabbit hutch, coal-shed and washing-line whirligig.

Now Owen let his eyes pan round familiar lawns, shrubberies and ornamental trees, as if for the first time. He knew he should disclaim responsibility for the landscaped elegance, but to mention a gardener who kept it in order two mornings a week must sound pretentious to the girl. Instead he nodded towards the neglected hanging-baskets on the house wall, which earlier had been crammed with bright flowers, but where prize fuchsias were now harsh brown sticks behind withered stems of blackened lobelia.

'They ought to be watered twice a day in this heat,' he told her, 'but nobody seems to have taken it on.' Gillian had planted them at Easter in a burst of optimism and then lost interest.

He remembered a time when his parents had spent winter evenings planning layouts, poring over nurserymen's catalogues and when, long ago, he had trailed after them with his own miniature trowel at planting time, haphazardly scattering seeds and dragging soil over, ignorantly pulling out anything he took to be a weed. Spuddling and diggling, as Guy had called it. Now there were no combined efforts, no family trio, no plans. He felt that the garden—like himself—had no future, was suspended in a prolonged and permanent *now* of semi-invisibility.

'I suppose it's too late,' the girl regretted, referring to the hanging baskets.

More than she knew, he thought. Too late for so much. 'Would you like to see over the house?' he asked abruptly to break the mood.

He carried the tray back and put their used crocks in the sink. 'I'll rinse them later,' Susie offered. 'I don't understand dishwashers.'

As he led her on the grand tour she didn't gasp with amazement or make gushing comments as some of Gillian's acquaintances did, but her eyes told him her delight. She had left her sandals on the terrace. Her narrow feet moved delicately over the woodblock floors, the hall terrazzo, the deep pile of pale carpets, as if they breathed in some of their perfection. Once or twice she reached out a hand and touched things: the brocade curtain looped at the tall landing window with its silver and peach tassels; the pale, blue-mottled tiles with their occasional motif of conches in the bath cubicle off his bedroom. And then, coming out again on to the landing she looked through the open door of Gillian's room and saw the long dress hanging on the wardrobe's mirror doors. It drew her, shimmering sea-green, through the transparent plastic of its wrapper and winking with scattered sequins of peacock blue and jade.

71

'A mermaid,' she whispered. 'It would make you look—like a mermaid.'

'If I fancied myself that way,' he quipped.

She smiled. 'I should have said "one". One would look like a mermaid. It's your mother's?'

'I guess so. I've not seen it before.' Even he could recognize it was something special, the top cut low and held up by one short, swathed sleeve, the other shoulder bare. And below the fine webby fabric of the bodice the skirt snaked tightly close, to break out suddenly in a foam of stiffened net. The whole thing danced with points of coloured light as facets of the scattered sequins moved under Susie's gently stroking fingers.

And he felt a sudden anger, that in all that he'd shown her she should be most allured by this bauble of his mother's. It had in a sense corrupted her.

But she had moved away and was looking around. 'This is a beautiful room.'

One he seldom came into, because he was now the outsider.

As a small boy he'd been brought here after nightmare terrors; he'd slipped in between the reassuring bulk of his parents, stretching his cramped toes down deep into their shared warmth and feeling his whole body soften and relax, the dragons depart.

Susie had gone to stand in the far doorway, looking into the dressing-room beyond. It was

72

more Spartan, holding a single bed, a dressing-table, one upright chair and a wall of glass-fronted wardrobes. A dinner-jacket was over a hanger holding an evening shirt with ruffled front. In a small box on the bed's coverlet were Paul Randall's black tie, his set of diamond cuff-links and studs, a birthday present from Gillian.

Owen confronted the dress-jacket as if the man were still in it. It did, in fact, still carry the shape of his body, in a slight puckering at the armholes. During the last year Randall had put on weight and his clothes had begun to pull.

'A bit of a do next weekend, it seems,' Owen said mockingly.

Susie stood, head cocked, her nostrils slightly dilated, and then he caught it too, the stale, musty scent of Randall's suit. It should have been sent to the cleaner's after last wearing, but he hadn't bothered. As escort he'd go scruffy like this while Gillian had splashed out on a pricey new number. Randall not caring all that much, with her still making all the running.

On an impulse Owen went close and slid his hand into the jacket pockets. A folded handkerchief in the left-hand one. In the other something rolled between his searching fingertips. With his back turned to cover his movements, he drew out the flattened square of tin foil. Inside it lay a slim tube of glass, one end blackened by smoke. The smell was now beyond any doubting.

Well, this was nothing new. Only, the man was getting more of a slob, bringing the things home. If Owen had been alone he might have left the stuff displayed on the bed to show that he knew, but there was no call to advertize to Susie how things were. Nor was he proud of having gone through the man's pockets.

He folded the foil a second time, enclosing the tube, and put both back. Go chase your dragons elsewhere, moron.

It was a habit experimented with and already discarded by the upper forms at Crane School before he'd reached them. Since Stephen Manders had been given the wrong stuff and was now an irreversible nutter, there'd been a barely hushed-up scandal, then a general acknowledgement that brains could pickle themselves enough unaided. The seniors had held a secret meeting, exacted an oath, agreed that no one was a wimp if he turned the stuff down.

Still Susie had said nothing. Perhaps she thought the smell hung about from some spicy oriental meal. Or perhaps she knew quite a lot already, had even experimented with soft drugs for herself.

He wondered if Ned was aware of dangers around his sister, and if so what he was likely to do about it. Once he was away to university there would be no one to keep an eye on things. Their mother was of another generation, a

74

teacher to boot, rather unimaginative and unquestionably straight. It looked as though he ought to hang around a bit, see Susie didn't get drawn into any kind of trouble.

He suddenly became conscious of her body as she stood with the window's light shining through the thin material of her summer skirt. Finely boned, she would later be voluptuous, with her mother's caryatid richness. Young, pretty—she instantly reminded him of the girl in Bardells Wood. Pretty and sexy, the Sergeant had described her. For a moment she was the same girl, scared and running from the male encounter. He felt a rush of bile in the throat. His forehead was moist. He closed his fists on clammy palms. Despite himself his body responded. He found himself walking towards her.

From Paul's dressing-room she looked right past him, at the dress still hanging on his mother's wardrobe door, and again he felt anger at her easy seduction by tinsel fabric.

'Try it on if you want,' he said abruptly, and removed himself into the passage before she could answer. Why not? So it was a bit tatty wearing other people's clothes, but hadn't he just gone through a man's pockets himself?

She hesitated before reaching the hanger down. The dress was new. Owen's mother would once have tried it on in the shop, maybe like others before her, so this wasn't really so bad. She had only to forget for the moment that it was already bought and paid for.

She carried it over one arm into the dressing-room and began to take off her blouse. She was too excited to notice Randall's wardrobe mirrors in which Owen now watched her strip to white briefs and bra.

They were no more revealing than the jazzy bikini she had worn with Ned and him to the lido. It was the whiteness of them that made the difference, the softness, and the invitation to touch.

Then she was sliding the sea-green dress over her head, easing it down over her breasts. She paused, one hand on the bra strap left exposed by the single bare shoulder. The dress came off and was laid over a chair back. She reached up behind her ribs and released the little strip of silky net.

Her breasts were so much bigger than he'd imagined.

Had he ever imagined? Yes, he thought he must have at some time, because this reality was a surprise. It left him slightly breathless. His fingers curled against the hardwood jamb of his mother's door as he lived the warm softness, stroked the pearly flesh in his mind.

She looked up and caught his eyes in the mirror, standing stooped with her breasts pendulous from the delicate hollows above. Instantly she covered herself with her hands, then mechanically apologized as he, confused, mumbled some sort of thing himself.

He moved away, leaning over the gallery rail above the silent hall, while she made faint swishing sounds of silk and net, settling the dress over her half-nakedness. And then, after a moment's preening, she appeared in the doorway, one hand behind her to gather in tight the fold of spare fabric at the waist.

'In dress shops they use clothes pegs,' she said, smiling. 'It's not much too big.'

No, it wouldn't be. His mother had lost weight steadily over the past few months, whether intentionally or not. Owen thought not: lately she'd seemed almost scraggy, which couldn't please her.

He stared at the transformed Susie. 'You *do* look like a mermaid,' he told her.

'No feet.' Laughing, she pulled up an excess of net flounces to display herself on tiptoes. 'I wouldn't be able to dance in it. Not without high heels. And I couldn't dance in heels anyway.'

He imagined her dancing. 'Do a twirl or two.'

He could have switched on a cassette from Gillian's bedside cabinet, but a memory of the obtrusive jungle-music escaping night after night from the scenes of Randall's love-making prevented him.

Susie lifted a handful of hem and pirouetted the length of the gallery, then back, stopping before him with a low, sweeping curtsey. Caught in the billowing gathers of the lower skirt, she wobbled and went sprawling, sat up hooting with laughter. 'Oh, I'm not ready yet to act the lady!'

All woman, though. Sombrely Owen reached out a hand and helped her up. She waddled off comically on her heels, the swathes of fabric bundled in both hands like a fat, paddling woman on a seaside postcard. And it hurt him, as though she mocked him rather than herself.

'I suppose,' she said coming back in her own clothes and serious again, 'I shouldn't—have done that. Mother would definitely—not have approved. But there's no damage to the dress—so no one will know, will they?'

Only me, Owen thought. Remembering forever. And as they went downstairs together he wondered if there was anything left that his own mother would have disapproved of his doing.

CHAPTER SEVEN

DS TURLEY DREW THE CAR in at the lower end of the Victorian terrace and nodded to Lew Duke. 'Get yourself something at the Chinese. While you're there find out if any strangers were seen around yesterday.'

'Uniform's questioned that lot already.'

'They'll have had a new crowd in since, and

time to talk about it.'

'Want me to get something for you?'

'No. I'll be back in twenty minutes. Got some phoning to do.'

Slipping off home, Lew thought. It's only round the corner. Maybe he thinks his wife'll be back. He should be so lucky.

Turley opened his front door, pulled the key from its lock and with his toe flicked apart the collection of post on the hall floor. Junk mail mostly, but the house insurance had come due. He picked up the crested envelope and carried it back to the kitchen. He used the wall telephone there to dial his mother-in-law's number in Hertford.

She took her time answering. He could picture her tight drawstring mouth and thin, hunched shoulders as she manoeuvred her wheelchair along the cottage passage with the dog's hindleg bend, scraping it past the longcase clock.

There was a clatter as she fumbled with the receiver. Then, querulously, 'Hello?'

'It's Don.'

A slight pause. 'I thought it might be. So you got round to it at last.' There was satisfaction mixed with the hostility in her voice.

'Is she with you?'

'Judy?'

'Marcia.' God, this was bloody silly, quibbling over what name to call her, but he wouldn't use the one he'd first known her by.

79

For a long time now she'd been Marcia to him, the second name on her birth certificate. Fleetingly he wondered if his wife had ever told the old woman the reason he'd made the change. If not at the time, almost certainly now, when she was seething with rancour, out to get him for every imagined offence.

'No, she's not here.' He hadn't been wrong about the satisfaction; the woman was incandescent with it.

'Stepped out for a bit?'

'My daughter has been staying with me for a few days, but she has moved on elsewhere.' It sounded rehearsed, hammed dignity.

'So where?'

'I'm afraid I can't tell you.'

'Won't? Or don't know?'

Another pause. 'She didn't say.'

'Left you in the dark too, eh?'

Reluctantly she started to justify herself, then the words poured out in anger. 'I know better than to press her about her plans when she's clearly unhappy. She told me she had a lot to think about and she wanted to be on her own for a while.' She paused, uncertain, then added righteously, 'There was nobody with her.'

Turley rested his head against the wall, considering this. The old woman was afraid of scandal on her daughter's behalf. It suited both women that all blame for the break-up should fall on him.

So, if Marcia was really on her own without

funds—which she would be because he'd emptied their housekeeping account into his private one—and since she'd not kept up with any other relatives, where would she be now? Stupid woman, she'd be somewhere back near home here, staying with one of her female cronies. Which had to mean somebody from where she used to work.

Silly bitch. How long did she think she could skulk around near Fords Green without him picking up her scent? He had only to wait. Wait and watch, keep his ears open. If he missed her himself, some cocky git back at the nick would bring news of her, if only to take a rise out of him.

'Right,' he said. 'I get it. So how much did she borrow off you?'

'That's not your concern. You should be ashamed of leaving her with nothing to fall back on.'

So she'd tried a withdrawal at the bank and they'd told her how things stood. Good. Her mother would have been obliged to lend her the fare home. But single or return?

He chuckled into the mouthpiece. Not that he felt that chuffed, but he had to show her he knew he'd scored.

He hung up the receiver without a goodbye, went over to the fridge and peered in at the empty shelves. How could the thing have nothing in it and still smell of food? He should have let Lew Duke buy him some chicken bits and bean shoots. There just wasn't time to go shopping now. That was a damn nuisance he'd have to face again tonight.

He swilled his face under the tap and drank water from his cupped hands, shook them dry and went out again into the afternoon heat, round the corner into Alma Villas to join his DC at the car. About to get in, he saw dawdling fifty yards ahead the Stafford lad they'd pulled in yesterday, and he was with a girl. Different clothes today, plus a baseball cap, but there was no doubt it was the same boy. And on his feet this time were a pair of blue and white trainers.

They hesitated at a house halfway up, having a discussion at the door. She seemed to be inviting him in, and the boy made out he couldn't decide. He was saying something about the bag he was carrying: an embarrassment of some kind, like it might have his overnight things in it?

She had a basket over her arm, with what looked like books. Yes, now she'd persuaded him to go in.

Turley scowled. The girl's hair was loose on her shoulders, the way Marcia used to wear hers, shiny in the sun, with a mixture of browns like the grain on a polished walnut table. There was something of his wife about her face too, heart-shaped, wide-eyed, the same kitten-like chin.

He clenched his fists, swallowing on his

anger, turned abruptly and climbed in beside Lew Duke in time for a crackle of static as a call came over the air. A brawl reported two streets down from the Green Man.

A patrol car leaving the motorway answered, but they were almost on the spot themselves. Another domestic, right up his street. He reached for the hand-mike and gave his call sign. 'This one's ours,' he said tautly. He'd sort them.

* * *

Paul Randall had been the third candidate for interview. A flabby, flannelly guy first, then a disgruntled-looking woman, so he'd felt pretty confident, prepared to charm the birds off the trees. And the interviewer *had* been a bird, but one of those charcoal-suited padded-shouldered masterly blonde women with icicle eyes. Asked all the wrong questions, wouldn't be talked round to the right ones, astutely pecking at the CV: why was there a year missing here, and before his present estate agency job had he really been sixteen months at the antique shop, not six?

He'd agreed. She was quite right; it must have been a typing error. And then she'd looked at him with an icy gleam, as though she guessed he didn't care for admitting she'd caught him out.

Well, chances were she'd hand out the same

hard act to them all. Except possibly to the female candidate. A dyke, probably, since she hadn't responded well to *him*; but in that case she could be looking for something more tasty than was on offer.

There had followed the usual ping-pong conversation and he remembered to ask a question or two of his own to which she gave short answers. Neutral, the whole thing. Gone a bit flat. On coming out he'd glanced into the waiting-room and seen there were two more candidates to follow; both male, one young and eager, the other middle-aged, pin-striped, casually reading the *Telegraph*. He thought his own first impression must lie somewhere between the two, but it was anybody's guess which image the headhunter would go for.

Head? That sounded good, or it would if he got the job. Headhunted as branch manager of a nationwide estate agency. No, he had to admit it was less of a headship than a knee-high job. Rather witty, that. Pity he couldn't share it, but Gillian had gone broke on the humour stakes of late, might even snap back about hammer-toe-hunting.

He'd be informed within ten days, the blonde had told him, whichever way it went. And no positive hint, so it didn't look terribly good. The longer he considered, the more feebly hope glimmered.

It was too early for the Pheasant bar to have cleared the lunchtime crowd, and he was in no mood for back-slapping company, so he drove straight to the office where he'd a bottle of malt stashed in his drawer for such emergencies. He would go elsewhere for some serious drinking later.

*   *   *

Gillian Randall was coping with a migraine, which is a thing nurses should be fit to cope with, but these days she seemed short on skills when the aches were her own.

She had arrived punctually at noon to check the luncheon tray which the domestic help had prepared for her client. There was nothing wrong with the menu; it was one approved by the patient's consultant, but the cutlery had been greasy, and the tray itself, clothless, bore smeary traces of an earlier meal. So she'd had no choice but to insist on it being put right.

The kitchen help had taken instant offence, thrown plate, lunch and all, into the dishwasher and herself into a fit of near-hysterics. Trouble at home apparently, but then who hadn't? And the end result was that Gillian had been left to provide a late, substitute meal while the woman was sent home by taxi. She would also be required to write a detailed report on the incident and, due to the delay, endure geriatric scolding from the very patient whose welfare she was protecting.

As further injury, since the only other help

due that day would be the senior nurse on night duty, it would fall to Gillian to clear up the broken crockery and food mess, although domestic tasks were guaranteed outside the duties of a qualified agency nurse.

Disturbance of sickroom routine had made the patient truculent. Normally he was equable enough, too far advanced in age and infirmity to take much interest in the comings and goings of those around him. But meals were the one remaining pleasure, so the torment of withdrawal, as he saw it, was worth a certain expenditure of adrenalin. He had become excitable, with patches of high colour on his cheeks and a rapid, stumbling, heartbeat.

'Don't you dare die on me today,' she threatened him silently, shaking down the thermometer, while his querulous voice went on and on complaining, and this after weeks of sleepy silence.

He did the next best thing, losing bodily control while his mind was totally taken up with offences suffered at her hands. She fancied, as she rolled him to change the sheets, that his expression owed as much to satisfied revenge as to temporary shame.

And when, with the kitchen straightened and the washing machine whirring, she went back to check on his sleeping, he was wide awake demanding she read to him. No, the taped story wouldn't do. It was a nasty book and the headset made his ears buzz. He wanted

86

one of his own from the library downstairs. *Pilgrim's Progress* or *Hearts of Midlothian.*

She consoled herself that in a General Hospital she might have had charge of a dozen patients just as difficult to please, but at least she could have handed the unsavoury jobs to a junior and escaped into clinical reports. With *Vogue* or *Vanity Fair* to read over her coffee.

Pilgrim's Progress!

*   *   *

Mrs Banks had taken Renata out shopping. Owen and Susie returned to find Ned stretched out on the scrubby lawn with an SF paperback open across his eyes. He grunted at their approach and hoisted himself on his elbows. 'The cavalry,' he said hopefully, 'their canteens charged with cola.'

'It's an idea,' the girl agreed. 'I suppose you're too idle to go and wait on us weary travellers?'

'How right you are, girl. How right you always are.'

Owen dropped alongside as Susie, grimacing, went back towards the house. 'It's a stinker. Hotter even than yesterday.'

Ned was regarding him with a sardonic smile. 'Must be. Over three hours to get books changed at the library?'

'We dropped in at my place for something to eat.'

'Ah.'

'What does *ah* mean?'

For answer, Ned rolled on to his stomach and poked at the canvas satchel Owen had dumped beside him. 'All your worldly goods? You had this with you this morning. I suspect you're on the road, bumming.'

'Not far short of it. Between lodgings, so to speak.' Since something more seemed to be expected of him, he went on, 'I had thought of staying a few days at Dad's.'

'—but . . .' Ned was watching with narrowed eyes.

'It wasn't convenient. Actually . . .'

'Yes?'

'I zizzed last night in his trailer, out at the building site. Know the place?'

'The intended pet foods factory? Crafty old you. Did you have a key, then?'

'Forgot to pick it up, but I did a bit of breaking and entering. Well, not so much breaking as diggling with a length of plastic tape at the galley window. Luckily the ventilator was unlatched.'

Susie materialized with a four-pack of alcohol-free beer. 'This is all there was. I only want a mouthful, so that leaves almost two each for you.' She popped the lid of one and sniffed at the contents. 'Did I hear you say you broke in somewhere, Owen?'

'Only my Dad's site trailer.'

'Short of somewhere to sleep,' Ned

explained.

Any intended sarcasm was lost on the girl. She was frowning, hesitated, then offered, 'If you're really stuck—you could have my room—for a few days. I could always bunk in with Renata.'

'Don't be daft,' Ned cut in shortly. 'Owen's hardly short of options.'

His sister looked from one of them to the other, considering. It hadn't escaped her that the only time she had been invited to Owen's home had been when he must have known it would be empty. It couldn't be a comfortable place for him with his mother's new husband there. There had been a funny sort of atmosphere when he stood looking at the man's dinner-jacket. 'Can't you stay at your father's?' she asked.

'Not at the moment.' He didn't feel like explaining why he'd be in the way there too.

'I'm sure Ma would say—one more here makes no difference,' she persisted. 'We'll ask.'

The girl tasted, made a face. 'I knew I wouldn't like this. Here, I'm going to do my music practice.' She put the can down between the others, rose and brushed dry grass from her skirt, then left them together.

In the ensuing silence Owen glanced across at his friend, conscious that something between them had subtly changed. Ned had gone coolly critical, and it had something to do with the implications of his own home circumstances.

'Dad's got so used to hoofing it on his own that I can't very well push in,' he excused himself lamely. It must have sounded crazy: that huge house up on the ridge, plus his father's flat, and still he had to be offered a bed by a friend's sister.

'At least you've got a father, semi-detached or not,' Ned muttered, between chewings on a grass stem.

Owen grunted, aware that he'd blundered. Mr Banks' death was so recent, and Ned never talked about him. It must mean the hurt went deep.

'I *never* had one.' The words were contemptuous, charged with resentment. Ned spat the grass out and pulled savagely on the second beer can's tab.

'He just wasn't there. At best a silent shadow, or a scene-shifter who scuttled on between the acts. Not that the scene ever actually shifted. No, we had a permanent Lady Macbeth upstaging everyone against an unchanging backcloth. Mother doing the double-parent thing, the ultimate authority!' His sudden bitterness was the more violent for seeming so out of character.

Shifting uncomfortably, Owen attempted to discharge the tension. 'The Scottish play without Macbeth? That's more impossible than Hamlet without the Prince of Denmark.'

Some of the fire went out of the other. 'Yuh.

A feeble analogy. But imagine if Shakespeare had written it as a one-woman soliloquy.'

He swallowed a mouthful of the beer and wiped a hand across his mouth. 'God, I can't wait to get away. It drives me up the wall, all the dos and don'ts, the why-did-yous and where-were-yous and when-will-yous. A household of females, you can't imagine the deadly bore of it! What genius called them a monstrous regiment of women?'

He slumped back on the grass, rolled on one elbow, pointed the can with mock severity under Owen's nose. 'Anyway, watch it, man. When I'm gone they'll likely start in on you. You'll need to creep past by the back street!'

Like I did last night, Owen thought, but then the real message behind Ned's words got through to him. *He's warning me off, doesn't want me calling here when he's gone. It really upset him, Susie offering me her room.*

Owen avoided his friend's eyes, afraid his own thoughts might show; at the same time embarrassed for Ned, that something complicated and private had suddenly burst through the surface. Complicated because even while he ranted against his mother— always competent, maybe a bit over-protective—he was admitting a need for the bond. He saw himself as the man of this female household, where seemingly his father had ducked out of the part.

It was devious and unNedlike. But there'd

be sensitive layers in him which remained invisible even when you'd known him half your lifetime. Increasingly Owen was discovering that people could be like that. He was, himself. But Ned? He was Mister Cool in person. Something had happened to rub him raw, rock him back on his heels, momentarily split his defences open.

Maybe, after the intensity of study, sudden success did that to you; spring-loaded, you fired off. Much as he himself had been jerked by failure into freak mode.

And then Owen's introspection was abruptly broken, everything eased up, with little Renata appearing at the top of the stone steps waving a carrier bag with her new sun-dress in it, and Mrs Banks was stomping down, hot and tired, but quite keen on the suggestion Susie had made about having him stay for a few nights.

Then Ned, for no known reason, was now backing her up, suddenly won over, affably insistent that it should be his room Owen had use of, and he'd camp on the day-bed in the lounge, because it would be far too hot at night for the girls to double up.

CHAPTER EIGHT

MARCIA TURLEY—NO LONGER JUDY because of the name's bitter associations—waited at the bus station until it was almost dusk. She had let down her hair and tied over it a drab silk square of her mother's. The borrowed off-white jacket which she wore made her thin form look more bulky. Even with these precautions she was frightened, seated on the varnished bench, feeling her heart pulse high in her throat.

She knew her fear was silly, because what could he do in the open street even if he caught sight of her? As long as she took care to go only where there were other people, and made sure he wasn't in the house before she called there.

It was awkward not knowing what kind of cases he was working on. He wasn't like uniformed police who had definite hours and a clamp-down on overtime. When there was an emergency, CID could keep you out until any time of day or night, so you went home in snatches when the job let up for a while. She'd need to keep watch and see what lights went on after dark. He had installed a rather elaborate system of automatic switching to fool would-be burglars, but she knew the sequences well enough to recognize if any changes were manual.

The best place to keep watch from would be the corner of the Andersons' garage. The street lights didn't reach there, and she'd only have a couple of yards to step out from cover to check on the house opposite and one down. Bob and Mina Anderson never went out at night, stayed glued to television from about eight onwards.

From that vantage point she would be able to see whether the garage door was left up, which meant he would be back at any moment. He always dropped it and put the padlock on when he was away for any considerable time. Overnight it was left shut, but unlocked because even after drinking he was a light sleeper and would wake to the sound of it opening. She was lucky that he was such a creature of habit, but he was also cunning enough to work out that she'd rely on his keeping to set patterns.

If the padlock was on and the lights set to automatic, he could either be away working late or off drinking with others from the job. In which case he'd not be back before closing time and she'd have every chance to get the things she needed. But he still might be indoors, expecting her back and setting a trap.

So many ifs, she thought, shivering. It wasn't just paranoia on her part; it had always been like that. She was the one who had to work out his programme and find some way to fit her own life in. It had never occurred to him to make allowances for her, not even when she'd

94

warned him something was going wrong after that last time; so she'd been alone there, unconscious for God knew how long on the hall tiles while the poor little baby slopped out with her life's blood. Well, hardly yet a real baby, but they'd told her it would have been a girl.

If Nancy hadn't dropped by ...

She'd ring Nancy the minute she got in, warn her she'd pick up some bits and pieces and be round there in half an hour. Maybe order a taxi to stand by a few doors down the road. She hadn't dared to make firm arrangements before, for fear they'd have to be cancelled. So used to having her intentions blocked, she'd no confidence any more in advance planning, even when he wasn't around to thwart her.

She peered at her watch, checked it against the hanging clock of the bus station, and knew action couldn't be put off longer. It struck her that two drivers opposite were staring at her. The older one could be about to come across and ask if she'd missed a connection. Under the high glass roof, buses had been coming in and emptying, waiting, refilling and starting off again for what seemed like hours while she hadn't moved. Her head ached with the throbbing of their diesel engines; her nostrils were full of the smell of spent fuel and overheated metal. Any longer here and she would be sick.

There was a cafeteria off the side of the bus

station, with brightly coloured plastic tables and chairs, but again the smell from inside had put her off. If it was tea, then it must taste of stale dishcloths. She had gone once as far as the door but there had been an old tape playing in there. *'Love and marriage, love and marriage, they go together like a horse and carriage ...'*

Other words had started up of themselves, and she couldn't suppress them. Even when she moved out of hearing of the jingle they went on revolving in her mind: *Punch and Judy, Punch and Judy ...*

That's what she'd screamed hysterically at him that first time he'd come home drunk and violent. It had been an eternity ago and she'd been young then, expected something better. It had unhinged her, the sight of his dull-eyed, brute, stranger's face, the stench of alcohol, the sound of hard knuckles on flesh and bone, the very thought of violation. Only later had come the pain and humiliation. She'd been furious, outraged, and imagined she could fight back. Then, over a period, she'd learned she couldn't. Could only scream, whimper, backing away until cornered and then made a rag doll of.

Punch and Judy, the whole disgusting show. And over and over ever after. Until that last time when she'd been taken away to hospital, victim of 'a fall downstairs'. Isn't that what the police always called it? In Casualty they hadn't believed her but she'd refused to change her story, couldn't because of the awfulness of the

96

truth. And that time it would have been murder, because he'd killed their expected baby.

The first time, eight years before, she'd thought that by morning his memory would have blacked it out, but he hadn't been that drunk. More out of his mind with anger over some frustration at work, and then the drink on top. He'd said he was sorry: it would never, never happen again. And it was from that night that he'd dropped her first name, in front of others referred to her as Marcia. He'd used clumsy endearments, swore she meant everything to him.

Until the next time.

The abuse went on and on. The apologies afterwards, the frantic endearments, became fewer, finally ceased. In the ever shorter intervals between these violent outbursts he had withdrawn into a new cold hardness. She knew he'd begun to regard her as the enemy. She grew wary, avoided the outside world in the same way that she tried to distance herself from him, became Marcia, someone alien even to herself.

Only Mother went on using the name Judy, because she didn't know, and now hearing it brought back the shame of the secret beatings. But she couldn't say anything to stop the old lady, for fear she might make the connection, guess what she'd never actually been told.

Marcia got stiffly to her feet, shook her head

at the nearby driver who had looked at her expectantly, and moved off towards the little local bus that served Fords Green. She gave the exact fare to the driver and sat on the long seat at the back where there was less likelihood of being noticed. At the stop just before the Green Man she got out, keeping her head down. As she made a wide circuit round the pub's rear she had to cross the car park, and it was there that she almost collided with someone she knew.

*   *   *

Paul Randall was wobbling towards the certainty that he'd not get the job. His couple of double brandies, meant to bolster his confidence, had stretched into four and he'd overshot, reached the doubting stage.

Not the desperate one, not that yet because, as ever, he had another ace up his sleeve. The Big One. He could still safely go back to Gillian with a glowing account of his performance at today's interview; all the more point to keeping her high on that, till the other dodge turned up trumps.

Eddie might not be quite ready, because he hadn't told him it was on for sure. He'd give him a bell. It would take a little juggling, but if he brought it forward so that the outcome of the estate agency application slid into oblivion—well, he could be on to a winner.

Worth trying.

He turned out his pockets for loose change, then remembered that the Green Man's public phone now took a card and his own was used up. 'Gerry,' he called to the barman, 'I need to make a call. Local one. Be a pal and lend me your phonecard.'

'Sorry, pal.' Was there unnecessary stress on that second word? 'Try someone else.'

Randall's mouth tightened. He glanced round, freezing the half smiles that had greeted Gerry's refusal. 'Money up front,' he promised, jingling coins. 'Fifty per cent agent's fee, howzat?'

There always was a wally. A pimply lad held out his card with two calls still on it.

'Tell you what,' Randall offered, all geniality. 'Only pennies in it. Double or quits, eh? I'll toss, you call.'

He had pocketed the coin almost as soon as the lad had agreed it was tails. 'Hard luck, chum, but thanks.'

He wasn't so broke that he'd had to do that, but it felt good to put one over when he was a trifle down.

Making for the corridor phone he jostled a stocky man pushing off from the bar rail. DS Turley rocked on his heels, made the other man sidestep and wiped the back of his hand over his mouth. He continued towards the door. Outside, the night was dark, briefly cooler, then a sultry air puffed on him with the threat of a summer storm. With over-deliberate movements he made for his car, took out the bag of provisions he'd stashed in the boot, slammed the lid and locked it again. No way would he be driving it back, tanked up as he was. And with the possibility of Marcia hanging around waiting for signs that the house was empty, he'd not risk her seeing him open the garage. Instead he'd go in by the back way, sit in the dark and wait. He hoped the storm would come in time and drop a deluge, wash some sense into the silly cow. He looked forward with grim satisfaction to the coming encounter.

Padding on crêpe soles down the empty street, he heard a car come up behind, then alongside. The passenger window rolled quietly down and PC Baron stuck his nose out. ''Night, Skip.'

He glanced coldly sideways. Was this a work call or some personal barb? Baron didn't live up to his name with fancy manners.

'You just missed your old lady.'

Turley went on walking, humping his bag of groceries in his arms.

The car kept pace with him. 'Been shopping?' Nothing offensive in the words, just the needling tone.

'Something you want, Baron?' He wasn't going to ask where they'd sighted Marcia, but then he was going to be told in any case. He could feel it building.

The driver leaned forward, staring past the other. He was a first-year, almost straight off training. 'She'll be along any minute, Sergeant. A bloke was offering her a lift, coupla minutes after you left.'

'So?'

'Thought you might be worrying. Smells like there's rain on its way.'

'I guess.' He turned at the corner and made for the lane that ran between the houses' backs. The patrol car was gunned, pulled away, left him to seethe.

As he dumped the bag to unlock the kitchen door the first drops fell, marking the concrete path with large dark stickers which, as he pulled out the key, spread and joined into a complete black cover. Thunder rumbled distantly. Rain rattled on the corrugated iron cover of the disused coalhole, struck cold and searching through the cotton shirt on to his muscled shoulders. Fiercely he turned up his face, letting water run over brow and cheeks and into his open mouth.

She would crawl back like a drowned rat. He didn't for a moment believe their story of some unknown man giving her a lift; she wasn't the sort to accept the offer. They'd made that up, were stirring it, that's all.

*   *   *

Rain drummed suddenly on the glass roof of

the Banks' extension, startling them as they sat with empty coffee cups on the floor beside them. Ned left his chair to close the patio doors, stepping over Renata's collection of farm animals confined in a palisade she'd built of dominoes.

His mother looked up from her mending, needle in hand, surprised at the darkness beyond her own pool of light from the standard lamp. 'We're in for a downpour.'

Owen was briefly distracted from the Scrabble board. 'Triple word score,' murmured Susie, fitting d-o-m-i-n-a-n vertically above the initial t of truant. 'And an extra fifty for using all seven letters.' She added her score to the pad on the table between them, then helped herself to more tiles.

At a growl of thunder her little sister sat bolt upright and pushed her knuckles in her mouth. Everyone went quiet, pretending things were quite normal. If the storm came any closer Renata could go off like a factory hooter.

'Let's have some music,' her mother said, getting up.

'Not the radio,' Ned warned.

'No. The old horn gramophone, if one of you men would crank it. I'll get out some old 78s, and you can all choose your favourites.'

Ned rolled his eyes at Owen but rose to wind the relic, a half-joke half-treasure which their father had once rescued at the music store's jumble clear-out. They had some discs which were of value now, pre-war Deanna Durbins and operatic numbers of long-dead tenors and divas.

'I guess you've won,' Owen conceded, shooting the Scrabble tiles back in their box and closing the board. Susie had scooped her little sister on to her lap and was poking at her ribs while the child struggled, trying not to squeal.

Ned turned up the volume of the Teddy Bears' Picnic until the sound of the rain was drowned out. The occasional flash of white light through the drawn curtains made Renata go stiff until the following rumble had ended. Owen saw she was silently counting in between. Someone must have told her about the speeds of light and sound. If she kept her mind on the counting she felt less helpless, seemed to have some slight control over events.

He remembered his own childhood fear of fire, how he'd believed flames could start up spontaneously anywhere, at any time. It was magic, an evil power. He'd lived in terror of it flaring up in his bedroom if he dared to close his eyes at night. Staring into the dark he'd sweated, willing it not to come, fighting to ward off sleep and not be left defenceless.

He'd had nightmares of burning, and once when he'd cried out in his sleep his father had come. Tearfully he'd confessed his fears, and it was all put right in a moment when Dad explained that fire came from people being

103

careless. Until then it had never occurred to the child that adults were ever less than perfect. So from that time he'd lost his fear of fire, started to have doubts about people.

He winked at Renata, knowing he could say nothing to explain away lightning, which was no one's fault. It simply was.

'It's electricity,' she said bravely, as if he had spoken aloud.

'Ah,' he said, 'I see. So that's all right then.'

The storm raged for over an hour, gradually rumbling away to nothing. When Owen went up to take over Ned's room he opened the window on to a world of gently dripping eaves and placid puddles. A powerful scent of grass and something like honeysuckle came up from the neighbouring gardens.

Just two feet below the window-sill was the ridge of the kitchen roof. He guessed that in this modest neighbourhood you hadn't to be afraid of anyone breaking in. Much more likely that Ned had used this as an exit to night jaunts in the past. He almost felt tempted to do the same himself, not having to take account of burglar alarms.

It would be good to slip out and walk the dark streets alone, looking for what might turn up. He could even go out to Dad's trailer for the night, and no one would ever guess. But it wouldn't be such fun slogging all that way on foot, then wading through the puddles and debris of the site with its sour stench of concrete and wet clay. Different, of course, if he had use of a car.

*   *   *

Marcia Turley gazed at the house front through the semi-circles cleared by the windscreen wipers. 'That *was* him we saw go round the back way. The automatic switching's been turned off. He's sitting in the dark. I'm not going in while he's there.'

'He can hardly stop you getting your things. Would it help if I came in with you? He couldn't do anything then to upset you.'

'He wouldn't need to. I just don't want him near me. Do you think he knows? That I'm out here, I mean.'

'Why should he? I never mentioned to anyone that you intended coming. Who else did you tell?'

'Nobody that it was today for certain. Maybe he waits like that every night. He's not a fool. He must guess I need more clothes by now.'

The man glanced at the dashboard clock. 'Why don't we leave it a while and get something to eat? We can drive out to a restaurant where you're not known, then back to my place. After you've seen your solicitor in the morning there may be a better chance to get inside the house when Turley's at work.'

'It's kind of you, but I'd better go straight to

Nancy's now and have an early night. I fixed it with her for whenever I came to you for the testimonial. She left it as an open invitation.'

'Ah, there's a difficulty there. Didn't she ring you? She called the office to say she'd be away. Her mother's had a stroke, not very serious, but Nancy felt she had to be there. Naturally I assumed you'd been warned.'

'Poor Mrs Webb! Such a nice old lady.' Marcia turned a worried face to him. 'Is that why you mentioned going back to your place? For the night? You know I couldn't possibly do that. There'd be such an awful row if Don found out. And maybe it could affect the divorce... I mean, not that there'd be anything wrong in it, but it's what people would think. No, I'd better get back to Mother's, try another time.'

'What about tomorrow's appointment?'

'Oh dear. It was good of Mr Etheridge to offer to come in at the weekend, but I'll not be able to get back here by nine. There isn't a connecting bus that early. I hardly like to ask him to change it, especially since it's already been put off once, but there's nothing else for it.'

'Put off for his convenience.'

'All the same ... Oh, doesn't it sometimes seem that everything's bound to go wrong?'

'You could stay for the night at a local pub. Then I'd collect you tomorrow and drive you to your appointment. Would that meet your objections?'

He watched her face as she worked it out. It was the cost, of course, and she would be horribly insulted if he offered to cover it. 'Look, let's discuss this over a meal. Everything may look simpler after we've eaten. I don't know about you, but I'm ravenous.'

She shot another glance through the streaming windscreen at the house that had been her home, and closed her eyes. Perhaps he was right. She had missed lunch, and last week when he'd suggested she should come over, she'd accepted dinner as part of the offer.

She's coming round, the man thought, switching on the car's ignition. And by the time we've eaten it will be too late to ring Etheridge to cancel tomorrow's meeting. I'll fix her up with something for tonight. She'll agree in the end.

CHAPTER NINE

GILLIAN RANDALL RELOCKED THE CLIENT'S conservatory door and splashed the fifteen yards to her car with a plastic nursing apron covering her head. The day had been one long series of disasters, the sudden summer storm only its most recent irritation. She'd been late on duty, missed the weather forecast and hadn't dared stop to tank up the car. Now she must do it in this downpour, and the Mill Lane filling-station had recently gone self-service.

White flashes lit the rumbling dark. She shot from a black tunnel of trees into the glare of the forecourt, stepped out under the inadequate canopy and unlocked the petrol cap. Over by the cash window a tall figure was signing a chit, his back towards her, raincoat collar turned up to tweed fishing-hat. His car stood two pumps ahead with the interior light on. She made out the outline of a woman passenger using a mirror to check her make-up.

The fuel meter flicked through the litres, built up the price to fifteen pounds and she replaced the gun, locked the cap, reached in her cardigan pocket for her Visa card. Heavy drips off the canopy edge forced her to do a detour round the other car. She glanced in and caught the woman's gaze. She stopped in her tracks.

'Hullo.'

'Oh. Nurse, it's you.'

'How are you?' She'd forgotten the name. Marcia something. Tower, Turner, was that it? Post-abortion, general bruising to jaw, shoulders, ribs and abdomen. As clear a case of physical abuse as any ever, but the girl wouldn't admit it. She'd been adamant, certainly had guts. Which made it all the less explicable that she'd let herself be made a punch-ball.

'I'm fine.' She was embarrassed, slumped low in the seat.

'And how—are things now?'

The girl bit her underlip, looking quickly towards the man's back still turned at the cash window. 'Fine too, really. I—'

'Yes?'

'It's going to be all right. Look, you were very kind. I got round to seeing it the way you said, so—well, I'm suing for divorce. Seeing a solicitor tomorrow.' The words rushed out, a plea for immediate privacy and oblivion.

The older woman nodded. 'That's the sensible thing: moving on. Good luck, then.' She smiled, splashed on towards the small window where the other customer stood.

As he turned away the man dropped his card, stooped to retrieve it, his face obscured, then quickly moved off before she was close. A pity, she'd been curious to see what he looked like. Staring after him she noted the stiff set of his shoulders under the anonymous garb. She hadn't imagined the furtiveness. A wife-beater, he carried uncomfortable self-knowledge around.

Putting up with that was something she'd never understand in a lifetime, and in Casualty she'd come across some appalling cases. For herself, she'd give as good as she got. Sometimes gave more, but with Paul it stayed mainly verbal plus a few open-handed slaps. If he ever went further, gave her a bit of the rough, she'd throw him out. Or would she? She grimaced. Maybe not the first time.

The point was that she wasn't one to take passively whatever a man chose to hand out. Fighting back had always been an essential part of her relationships—and maybe that was why she so often loused things up, why eventually Guy had walked out, why Paul got the sulks and Owen put the shutters up?

You were what you were. Yet now it seemed that this Marcia girl had moved from passive to active, or at least was on the way to it. That could be an easier transformation than herself going soft and assuming the little woman act. Somewhere between that girl's submission and her own over-aggressive reaction there'd be a way of getting it right. Or else—get shot of men altogether, opt for a nunnery? No, that certainly wasn't on.

She nodded at the man in the booth. Attendant he couldn't be called, cut off by his Walkman, twitching to some ceaseless tinny rhythm that leaked from under his over-long thatch. He barely glanced at her signature, not at all at her. Robotized.

She pocketed her card pushed through with the receipt, splashed back to her car. The other, with the two in it, had slid off into the night, its twin red rearlights disappearing down the country lane in the opposite direction to her own.

Home and a lazy bath, she promised herself. Something reheated by microwave, then a book in bed. Or Paul. Well, *and* Paul, she

110

supposed.

She wondered—for the first time since leaving the house that morning—how his interview had gone and what mood it would leave him in. Elation if he saw the job within his grasp; some wild alternative cockily conceived if he'd been turned down out of hand. In which case he'd not show up until he'd wooed his self-confidence back. Normally he had his ups of an evening, when she was feeling drained. The few brief occasions when he soberly faced reality were on first waking, once her favourite time of day.

Tomorrow was Saturday: only a four-hour shift, eight till twelve. Then she could rest until the big occasion, the annual Charity Hosts' Dinner Dance, to be held this year at Chardleigh Place. Very exclusive, with the cream of three counties' professionals gathered to preen and congratulate themselves on their eligibility. She'd been going for more years now than she could number. The subscription tickets still turned up with her old surname on them, and Paul went along as consort, as though he'd stepped into Guy's professional shoes as well as his bed and board.

But that was a cynical way to look at it. She'd have to watch herself more carefully if the evening wasn't to come to a shambolic end.

She sighed, staring through the raining dark. Recently relations with Paul hadn't been all that easy. And then there was Owen. Some

111

time tomorrow she must get a moment alone with him to sound out his plans for college.

She changed down to third gear at the top of Maze Hill and the sensor lights came on at the entrance to the driveway as she turned in. The double garage doors swung up at her approach and closed behind as the car came to a stop. She saw the second space was empty.

By the connecting door she went through to the hall and called up the stairs. 'Owen? Are you home?'

There was no one there. Part of her was relieved that she need make no social effort. And part quietly appalled. There was nothing, she knew, which so petrified her as the thought of sometime being left utterly alone.

*   *   *

Don Turley stowed the groceries and went back to the darkened lounge where the open curtains allowed an uninterrupted view of the brighter street outside. Slanting rain shone like metal stair rods, beating flat the godetias Marcia had sown in the small front garden last Spring. There were parked cars along the kerb to either side but no movement. He went back to the kitchen to make coffee, brought the pot in and set it with a mug on the floor beside him, prepared for a long vigil. The rain continued drumming; the thunder roared overhead and slowly receded. After the rain there was still a sound of gurgling gutters and dripping eaves. In the row of small front gardens damp evergreens sparkled under the street lamps.

At a little after midnight he decided it had been a waste of time. Maybe she hadn't come to Fords Green at all, and either the two patrolmen had mistaken another woman for her or they'd made up the story to needle him. By now the coffee had settled the booze, leaving him empty and irritable, but steady enough to go and fetch the car. He fetched his oilskins and pulled on rubber boots, then set off to plod his way back to the Green Man's car-park.

There were still lights on inside the pub for cleaning up, but the outside ones were cut. Only three cars remained, separate dull outlines catching an occasional metallic reflection from passing traffic on the road. He splashed through puddles, fumbled to unlock and eased himself bulkily in. When he switched on, the dashboard clock lit to show 12.50 a.m.

He sat a while, not so much thinking as brooding, perversely almost enjoying the acid discomfort of frustration. Then he put the car in gear and swept out into the roadway.

The rain had killed what little night life Fords Green boasted. At its most vigorous this was limited to a social few with upmarket ambitions, and the more familiar criminal fringe. Vaguely bent on looking for trouble, Turley took a roundabout route, encompassing the older part of the village. Not until he turned back on the Barrowmead road for home did he see any pedestrian, and then, slipping from the house he'd earlier seen him enter with the girl, it was the lad he'd picked up at Bardells Wood. From the darkened doorway he slid out, hunched in a dark anorak and with the baseball cap over his hair.

So was he bent on mischief after the witching hour, or slinking home from his tomcat session with the girl?

Turley slowly passed the hurrying figure, pulled in to the kerb, cut his lights and watched in his driving mirror. Fifty yards beyond the terrace was a dead-end alley leading to a row of lock-up garages. The boy disappeared inside and the waiting policeman heard his receding footfalls stop, followed by the sliding of a metal door. A pause, then the sound of a car engine starting. A bar of light yellowed the dark brick wall as he drove cautiously out and turned left, away from the silent watcher.

In itself, nothing suspicious. But there was always a chance. The boy had said he'd no car of his own, so whose had he taken, and with what key?

'Stafford,' Turley reminded himself, easing off his brake. A cub of that presumptuous git from the architect firm. It would be quite a lift to have the rise on him.

He let the other car disappear before he switched on his headlights, made a three-point turn and followed at a reasonable distance behind. Two small points of red showed ahead on the Barrowmead road.

After barely a quarter of a mile the first car slowed and pulled off on to the forecourt of the Martinez Caff. Turley held back under the sheltering trees, cutting his lights. The building's white façade was no more than a smudgy grey.

Stafford's car made a slow circuit, going close enough to the building for its driver to ascertain whether there were signs of life in the restaurant or the cramped living quarters in its eaves. Then the engine was gunned and the car swung back on the road, continuing in the same direction. Turley tossed in his mind whether to resume pursuit.

Hell, why not? The boy was way off his home ground. There had to be a reason. After the fiasco of waiting for Marcia to turn up, this might be the only chance tonight of making a positive score.

Another mile and a half showed up on his trip-meter when Turley discovered he'd lost him. Rounding the wide S-bend above the river, he saw the road stretching dead straight ahead. And empty. So somewhere in the last half minute the other car had turned off.

There was no village near. As far as Turley could remember, no houses either. Just the site works for the proposed new pet foods factory, hardly progressed far enough to have valuable stock installed. And wouldn't there be a night watchman?

He turned the car and drove slowly back to the concreted turn-off with the staring white notice-board which advertised the project. With the engine cut, he sat listening, his driving door ajar. The rain had restarted but was less heavy now. Above the sounds of it striking on tarpaulins and steel scaffolding there came the growling of a car in low gear ploughing across uncertain terrain. No lights though, as far as he could see. Unless ahead there was a short row of small squares beginning to show up paler than the surrounding darkness. Like curtained windows at some distance.

Turley was still in his oilskins. No sweat to take a look, see what kind of rendezvous the boy was so furtively keeping.

He ran the car under overhanging trees and took to his feet. The concrete road was solid enough but just past the empty site hut a second track went off, roughly shingled, in the direction of the row of windows. He could see now the oblong shape of the construction, like a prefab or a trailer. Then, as he watched, a door opened and a woman stood in silhouette against the sudden rectangle of light. He heard her voice rising in pitch as she called out to someone in the dark. A male voice answered, but he was too far off to catch what was said.

He stepped swiftly forward and found only space. His leg crumpled under him and he fell face down in several inches of water, grazing his forehead on the edge of a pile of stones. He heard the woman's voice again, angry or frightened, then the slam of a door, and everything went still.

He stood up, muddied and shaking, barely with breath enough for the oaths that choked him. What in buggeration was he doing here playing Peeping Tom on an adolescent Casanova when he could be at home shoving good malt into his hollow belly? In disgust he turned back the way he had come, moving more carefully now and his eyes better adapted to the dark.

Arrived at the car, he opened the driving door and the courtesy light shone out on the muddied state of his shoes and trouser ends. Beside them water gleamed in deep impressions of turning tracks in the soft topsoil.

But not made by the small banger the boy had driven here. These tyres had been wider, for a heavier model. And the tracks were recent.

So just what was going on out at this building site? It seemed there was night life in the Fords Green area after all.

CHAPTER TEN

Saturday, 22 August

SATURDAY DUTY WENT MORE SMOOTHLY for Gillian. Old Mr Judge—the tender-loving-care service required that she address him as Stanley—had been exhausted by the previous day's comparative excitement and remained totally unresponsive to handling. She left him snoring gently on his side with a clean tissue tucked loosely in one hand. The relief nurse saw her out and turned the dead lock after her.

In the car, reaching for the ignition, she thought suddenly, no. Back home there would be only hassle. If she opted to rest, Paul would want to get in with her. If she sat in the garden, Owen would surely be mooning around and there'd be his problems to get started on. Tomorrow would be soon enough, after the big evening was through.

She realized that she had been looking forward to it as some kind of endurance test. This year the Charities Ball seemed to have a sinister significance. Something like a premonition haunted her, keeping her on edge. She had to be ready, rested, and the idea of not making the grade had her near panicking. And there was no reason for feeling that way, none at all.

What she needed was to be on her own for a while, get her mind to herself. Paul could manage his own lunch. Let Owen see his father about any problems. Right now she didn't need any of them.

All the same, she'd have to check back, make certain things still stood for this evening. With Paul you could never be one hundred per cent sure, and last night she'd had this feeling he was up to something dodgy.

She stopped at a public phone and used her card.

'Yeah, yeah,' he answered impatiently. 'All OK. Oh, and your mother rang. She wants you to call in, said it's important.'

'What kind of "call in"? Visit or phone?'

'Drop by, I guess.' Imprecise as ever, she thought. Yet not vague: there was always a gleam of motive keyed in behind his apparent casualness. Bright and foxy, with lazy eyelids. She could see him as clearly as if it were vision on sound.

'Is Owen there?'

'Not at the moment.'

Implying he'd been in and left again? Her mouth tightened. Why couldn't he see she needed to know the boy's movements? That wasn't a rhetorical question. The answer to it was that she'd a bad conscience about Owen, and bad consciences were something Paul was constitutionally incapable of recognizing.

'Right. Expect me when you see me, then.'

119

She hung up before he could reply, backed out of the phone booth and returned to her car.

So, just when she needed to be on her own, it seemed that she was booked for a session with Mother. And that could lead anywhere.

*   *   *

From the roadway she could see her on the top balcony, fiddling with a trowel in her tub of geraniums and trailing ivy. Couldn't miss her in that jade and white outfit striped like a seaside tent. Gillian made her way up the two flights of exterior stairs. 'Hi,' she said, and her mother nodded. It was their customary greeting. They never kissed.

Mrs Francis ran her eyes over her daughter and turned to the open doorway. Stepping into a pit of memory, Gillian caught herself wiping her shoes on entering, as if she'd been playing in mud.

'Let's have some coffee,' her mother said brightly. Then, abruptly, 'No, maybe a glass of wine.'

Well, that was something fresh. Gillian watched her disappear into the tiny larder off the neat, bright kitchen. She came back with a bottle of red. No need for a corkscrew; a third of the bottle had gone already.

Or two thirds remained, Gillian reminded herself: opposite interpretations of pessimist and optimist. And she knew which she was.

'Are we celebrating, or drowning sorrows?' she demanded.

Mrs Francis placed two cut crystal glasses on a silver tray beside the bottle and waved her towards the front of the apartment. Not for her to entertain in the kitchen, however well-known the visitor.

And she does know me, through and through, Gillian thought flatly. She looked at her mother, cool, distinguished, competent, and reflected that in the face of such schooled perfection how could she ever expect to feel other than a mess?

Yesterday's summer storm had cleared to a hazy dawn that built to the present midday heat. In the south-facing lounge the vertical blinds were adjusted to make tiger stripes over the cool grey interior. They sat opposite each other, Gillian on the chintzy settee, her mother in a matching armchair, the low table between them.

Mrs Francis poured and rotated the tray. Gillian reached for her glass and sipped. 'Lord, what's this?' She leaned towards the bottle and read the label. '"Bulls Blood"?' Strong stuff. Surely this was a day for chilled white Bordeaux?

'I thought I'd try it for a change.' Yes, there was definitely something different about Mother today. A satisfied little smile hovered on her lips. She put up a hand to her exquisitely sculpted hairstyle and left a dark particle of

121

something suspended there. Potting compost? Coming in, Mother had forgotten to rinse her hands.

'How are your menfolk?' Mrs Francis inquired.

'Fine.' Pointless to mention that Paul had put in for a different job, and she didn't know enough about Owen's plans yet to venture on that topic.

'Mmm.' It sounded dubious. Maybe she had a right to be. 'I had lunch with Guy last week. Wednesday, it would be.'

'And?'

'Very pleasant. That new French place in Amersham. *Sole Dugléré* followed by *Ananas au Kirsch*. Rather good, I thought.'

Gillian was suddenly impatient at being played with. She wasn't in the mood for implicit comparisons between her two husbands. 'Paul said you wanted to see me. Something important.'

'Important to me, yes.' Mrs Francis took a deeper breath. She let a short silence build up before stating abruptly, 'I've sold this apartment. I thought I should tell you in case you dropped by and found everything upside down. The removers deliver the tea chests tomorrow.'

She relaxed enough to look amused at her daughter's amazement, ready to startle her further. 'I'm moving in with a friend. You haven't met him. George Winterton, he lives

122

over Reading way.'

'*Moving in?* You mean—'

'Co-habiting, yes. I understand that's the correct term.'

'I don't believe this. I mean, why—?'

'Why what?' Mrs Francis opened her eyes innocently wide.

'Well, why not wait and get a divorce—'

'From your father?' She rolled the stem of her wine glass between thumb and forefinger, letting a few drops spill. 'I could say it would take too long, but neither George nor I is particularly impatient to remarry. No, it's simply that I couldn't do it to the poor old thing. I doubt if he'd understand at all when they served divorce papers, but there's a chance that it might get through to him. Having lost so much already, then a final insult like that . . .'

'Need he know?'

'*I* would know. And I remember, you see, what he once was. Before Alzheimer's. When—we first met. Such a man. There will never be anyone again like him. It never made a patch of difference to me that he was over twenty years older.'

Gillian gazed at her mother. This was someone she'd never known. 'But he was such a drag.'

'When—it struck, rather suddenly, I arranged for you to go away to school, and in the holidays I invented distractions. You

123

seemed not to notice things were going wrong. Youngsters can be very wrapped up in themselves.'

'We didn't relate. He was so—distant. Like other girls' grandfathers.'

'Distant, yes. He had *gone* a long time before he had to go away. For short periods he had enough control to keep up a front. Front was all he had. A show of wounded dignity, and sometimes, when he was able, a pathetic burst of desperate geniality.'

'When he disappeared, I couldn't understand what you'd done. I told myself it was some idea of Dr Payne's. I thought that you and he might be—fond of each other.' Even now she couldn't say 'lovers', meaning her mother.

'It was on Dr Payne's insistence finally. I didn't give in until—well, at the end he got so difficult. The mess ... you wouldn't have understood. Faeces all over the curtains where he wiped his hands. I mean—'

'I never guessed.'

'That's how I wanted it.'

'But suddenly he was in that awful place and you were away on holiday—'

'It was taken out of my hands. I was distraught. Dr Payne sent a geriatric specialist. I agreed he could go away for a week, for tests; there were new drugs they could try on him ...'

'And he never came back.'

'Afterwards I saw how they'd taken the

burden of choice off me. They explained I must accept it that way, for your sake as well as my own.'

'I had no idea. I got it all wrong.' Shakily she held out her glass for a refill.

'Why should you have guessed? At that age one's parents are peripheral. But I'd loved him once. Deeply. By that time I couldn't even remember what love had felt like.'

There was a long silence. Mrs Francis rose and adjusted the blinds so that the whole room was in shade. Like drawing the curtains round a bed where someone's dying, Gillian thought. So often as a nurse she had been the one to break bad news. Now she seemed to be back in a strange visitors' room and the roles were reversed.

How could she, with her nursing training, have remained blind to what had happened in her own home? As a child she'd taken one frightened look, read the scene wrongly and, self-absorbed, firmly closed her mind to it from then on. Not only had she failed to notice her father's failing mental condition but she had never recognized her mother's vulnerability, seeing her as authority and not a real person.

'You should have explained all this to me long ago,' she accused her.

'It hurt too much.'

'And this new man. This—what is he? Do you love him?'

'Need him.'

Ah, yes. There was a difference; Gillian knew this herself. She watched her mother's flushed face with wonderment as she went on.

'I want to come alive again. It's been a long time. He's younger than me, quite a bit. Out of a job, and he isn't blessed with worldly goods. But he's—vital. I want what I've missed for so long.'

Gillian looked at her and tried to see the whole woman: a third of her life single, a third with Father—much of it sterile duty—almost a third alone again. A long time, yes.

'Which is my reason for this.' Rather wildly Mrs Francis lifted the bottle turned to display the label. 'Bulls Blood. The male thing. It's what I once knew and lost. And I want it again, before it's too late. I'm tired of the tidy perfection of being alone, the empty repetitions. Every day so longdrawn, and always the same. Getting up, keeping house, going to the shops to escape the awful silence. In the daytime watching neighbours through the windows, and at night the made-up lives on television. Glad to be going to bed at the end of it. But it's empty there, and I can't sleep.

'I've always admired the way you lived, the decision to get up and go whatever the consequences. Envious perhaps. Well, *I'm* going to be rash and impetuous now. Before it's too late. A new infusion of life's blood. Even a bit of the rough.' Her voice broke.

Through pricking tears, Gillian stared at the

human being rawly revealed. Gently she took the bottle from her and reached for her hands. Across the hard rim of the little table they clung to each other, desperately hugging, as the girl never remembered holding her before.

*   *   *

There had been conveyancing documents to catch up with, so for a while Brian Etheridge hadn't fretted that the client wasn't on time. Young Sheila had offered to come in for an hour but he'd assured her that he could manage the coffee machine and anyway the client was sufficiently respectable for a chaperon to be quite unnecessary.

By 11.15 a.m. he had to recognize that Mrs Turley would not be turning up, and he was justifiably annoyed. In future he'd follow the senior partners' example and put Saturdays firmly beyond his clients' demands.

He poured a third cup of coffee, and with the machine's burbling switched off, the sunlit rooms of the law partnership were unnaturally still. He riffled through the Turley file for the woman's telephone number and found he had only her mother's in Hertfordshire. There was no girl on the switchboard and it all seemed too much effort when he'd already been put to unnecessary trouble. He made a note on his desk-pad to ring through on Monday if an explanation—and apology—hadn't been received by first post. Then he reclaimed his golf bag from the cloakroom and went down to the firm's rear yard for his car.

*　　　*　　　*

Ned had almost physically dragged Owen out to join him jogging and they arrived back at the Banks' terrace house when breakfast was being cleared.

'A couple of rashers for you, Owen?' Mrs Banks asked. 'They're only streaky, but nice and lean. Do you want them with an egg or in a sandwich?'

Owen dropped on to a chair. 'Just a drink, thanks.'

She turned to observe him. 'Are you feeling all right? You look washed out.'

'I'm fine. Ned's idea of jogging is my idea of sprinting, that's all.'

'How did you sleep? Was the bed comfortable?'

'Great. Slept like a log,' he lied.

'Going into a decline,' Ned mocked. 'Like a Victorian Miss with the vapours.'

'How about some toast?' Mrs Banks tempted.

'OK, then. Thanks.' It was easier to give in. He didn't want to offend her when they'd all been so decent.

'I'll shower first,' Ned said. 'You can have the bathroom when you've eaten.' Despite the exercise he was bright-eyed and bushy-tailed as ever, even extra cocky.

Might be better company if he wasn't quite so high on his successes, Owen thought wryly. Unlike himself. Uncomfortably aware of his own social shortcomings in this dejected state, maybe he should bow out, thank the Banks family and trek off back home. He'd do that as soon as he could without seeming abrupt.

It wasn't difficult. The two girls left with their mother, bound for Renata's Saturday dancing class, and he explained that he'd have left before they returned. Ned had taken his paperback into the rear garden and was stretched out in the sun, making no effort to hold him back. Owen said goodbye, reclaimed his canvas satchel with his spare clothes and let himself out into the street. With luck there'd be no one at home and he could get to his own room unseen, sleep off his weariness.

Paul's red Sierra hatchback was standing out front, the wheels and lower bodywork splashed with dried mud. As Owen tried to slide by unobserved, his stepfather called out of an upstairs window, 'Care to wash the old bus over for me? I need it for your mother tonight.'

He trudged on silently, let himself in with his latchkey and met the insufferable man in the hall. 'I'm not a boy scout.'

'I'll say. And then some.'

As if appealing to Owen's obligations to

129

Gillian would have made him eager to do the bastard's dirty jobs for him! But at least he'd learned that they'd be out tonight. If it was the mermaid dress and dinner-jacket affair, then Owen would have the house to himself and they'd not be about until lunchtime at earliest tomorrow. All he had to do was keep them out of his hair until they left this evening.

CHAPTER ELEVEN

BEFORE THEY WERE QUITE DRESSED for the evening there was the customary upsetting disagreement, Gillian offering to ring for a taxi, but Paul tetchily insisting that he'd be perfectly capable of driving there and back. It was no distance anyway.

Much more sensible to take a cab, she claimed, but he wasn't open to reason, glaring viciously at her as if she took delight in crossing him.

She watched him in the mirror as she clipped on the emerald ear-studs which Guy had given her on their first anniversary. She'd turned down Paul's offer of a preliminary snort to get them in the mood, and then he had seemed to think better of it himself, so she couldn't be sure that he'd taken anything. Either coke or hash, it didn't appear to matter any more to him which, so long as it gave him a lift. He'd got as casual about taking speed as taking a drink, and it frightened her, which was what had made her determined to pull out before it became an unbreakable habit. The ups weren't so good any more, and the subsequent downs were appalling. As a nurse she'd known all the theory, and practice was beginning to bear it out.

Yet at this moment she was half inclined to give in. It would be a long evening and already she felt drained, intimidated at the thought of the formidable personalities she had to face on these annual occasions. Presumably because she wasn't important enough to be gossiped about at fogeyish county level, many of them were still unaware that she had remarried, and took Paul for Guy Stafford, the successful architect. Others knew and were patronizing, seeming to renew acquaintance grudgingly on a trial basis.

It meant a lot to her, raised a small-town girl, to be numbered among the county's elect. If next year the ticket application failed to arrive she would be mortified by the intentional snub. It was ultra-important that tonight she and Paul should make a good impression as a couple.

He came through from the dressing-room to have his bow tie fastened, and she turned round to show off her dress. 'How do I look?'

'Sexy,' he said, barely giving the outfit a glance. It had, after all, been hanging on show for a couple of days now. 'Bet it cost you.' He ran his right hand under his left armhole, easing the tight fabric. 'Have to get a new dinner-jacket. This one's bloody uncomfortable.'

She observed him critically. Yes, he looked—slightly seedy. She couldn't put a finger on what specifically was wrong. It was an overall impression, perhaps centred on the pink puffiness under his eyes. The present petulant droop of his mouth didn't help. And he was right about the tailoring.

But suddenly he whirled, snapping his fingers above his head as he pranced.

'Gonna getta brand new jacket.

When I've made myself a packet,

Oh-ho-ho—' he sang out, and she knew. He was away.

If they were to handshake their way safely past the Charities' Ball reception line before exuberance burst into recklessness, they'd best leave at once. She stepped into her high heels, picked up her purse and preceded him down to the car.

*   *   *

There had been more than one snigger when word got around that DS Turley had drawn the short straw to represent divisional working force over at Chardleigh Place. He faced the news with only a slight tightening of the jaw muscles. It hadn't surprised him. Nobody at the local nick wanted to spend an evening within possible scrutiny of the Chief Constable and Lord Lieutenant, even less of their starchy wives.

It was common knowledge that he was a loner, wouldn't take a partner along, and so would be available for any dodgy jobs that cropped up in the course of a snob knees-up. But they needn't imagine he'd be arse-licking round the notables into the early hours. A cold buffet and two glasses of bubbly were included in the free ticket. He'd look out the caterer and trade in the dry champagne for a bottle of scotch, then find himself a snug corner to watch proceedings without being obliged to take part. Security worked both ways. When the party broke up he'd call in a patrol car to get him home in one piece.

His dinner-jacket had gone missing from the wardrobe. It would be just like Marcia to have sent it to the cleaner's months back and forgotten to pick it up. He was on the point of ringing the hire shop in Great Missenden when he remembered her habit of folding things away in boxes. It came to light on the top of the spare room wardrobe and he shook it out of its tissue-paper wrappings, disturbing a vague scent of verbena. Well, a big fat freebie cigar would soon drown that out.

He thought he looked pretty good in the mirror, however much he despised the dressing-up mania. Even if the shawl revers were a bit old-fashioned, it was a good quality

133

suit which Marcia had found at a Barnardo's charity shop; and nobody would notice that the bow-tie was a pre-fab.

* * *

Guy Stafford arrived back with little time for dressing. While he showered, one ear cocked for the news from his portable radio on the bathroom stool, he wondered whether Owen might have called while the flat was empty. He had meant to contact Gillian with a view to discussing the boy's plans, but a sudden emergency with builders out at Hatfield had filled his day.

She would surely be at the charity affair tonight, but he doubted whether she'd welcome the subject's intrusion on a social occasion. On the other hand, since they were bound to run into each other, it might help to be able to converse about something outside their personal interests.

He had happily given the annual summer ball a miss since he'd been on his own, but one of his major clients had left a message at the local office, hoping for a word with him there tonight. The unanswered invitation was still among junk mail on his desk, so he'd no excuse to default. He could hand it in with a cheque at the door.

He smoothed the pin-tucks of his dress shirt and debated the wearing of a cummerbund. It always struck him as a trifle *outré*, but Gillian had considered him a timid dresser (whereas he knew he was merely indifferent). Tonight, having steeled himself to run into her socially, he felt bullish and the slight affectation appealed to his sense of humour. He unfolded the silk cummerbund and clipped it round his waist.

* * *

At some point before supper Gillian lost sight of Paul. He'd been acting pretty high but admittedly with some attempt at restraint. In the artificial gaiety of this social mix she hoped he would pass as unremarkable.

Tonight she was more than usually aware of the pretentious self-advertisement the occasion demanded, and was hating it. Twice she had been glassily stared through on attempting to join a fresh group, and Dr Mayhew had been stupid enough to compliment her on her appearance in front of his vinegary wife.

It had been a mistake to choose such an eye-catching dress. In Thames Valley ancient prejudices were cherished, and this was a mixed gathering of establishment and glitterati, to neither of which groups did she any longer belong. Other women would be telling each other that she didn't know her place.

Coming from a powder-room session with the Public Health Officer's unmarried sister, she had glimpsed Paul's taut, glazed face on the edge of the dancing throng and feared that he was about to lose control, either going into rave mode or out stone-cold. It was at that critical moment that she was confronted by her ex-husband with an amused smile and two full flutes of champagne. He looked so sveltely confident, and this was someone she had always considered countrified, a craggy man in shaggy tweeds.

It was impossible to admit to him that she must go urgently and sort out husband number two, so she accepted the glass, to sip genteelly while he asked her intentions regarding their son's future. To admit that she had none must make her appear callously indifferent, but in fact she hardly knew what the present situation was. From what Guy was saying it seemed that Owen had done so badly that he would be staying on at school another year.

Not school, Guy insisted: Owen wanted to continue studying on his own at his own speed. He approved of this as a good introduction to the university system, where initiative and responsibility lay with the students themselves. The main question, she gathered, was where Owen should live while he caught up with the required academic standards.

'What's wrong with how things are?' she asked defensively.

'Owen seems to want a change. I'm looking for a studio flat he could take.'

'No,' she said abruptly. 'He's not ready for

136

that. It's quite out of the question.'

Guy looked at her from under thick, sandy brows, waiting for her to expand on this, perhaps give some hint of why Owen shouldn't be in charge of his own living arrangements. She couldn't surely mean that the boy was unreliable, some kind of deviant.

'There's nothing wrong with things as they are,' she said weakly. 'It isn't necessary. And a studio flat means more expense.'

She was conscious of Guy watching her over the rim of his glass. He didn't attempt to reassure her that the boy's allowance would still be paid to her. 'Would you truly say it was a satisfactory arrangement, the way things are?' he queried.

She looked around wildly but there was no one near who might come and interrupt them. 'Look, this isn't the time or place to discuss Owen.'

'Maybe not. So when and where?' He was suddenly crisply detached. 'Ring my office Monday, will you? Tell Annette. Then I'll try and fit in with you. Evenings are my best time. But don't put it off too long, or we may have to set something up without consulting you.'

He gave the merest inclination of his head, turned and as he moved away into the crowd, his sleeve was plucked by a middle-aged woman in black with a necklace of rubies.

He didn't even ask how I was, Gillian thought hollowly. I might have been a

137

stranger. She threaded her way back to the bar and put down her empty glass with an unsteady hand. She had lost sight of Paul again. Perhaps he had stepped outside for some fresh air; it was intolerably hot in here.

Over by the double doors a toastmaster type in a red tailcoat announced supper, and there was a shifting in the mass of bodies round the dancing space as the awaited summons freed them from the obligations of small-talk. A short, red-faced man over retirement age appeared at Gillian's elbow and offered his arm as if it were a formal dinner. She let him lead her through the archway, though the thought of food was stupefying. Fortunately he didn't have a line in social pattern or seem bothered to find out who she was. It wasn't until they had loaded their plates and were seated together at a table among loud, laughing strangers that she realized he was trying to insert his fingers between her thighs.

*   *   *

Sourly, from the gallery above the ballroom, DS Turley surveyed the assembly. He could pick out a few faces, some from contacts locally, others from press photographs. They weren't impressive. A few years back he'd have envied them their money and influence, but even at second-hand they were useless to him now. Whatever unwholesome little secrets in their background, they were invulnerable to

138

anyone like himself whose word was already discredited. Too clever to leave tracks, most of them. And the rest? Out of his range, he guessed.

All the same, from habit he kept watch, nodding to himself as he put names to faces, fitted partner to partner, activities to individuals. And by halfway through the evening—and the end of the half-bottle which was all he'd been able to extract from the catering manager—he had recognized connections that were new to him and well worth the interest.

*   *   *

There was enough loud badinage going on for Gillian's escape to pass almost unnoticed. She pushed back her chair, extricating herself with the excuse of going for more cutlery, having spilled her own from the napkin wrapper to the floor.

'Let me ...' 'Shall I ...?' two male guests offered simultaneously, but she brushed past behind as they half-rose, then sank back to be reabsorbed in the social banter.

Again taking refuge in the powder-room, she fixed her smudged eye shadow, glaring defiantly at the image of outrage which confronted her in the mirror. Enough had gone awry this evening without her being reduced to the prey of a geriatric lecher. God, where was Paul? Didn't he realize he had a duty to her, a need to help create a joint favourable impression?

From the foot of the grand staircase she saw him leaving the bank of telephones in the foyer corridor. The tilt of his head was jaunty but his legs pumped like an automaton's, and his eyes as he came close, were half-hooded.

'Paul,' she said sharply, 'we ought to keep together, talk to people. You miss opportunities going off on your own like that.'

'Together, yes.' He nodded slowly several times, like a toy dog at a car's rear window. 'Let's dance, then.'

But in the ballroom the orchestra had been replaced by a lone piper, and the floor was occupied by a formal *contre-danse* team, the men in soft pumps and immaculately kilted, the women with plaid sashes over one shoulder of their long white dresses. Those of the guests who were not at the buffet supper stood around clapping to the rhythm as they admired the elegant movements, active legs, the controlled level balance of shoulders and hips.

'The only thing the Scots are good at is Scotch,' Paul muttered sourly. 'What's this? Breakdance by zombies?'

She pulled him past a group who half-turned to observe him, eyebrows raised. He'd goofed again, misjudged his audience. That might have gone down as a joke among the buffet crowd, but these were *aficionados*.

She found a corner table half-hidden by a

140

potted palm, and they settled there to wait for the demonstration to be over.

In the wall of onlookers which screened the dancers she recognized Colonel Wilder's wife, red-faced and pudgy-armed in an off-the-shoulder obscenity of bright yellow taffeta. Loud of voice and over-exuberant, the woman was unashamedly vulgar. Yet popular. Everyone accepted Hetty Wilder for what she was. What did you have to do to achieve that sort of success? It wasn't just that her husband restored the balance by being socially correct.

She thought, still dazed with amazement, of her own mother's sudden decision to throw up respectable obscurity for 'a touch of the rough'. Maybe in your fifties, impatient with a lifetime of voluntary service, coffee-morning charities and flower-arranging classes, you could afford such a volte-face. Envying Gillian's freedom, she'd said. God, what was free about the present wretched hassle to get her new marriage accepted in narrow-minded country-town society? She would almost welcome being middle-aged and no longer a target for others' stuffy censure.

Eventually the dance band returned and struck up a quickstep. The floor refilled with couples, some staying conventionally paired, others breaking away to perform the neurotic contortions of the self-absorbed. She and Paul joined in, almost physically supported by the crush. They applauded politely at the music's

141

end, seated themselves, came back again to dance, went on and on partnering each other. No one broke in.

They had nothing to say to each other. Only in the powder-room, she realized, had she had any conversation at all. Apart from her brush with Guy.

Paul disappeared towards the bar and came back with a bottle of St Emilion. She didn't ask what it had cost, but began to match him glass for glass until it was gone. When at last they went out in the cool of the early hours to locate Paul's car, she knew that neither of them was capable of driving.

CHAPTER TWELVE

Sunday, 23 August

GILLIAN STARED AT THE RING of keys Paul thrust on her. 'Go on, woman, get in,' he said savagely.

It was no time to argue. At least if she drove she could exercise some control over events. Paul had parked at some distance from the floodlit courtyard, tight against a wall of rhododendrons, which didn't help. The car interior was stuffy and sour-smelling. The glass seemed misted, or was that muzziness just due to her eyes? She rubbed at the windscreen with the back of one hand.

Grateful for the delay as cars clogged the exit gate, she turned her long skirt back over her knees, wound down her window and sat back to await her turn to draw out.

'Go right,' Paul growled impatiently, 'back past the old stables. There's a track that leads through to the Slough road.'

She switched on and fumbled with the gear shift.

'Lights, you fool,' he snapped, leaning forward to flick them on. He seemed suddenly recovered from his torpor and had a new tautness which scared her, because if he'd taken a fresh fix he might at any moment go wild and reach for the controls while she drove.

She took a deep breath, centring her mind on what her hands must do. It wasn't easy because the heavy effort seemed to split her brain, making her struggle uncertainly against, rather than with, the demands of habit.

The way ahead sprang out at her, a yellow tunnel through dark evergreens and, as she turned, the car's beams caught and held a man teetering on the track's edge. Some part of the front wing struck him as in panic she trod on accelerator instead of brake. Over her shoulder she saw him thrown back, arms flailing, to be swallowed into dense, black foliage.

'Go on,' ground out Paul. 'You can't stop now.'

She found it was impossible. She let the car take her, her whole mind forced to holding

143

back rising panic. And now as they bucketed down the rutted track there came headlights behind, striking at her eyes in the driving mirror, as other cars began to follow, trying for an alternative exit.

By an effort of will she lifted her foot to cut speed. The twisting track came at her more slowly, but still giddying as she leaned shortsightedly over the wheel, clinging to keep steady. Her feet on the pedals felt so far away, almost separate from the rest of her. Messages sent down had a long delay.

Close-tunnelled S-bends gave way to a short open stretch with fenced grassland to either side. Ahead loomed a high wall with tall brick pillars. Beyond open iron gates traffic flashed past at speed and somehow she had to break into its flow. The cars behind her were stacking up pressure to take a chance.

'Go right here,' her husband snarled.

'Do as he says.' A second voice spoke flatly from the car's rear. 'And after that I'll give the orders.'

As a cold, hard object was pressed under her left ear, fresh terror flooded her body.

'Watch it! Steady, missus. No mistakes or this might blow your head away.'

Instantly she was wide awake, heart hammering, mind silently screaming. Of course, of course: there'd been mist on the windscreen. The man had been lying hidden in the back, waiting. They'd got themselves a

144

stowaway.

It was fantastic. They were a hijack statistic. Unreal, but she had to believe it because of the gun pressing hard against her neck, angled up to blow out her brains.

Paul spluttered something.

'Shut it, you,' said the hard voice. 'Shut it or she gets it. Her first, then you. Sit tight and you'll stay whole.'

'Do whatever he says,' Paul muttered. 'Gill, for God's sake watch how you go.'

There was a dark break in the bright stream of passing cars and she was out on the main road without thinking. She bit on her lip and steadied the car's bucketing in the traffic flow. Quite soon the traffic began to thin and, at the man's directions, she turned off into side lanes, avoiding the villages.

Travelling westward, away from the motorways. Crossing the Farnham road, leaving all the lights behind. Oh God, no! They were making for Burnham Beeches. The man was a maniac! Out there, miles from any help, he would rape her, then kill them both!

The last houses slid away behind. Ahead lay only darkness and thick woodlands. But theirs wasn't the only car out there in the early hours. Twice, as she followed the twisting route, her headlights glinted on metal or glass where lovers had parked off the road, half-hidden among the old beeches. Wildly she thought of leaning on the horn, switching on hazard lights, but no help could possibly reach them before the man acted. She couldn't risk hastening their end.

The voice said, 'Pull off on the left there. Lights off,' and then as she dowsed them she saw the bulky outline of another vehicle ahead under trees, a dark van. Surely there'd be a chance now?

'Out,' he ordered.

She opened her door and twisted to get down. Intending to run, she felt her legs collapse under her. Hobbled by her long skirt, she fell forward, landed on both palms, bruising her breasts. Her face went down into soft earth. Soggy mulch and harsh heather stems forced themselves past her teeth. A graveyard stench. She tasted mould and was violently sick.

The paroxysm over, she sat up shaking with cold. Dimly a few yards away she saw Paul facing their car with his hands on the roof. He stood with legs wide-spread as, incredibly— like a TV cop—a dark figure patted his way over him, searching for a weapon.

But this was real, and her first sight of the man threatening them was further shock. He had no head. Instead, his shoulders were topped by a huge beige onion. She realized he must be wearing a nylon stocking to hide his face, but knowing that didn't dispel the sense of hideous madness.

Beyond the two men she sensed a movement

146

beside the dark van as a shape detached itself, moving forward. Surely this was the moment help would come. Even armed, there'd be only the one attacker then against three of them. It was her only chance. Unsteadily she got to her knees. A feeble croak escaped her as she reached beseechingly out to the figure loping towards them.

He came close, not a black man as she'd at first thought. As he leaned over, she made out a dark balaclava that allowed only his eyes to appear.

Only his eyes, and they were jeering at her. He grabbed her hair and dragged her to her feet. He never spoke, just nodded in the van's direction and started towing her towards it.

'Leave her alone!' Paul shouted. 'Listen, I'll...' There followed a dull thud as his head was smashed into the car roof. Falling again herself, she twisted to see him slump to the ground, then she was dragged on towards the van's open rear doors and slung inside. She fell on sacks, yielding but prickly with some filling like straw, and a few moments later Paul was hauled up and thrown in beside her. With the slamming of the doors all light was cut off.

Painfully she crawled to her husband's body. Her hands felt for his face, found his eyes closed, his forehead sticky with blood. She tore at his tie and thrust her fingers under his collar. A slow pulse beat in his neck. He was breathing.

A door slammed in the cab ahead. The diesel engine coughed into throbbing life and the van began rolling over grass, lurched out on to the roadway.

So this wasn't where it would happen. The men were taking them on somewhere else. Two of them in collusion, because this must be a thing they'd set up. The man hiding in Paul's car had brought them here for a rendezvous with the other.

But if it was a deliberate plan, for revenge or kidnap, they'd got hold of the wrong people. They'd meant to pick on one of the influential couples attending the ball.

What could they hope for from Paul and herself? Nothing, unless it was quite haphazard viciousness. And if they were out to rob them, why had they kept their old van and not taken Paul's Sierra?

No, she'd got it wrong there. Only one cab door had slammed. Which meant that the first man wasn't with this balaclava one. Onion-head could be following in Paul's Sierra. Its quieter engine would be covered by the van's noise.

She lay half-stifled in the prickly sacks, jolted with each of the van's erratic movements and waited, desperately counting *one-and, two-and, three-and*, with some vague idea of later working out how long they'd travelled. But somewhere among the 180s she lost her way, counted herself out into sleep, only starting

148

awake as the van stopped with its engine still throbbing.

There was a short wait and again a cab door slammed, followed now by the low mutter of voices beyond the partition. It seemed the first man had rejoined them.

She crawled back and felt for the rear fastening as the van began moving off. She threw herself against the doors. There was a sharp click and they gave a bare half-inch.

There had to be a bar across the outside. She fell back and the van again gathered speed.

Stupid! she told herself. Even if she'd been able to get away, she couldn't have left Paul unconscious for them to take it out on.

She crouched down, huddling close, one arm across his body, as if by that she could cancel out the momentary thought of desertion.

* * *

Towards dawn on Sunday morning Owen came half-awake to the sound of a garage door rumbling open. Steps crunched below on gravel, and then the Sierra was being quietly driven in. Which was unusual, because after a heavy night it was usually abandoned in the drive. And then came none of the customary whoops and stumblings as the revellers let themselves in.

But it didn't concern him. He turned his pillow, buried his face in it again and had

149

forgotten by morning.

He guessed his mother and Paul would rise late but, rather than risk running into them, he came down soon after seven, breakfasted on cereals, then pulled out his racing cycle from the garden shed and set about mending a puncture in its rear tyre.

He hadn't ridden the bike since the school's Easter break, and wasn't sure that the rubber solution, already half-used, would still work. He took out the inner tube, checked for the hole with a basin of water and made a neat patch. While it was setting he returned to the kitchen, filled a Thermos flask with coffee and made up enough ham and chutney sandwiches to last him all day.

At a little after nine o'clock he set off in shorts and string vest to follow a route he'd marked on an ordnance survey map of South Bucks. As he crossed the hall he heard the phone begin to ring persistently. He stood with the front door open and listened, half-tempted to go back and answer it. But why the hell? He left it to wake the sleepers.

* * *

In Hertford Marcia's mother slept on well after her usual hour, and it was only the neighbouring church bells announcing Mattins that woke her. She made her way stiffly from bed to bathroom, then, still in her

150

nightdress, took the invalid lift down to where her wheelchair waited in the cramped little hall. Her sleep had been punctuated with disturbing dreams and worse awakenings when she had tossed and worried and tried to make up her mind what action to take, if any. By the coming of light she now felt enough exasperation to risk facing anything. She wheeled her way along the narrow passage past the longcase clock to the telephone and pressed out her daughter's old number at Fords Green.

The ringing continued unanswered, but she persisted. Eventually the receiver was lifted at the far end and she heard a grunting breath. 'Judy?' she quavered.

It was him, of course, probably answering from his bed.

'What is it now?' he demanded.

'I should like to speak to my daughter.'

'She's not here.'

'I'm afraid I don't believe you.' Although he terrified her, she pressed doggedly on. 'Perhaps you would give her a message. Will you ask her to ring me later this morning if it's not convenient now.'

'Get this, I haven't seen your daughter. I don't *want* to see your daughter. I don't know where the hell your bloody daughter is. Now will you just get lost and give me some peace?'

'But Judy came across to Fords Green on Friday. You know she did, because when you phoned me I told you so.'

151

'Listen, what you actually said was that she'd left your place and you didn't know where she'd gone. Now, when *you* phone *me*, that's all *I* can say. I don't know anything about your crazy daughter, haven't heard anything, don't want to hear anything. As far as I'm concerned she could be dead and buried.'

'That's a wicked thing to say!'

His contemptuous reply was mercifully lost to her as he slammed down the receiver. She sat listening to the prolonged buzzing of the instrument in her hand and had no idea what to do next.

*   *   *

Gillian Randall was aware of half-waking three or four times before becoming conscious, and even then her senses were slow to pick up their functions. There was a harsh sawing noise, and as she held her breath to listen it ceased, leaving a confusion of sounds in her head and the hammer-stroke of heartbeats. Her throat was sore and she knew the sounds she had heard were her own breathing.

Behind the pounding headache there was something more than her normal foggy wretchedness on waking after a heavy night; an insistent dismay, a memory of terror. It rushed back then like a rapid sequence of photo-stills—the charity ball, and a wall of evergreens

152

with a man falling away into darkness; the windscreen looming like a lit TV screen; the horror film flashing across it, starting with an invisible voice; the violent onion-headed man; the other who threw her like a sack of potatoes into a van ...

Her eyes came open on a totally unfamiliar dimness. From a grimed ceiling above her hung a feeble, unshaded light bulb that sang on a constant high-pitched note, as if about to go out. A flock mattress separated her from the concrete floor. Against one shoulder she felt the chill of a brick wall with flaking distemper.

She seemed to be lying in a recess of a large cellar with vaulted openings that must correspond to room walls in the building above. At the dark far end there were stone steps leading upwards and, beyond them, the bulk of an old boiler with pipes extending through the ceiling, its furnace dead. No window, so she couldn't tell what time of day it was, and the little diamond-studded watch she'd worn last night was gone from her wrist. It had to be Sunday, though. Sunday at earliest.

Paul! Where was he?

The room swam dizzyingly as she forced herself up on her hands and turned. Along the wall from her was a second mattress on which her husband lay sprawled. At least she assumed it was Paul. His back was towards her. He had been stripped, and a grey blanket covered his lower half.

They were prisoners here, but at least together.

They hadn't removed her clothes. She still had on the remains of the sea-green evening dress. It was ruined. She ran her hands over it. The single shoulder had torn away and there was a long split in one side of the skirt.

God, what did a dress matter? She must be out of her mind. What about Paul? He'd taken an awful slamming on the car roof and he'd gone out cold. Maybe she had too, but from the jumble of memory there rose an impression of someone jabbing a needle in her arm.

She had a nurse's distaste for receiving injections, and her fingers went probing for the puncture on her flesh. There was a red point in a slight lump and some soreness. Histamine reaction. She tried not to think of the worst possible outcome from an infected needle.

She rolled on to her knees and started to crawl across to Paul—yes, it *was* Paul; she could make out the pattern of moles across his ribs—but was suddenly aware of her bladder strained to its limit.

No place to go. Desperately she looked around, considered shouting for someone to come and let her out, but even with an immediate answer, the need was too urgent. She pulled herself up, steadying herself on the cold, flaking surface of the wall. No convenience had been left for them, no screen, nothing. She stumbled to the far side of the cellar and in the recess after the steps squatted with her skirts about her waist. This was humiliation enough; she should be thankful there had been no rape. Her briefs were intact. There was no bruising there.

She straightened and limped across to where her husband lay. 'Paul,' she whispered, pressing on his shoulder. 'Paul, wake up!'

His head rolled back as, kneeling, she pulled him towards her. A dark stain had dried on the farther edge of the mattress and the floor. But not blood. He had vomited while he slept. But for the lucky angle he'd lain at he could have choked on it. But he was breathing, his body was clammily warm. Perhaps the vomiting was why they'd removed his jacket and shirt. But didn't they know about the dangers of concussion?

Still he made no voluntary movement. She cradled his head on one arm, lifted one of his eyelids, but in this dim light the pupil showed no vital reaction. She needed a torch. They must get him to hospital for an X-ray at once.

He gave a long gasp and she eased him back. 'Paul. Paul, can you hear me?'

He groaned, a spasm twisted one cheek and his eyelids flickered.

'Come on,' she urged. 'Wake up, Paul.'

He groaned again, opened his eyes and pushed her away in one movement, tried to sit up and fell weakly back.

'Paul,' she insisted, 'do you know me? Who am I?'

Fleetingly some emotion flickered in his eyes before they closed again. Then he said flatly, 'Who the hell do you think you are? My wife, of course.'

She gave him a few moments to sort out where they were and go through the stages of waking recollection. When he tried to sit up, protesting, she eased him back. 'You have a bad gash and an egg-sized bump on your head,' she told him. 'Don't make any rapid movements. Just take it quietly, while I look whether there's any way of getting out of here.'

He gazed blearily around. 'How did we get here? Where is it?'

'They slung us in a van. I think one of them went off in your car.' She spoke breathlessly, already steadying herself along the wall towards the steps. She pulled herself up them, hanging on to a thick rope threaded through rings alongside. At the top she paused before reaching for the door. It was a steel fire-door, with no handle on this side. Whoever owned this place had a taste for security. But if it was an old cellar, maybe there had once been a chute for coal.

She would have to go feeling above the walls for some wooden trap-door, strain her sight for a glimpse of outside light. If there was even the slightest chink she would know where to start forcing a way out. But the cellar walls were a good eight feet high and there was nothing here to stand on to help her reach the top. She must wait until Paul was able to get on his feet, then hope he could lift her up.

'One of them?' He sounded puzzled. 'There was a man with a gun. Hiding in the car. He told you where to drive.'

'To Burnham Beeches. D'you remember? There was a van there waiting.'

'How many of them?' He sounded uncertain. Probably he hadn't seen the second man. Onion-head had already had him facing the Sierra with his arms spread on its roof before knocking him cold.

'I saw two. They both wore masks. And gloves,' she suddenly remembered. Details were beginning to re-emerge. 'Do you think they just wanted the car and they've dumped us?'

'Are we locked in?'

'Yes.'

He didn't have to explain what difference that made. Car thieves could have dropped them off anywhere and concealed the car until its colour and registration were changed. But bringing them to this place meant they had some reason for hanging on to them as prisoners.

Prisoners, she repeated in her mind. It was incredible. What use could they possibly have for Paul and herself?

'So we've been kidnapped,' her husband said

in a voice of disbelief.

'Yes. They must have mistaken us for some other couple.'

A flicker of some emotion crossed his face, he was silent a moment, then, 'I guess so. But in that case—what happens next, when they find out they're wrong?'

CHAPTER THIRTEEN

'STAFFORD,' GUY SAID, LIFTING THE receiver on its third ring.

'Challoner here. Voice from the past, eh? How are you, Guy, you old dog?'

'Pete? It's certainly been a time. I'm well, thanks. And you?'

'Got a little query's bugging me. Otherwise on top of the world. Wondered if you'd be free to tootle down and wise me up on something.'

Guy grinned wryly. 'I should have known this wasn't purely social.'

'Consultation. All legit. Double fee and expenses if you'll make it today. Seeing it's Sunday.'

That was typical Challoner: vanish for a decade, surface—all *bonhomie*—demanding compliance on the dot. But genial, confident, generous, and probably in a position to put some interesting business in the firm's way. Nevertheless, softly, softly; bad policy to seem grasping.

'I'm a bit tied up at present. I could possibly drop by next weekend.'

'Won't do, old chap. Local eggheads are into dazzling me with science. Need to know what the words mean. Decision by the board tomorrow.'

'Board, Pete?'

'No. Never bored, too busy. Sorry about that. Board, yes. We're buying Hobden's Holdings, and I'm the dummy in the chair. There's an ongoing contract, lot of technical hoohah—complete double-dutch. Confirm or bin it tomorrow. Need you to read some drawings, make sure the drains don't run upwards, sort of thing.'

'Complicated?'

'Big industrial development. Pitfalls could be costly.'

'Mmm.' If Challoner admitted so much, then his need was a real one. The man was clued up enough technically, for all his vague waffle.

'I'd say bring the wife, celebration dinner afterwards and stay overnight, but I don't want you seen. No whispers that I've consulted outside. A personal job, no company receipts. You got it?'

Challoner shorthand for a spot of undercover. Second-opinion insurance in a face-saving operation.

'Completely according to the book, mind.

159

All kosher and VAT-inclusive.' Challoner was beginning to sound slightly anxious.

Guy glanced at his watch. 'Be with you in—three hours, say?'

'Make it two and a half. My Bristol number's in the phone book, but we'll have to meet on neutral ground. There's this little pub out on the Westbury road. The Three Pheasants. Does a tolerable lunch. I'll be waiting. Thanks, Guy. You're *the* stroke, man. See you.'

He rang off and left Guy with memories. *Stroke.* They'd been final-year men together in the Oxford eight. Challoner, cox; Stafford, stroke. How could he forget such a climactic experience? All along the Thames' banks the crowds wildly cheering as the dark blues and light blues fought it to the bittersweet finish.

Collapse and the agony of exhaustion, with the supreme knowledge that you'd given your all and won through. And—face to face, only a searing breath away—the never-to-be-forgotten face of the driving force, like a wizened little monkey, waving a jubilant fist under his nose, mouthing specific obscenities.

Peak point in their young lives. And Challoner, it seemed, was still up there, manipulating the effort, forever demanding the last gasp of his crew, gobbling up victories.

Guy had had some modest successes himself, but of late they'd lost their magic, blips on the downhill emotional graph since his first

160

big contract signed on the day his son had been born. In view of the recent recession he hadn't done badly, but he was conscious of a diminishing ability to meet challenges with relish. Since that student glory of the big race, few sublime moments, no calls nowadays for the ultimate effort. Life without balls. Even a tendency to consider ambition vicariously, as something for the next generation.

He wanted equally big moments for Owen, but the boy was physically slight, not built as an oarsman. His peaks must come in some other sphere. Perhaps not even academic, to judge from present form.

He stared from the window at a predictable view of right-angled walls and lacklustre evergreens. The gloom of the sunless Sunday morning had got through to him. There seemed no real point in his trekking down to Bristol. He and Challoner owed each other nothing. They'd gone their separate ways with separate aims. Why should he trouble to involve himself again? Except that what Challoner proposed was work of a kind, and he had to admit that for some time work had been his sole obsession. And what alternative was on offer?

He could go and see what was bugging old Pete, sort him out if need be. On his way there he'd pick up some stuff from the trailer, data and photographs which might prove relevant to the 'big industrial development' the financier had in mind.

*   *   *

The fire door at the top of the cellar steps was
so solid that no warning had come of the man's
approach. It swung inwards and he stood
there, silhouetted against a more powerful
light, with a sawn-off shotgun cradled on one
arm, and peered over to make sure they'd
prepared no reception for him. As he came
slowly down she could sense the tension in him
matching her own. She remembered then
something from a hospital lecture in student
days, when they were warned of break-ins,
burglars and druggies: 'You will be scared, but
remember—so are they. Keep everything low
key for everyone's safety.'

Paul hadn't had that warning, wasn't in any
fit state to think straight. He raised himself on
one elbow, got his back against the wall and
tried to stand, shouting all the time, filth and
obscenities, as if the man was someone he
could control, some stupid oaf who'd got his
wires crossed.

She moved across in front of him,
protectively, as she saw the man's gun come
up, and Paul reached out, took a handful of her
dress to drag her aside. She heard it rip as she
stumbled to her knees, and the whispering
menace in the man's voice as he bent over,
ready to club her husband down.

She stared up at the black balaclava still masking his features, but the face had changed. She remembered last night's jeering eyes, the vicious laughter at her plight. This wasn't the same man who'd thrown her in the van. Maybe it was the other, and they'd swapped masks, or yet a third man. God, how many of them were there? Some kind of gang, organized crime, real professionals.

He'd stopped just short of hitting Paul, stood over him threateningly. Through the sewn-up mouthpiece his voice came out muffled by the thick wool. 'You're gonna make a phone call. Giddup.'

'Look,' she said desperately, 'you've made a mistake. We're not important ...'

He turned his head towards her without moving his body, and at the same time he jabbed forward with the gun's butt. It took Paul in the chest and he doubled up backwards, slid down the wall. 'Tell yer woman to shut it. Git back on yer feet.'

She forgot all warnings, began to shout, fists clenched, standing over her husband's fallen body. 'Who the hell do you think we are? We're nothing to do with you, nothing!'

The man started to turn, ready to swing at her and she leapt away, caught her heel in her torn dress hem and went down on her back, her head hitting the concrete so that she felt the brain inside shaken loose like jelly. For a moment she could see nothing, feel nothing, then agony in her ribs as he kicked her, not seeming bothered to hurt but almost absently, clearing her out of his path.

Paul was rockily on his feet being prodded ahead towards the steps. She was too scared to cry out now, too damaged. She wound her arms round to hold herself in one piece, and when the steel door slammed shut again her body began to shake like an epileptic's.

It was then that the singing light bulb gave a soft final ping and went out, leaving her in total darkness.

*   *   *

The puncture kit *had* been time-expired. And it was Sunday, so in this medieval rural backwater there weren't any shops open. Owen wheeled the bike for two miles with the front tyre flopping on its rim until he came on a few houses with a pub. There he propped the useless thing against an ivied wall and went in for help.

When he asked—as he felt obliged to—for a half of shandy, the innkeeper gave him a surly look as if he might be a fourteen-year-old trying it on. But he sloshed the drink out and passed it over with no remark but the price.

At his arrival whatever conversation there had been stopped automatically. They were all old men there, three drinkers and the one behind the bar, chemical enemies of youth from the word go.

But they must have ridden bikes at some time. What else would there be here? Definitely not Porsche country. Tractors maybe, or the odd banger stinking of calf shit. They might have grandchildren who mended their own punctures. It was worth trying, so he asked.

You'd have thought he'd said something dirty, or spoke a foreign language. They all went on staring at him, then two of them looked at each other and nodded. The third giggled geriatrically into his half-empty tankard.

The man who'd served him with the shandy said, 'Best drink up, and be on your way. We don't serve your sort in here.'

So he downed the shandy, wiped his hands on his pants seat and considered spitting on the floor. But they weren't worth good spit, so he went. He wheeled the damn bike for another half-mile then hid it in a spinney.

Across a sloping field he made out the glint of water threading past willows and recognized where on the map he'd reached. Three miles across country and there should be a train halt, if it hadn't been closed down. If it had, he could always walk the rails as the shortest route to some place where there'd be buses.

*　　　*　　　*

Don Turley's Sunday had begun with the old

165

hag ringing up and demanding her daughter. It was late and he still had on his rumpled clothes from last night, and his mouth tasted of ashes and stale drains. When he'd hung up on her he stood under the cold shower as he was, then peeled his clothes off and let the shock of water drum on his cooling body. His head still lurched on a fairground swingboat.

He made strong coffee, drank some and vomited. Then he put on trainers and tracksuit, took a string bag and went out to find a supermarket which opened on Sundays, to replenish his stock. Hair of the bloody Baskerville that bit him.

Walking jarred his head, so he retraced his few steps, unlocked the garage and got out the Escort. While he was out he might as well pick up a decent load. He shopped, transferred it all—twelve of beer and two bottles of Bell's—to the car boot, slammed the lid shut and made it back to the house, all in under three-quarters of an hour. Which left twenty to fill before he was due in on Monday at the CID office.

He wasn't feeling up to squash or a swim. The booze would help him fill in the vacant time. He lifted the sopping garments from the bath and hung them over the garden's washing line to dry.

*   *   *

166

Without her watch Gillian couldn't tell what hour it was. She had hoped at first, as her eyes adapted slightly to the darkness, that loss of the bulb would help show up some chink of daylight from outside. But there wasn't even a pinprick. She tried believing that it was night, and managed briefly to persuade herself to sleep.

When she awoke the darkness was still there but over-printed spasmodically with moving coloured patterns, which she knew must be due to a trick of her brain, a consequence of having no solid food after Saturday's alcohol and whatever they'd used to drug her.

Yet one oblong of greyness stayed unchanging. It was high to one side of the boiler, and it struck her then that no furnace could ever have burned in a hermetically sealed cellar. Not only must there once have been a coal chute but adequate air vents too.

She groped her way along the wall and pulled herself up on the boiler's top. The flue was walled in, and after she had torn her nails prising loose a half-brick from the crumbling cement she found a metalled duct behind. Hopeless.

But the grey oblong was above her, just within reach. She used an edge of the brick to beat at it. It clanked and gave a little, letting in a thin trickle of cool air.

She went on doggedly beating at it above her head, frequently resting to let the blood flow back in her arm. Then, without warning, there was a metallic screech as the grey screen fell away, swinging by a corner. Behind was revealed a solid Victorian barred grating. There was no way out here, but at least a dull twilight now reached through. She could make out the walls again and across the cellar her own and Paul's empty mattresses.

He had been gone for an age already. What were they doing to him? The man who took him had mentioned making a phone call. What about, and to whom? Paul hadn't been capable of arguing or demanding why. He'd been led away like a zombie. They should have taken her. Paul really was in no fit state ...

But when he was pushed back through the steel door, to stumble alone down the steps, she shuddered at the thought of what they might have done to her. His face was marked with fresh blood, the lower lip split, and already a swelling on one cheek was closing the eye above it. It needed a cold compress.

Water. The men had left them a metal bowl with less than a pint on the floor in one corner. As if they were dogs. She had kicked against it in the dark and spilled half of it, but now she tore away part of her ripped skirt, soaked it and made a wad to clean off the blood.

Paul was mumbling and tried pushing her away. She held him steady, digging her fingernails in the flesh of his bare arms, and insisted he listen to her. 'What happened?

168

What did they want? Did you explain who we were?'

No, she had to give him time, let him lie still a moment and get a grip on himself. She let him fall back on his mattress where he curled up on one side, hands defensively covering his head. She could see only his mouth, a single tight line, the ends quivering like a child's when it's trying not to cry.

For the first time, seeing him defenceless, she recognized his weakness and felt doubt. Suppose it really was Paul these men were out to get. Something he'd done, and they meant to punish him.

Or something he'd not done. That was more likely: some debt he'd put off repaying. Men were like that to each other, weren't they? She'd seen TV plays where gamblers had sent out hit-men to beat up the debtors until they'd agreed to settle up.

But this wasn't like that. They hadn't just duffed him up and left him in a back street. They'd brought him here, and with herself along. They must have something else in mind. If it really was Paul they were after.

'Paul!' she appealed, desperate now for the truth. 'Paul, who are these men? Why are they doing this? Is it for money?'

'Money,' he repeated stupidly. 'Yeah, they want money.'

'How much?'

He mumbled, but she couldn't catch the

words, his voice was so slurred. Despite his condition she shook him, and momentarily his eyes met hers and held.

'Three hunnerd kay.'

'Three hundred *what?*'

'Three hunnerd thou—'

'*Three hundred thousand pounds?* Oh my God! How would we ever get hold of money like that? What the hell have you been up to?'

Paul was making an effort to sit up. He frowned in concentration. 'Not us, no. Stafford. He'll hafta pay.'

'What for?' But as she said it she knew. These goons were holding her and Paul for ransom. And the fools thought her ex-husband would come up with the money!

'Is that who they made you phone? Did you tell him that? He must have thought you'd gone out of your mind!'

''Sgot plenty. Still got the hots for you. I saw you both last nigh'. Try again later.'

'Try what? Paul, you've got to stay awake. Who will try what later?'

'Phone'm. No one home. Went on ringing.'

'But he's got a machine. Didn't you leave a message?'

Paul closed his eyes, shuddered and stayed silent.

Of course he hadn't left a message if the phone went on ringing. Guy must have forgotten to switch the machine back on before he went out. Part of his Sunday privacy. So

170

bloody civilized, while they were here in this awful place with these savage brutes. Small wonder they'd beaten Paul up some more, out of sheer frustration.

Suppose he's away on a job, gone for days, she thought. We'll be rotting here, the men upstairs getting more and more nervy, taking it out on us. Fools, fools! They should have made sure the man was available before they set this up.

Only what would Guy have done if he had answered Paul's call? She just couldn't see it. There was no love lost between the two men. He thought Paul was a shyster. He could have thought it a hoax, or at least a put-up job. If he'd accepted it at face value he might have called the police. But not if he thought any scandal over Paul would rebound on her.

This was useless: too many unknowns, too many ifs. Paul had rung, but Guy hadn't received the message. So what was due to happen next?

They had to find some other way to get to him.

She left Paul resting, gathered her torn skirt over one arm and hobbled up the steps, beat with her fists on the steel door. No good. It needed something harder. She went down again for the metal dog bowl, resoaked the cloth and laid it on Paul's cheek, let him drink the bowl dry, then went back to beat it on the door.

When the door swung inwards it caught her off balance but the man reached out and clamped his hand about her arm. 'Listen,' she said, 'it doesn't work your way. I've got a better idea.'

The second man was there in the lighted room behind him. She let herself be pulled into a stone-flagged kitchen. There was just a glimpse of a small, shuttered window and an old range in a bricked recess before she was pushed into a hard wooden chair and a cloth whipped over her eyes. She heard the steel door slammed shut again.

'So?' one of them demanded.

'You're holding my husband and me to ransom. Well, he's of no value to you. My ex-husband—Guy Stafford—wouldn't give a ha'penny for him. It's me he might pay for, so it's me you need to hang on to.

'You could let Paul go. He's no idea where we are or who you are. But he could go to Guy's flat with a note from me and wait till he gets back, explain that you'll be in touch and he mustn't tell anyone.'

She waited, praying desperately inside. The men said nothing. Blindfolded, she couldn't hear any movement from them. She guessed they were looking at each other, sizing up the odds.

'Guy will see what you've done to Paul, and that you're in earnest. He's badly hurt. He needs medical attention. Let him go. I'll write down whatever you say. And later I'll talk to Guy on the phone. He'll believe me when I tell him—how things are.'

They put her back in the cellar while they made up their minds. When the balaclava man took off her blindfold she complained about the dark. He went off to search and came back with a fresh light bulb which he went down and fixed.

Insisting on that and getting it gave her confidence. She began to think that after all she might find some way of getting them both out alive.

She had never before had to set a money value on herself. They were asking for three hundred thousand, which sounded a terrible lot to have loose in your hand. But it was just the price of a rather nice modern detached house. Their home, which Guy had made over to her on their divorce, was worth far more. Would he value her more highly than bricks and mortar? Only a second-hand wife. But a human life after all.

More to the point, could Guy get his hands instantly on a sum like that? It was only a small percentage of the value of buildings he was involved with, but his professional fee would be only a minute part, and he had to live on it, provide maintenance for Owen and cover overheads. She had never bothered to think before how much was available and where it had to go.

She'd supposed Guy was wealthy because two years back he hadn't begrudged her the settlement her solicitor had asked for. But when you looked at it another way, that was money he'd got rid of, so he was short of it now. He'd have to borrow, go to the banks or a money-lender. They'd demand collateral.

If Guy couldn't raise the money, where else could she turn? Not to Mother. What little she had might have to support two from now on, since she'd implied the new man had nothing. Mother would want to help, but wouldn't be able.

No, it all turned on what value Guy still put on her. Once it might have been worth a lot to have her returned, but would he pay that much to have her handed back to Paul?

It was bitterly ironic, and there was only one person to blame for this stink she'd got herself into. She'd loused her chances up, like she ended by lousing everything up. But this was worse than anything before, the final result of the trail of all her messes leading up to now.

She must have slept, because she was disturbed by the man coming down with Paul's clothes. No jacket, just his singlet and the dress trousers. He still seemed lethargic as she helped him put them on, but mentally he was pulling himself together, understood all right what he had to do. There was a tipsy cockiness about him. Of course, he was the optimist; saw the glass half-full when she saw it half-empty. Just because he was going free, he thought it would all work out. Well, she didn't, despite the persuasion she'd frantically employed on the men who held them.

He lay back to rest while they allowed her up to the kitchen to copy out the note they had ready. The men were both hooded again, so this time they didn't cover her eyes.

She would have corrected the grammar at two points, but then realized that the mistakes would show she hadn't composed the note herself but written it under dictation. And these were clues, after all. Even if she never got free, Guy would have something for the police to work on after they found her body.

She was sent back to the cellar before they were ready to leave with Paul, but not before Onionhead took kitchen shears from a drawer and chopped off a chunk of her hair.

It made her feel sick, because she recognized the cliché. First they'd send a lock of hair. After that, a finger.

CHAPTER FOURTEEN

Monday, 24 August. 11.00 hours

WHILE THE LAST ARRIVALS FILED in and found places, Superintendent Yeadings slowly scanned the gathering. There was something

175

here beyond the normal tension arising from the opening of a murder investigation. An undercurrent that was more immediate, almost personal. Accentuated perhaps by the clear dichotomy between uniform and CID? There was a watchful relish on the part of the former, while the two local Detective-Constables displayed a definite unease.

So where did this tension spring from? Some gossip among the lower ranks which he wasn't yet privy to? There were times when he would give a lot to be an informed fly on the canteen wall. Well, doubtless any mysteries would surface by themselves and shortly be made plain.

He cleared his throat to begin. 'Some of you I've had the pleasure of working with before. For those others, my name is Superintendent Yeadings. On my right, soon to brief you, is Detective-Inspector Mott, and on my left Detective-Constable Zyczynski—who may allow any of you with severe speech difficulties to address her as "Z".

'Throughout this investigation you will be working under DI Mott—in the absence on sick leave of your DI Hadden—assisted by DS Turley when contacted.'

There was clear body language in reply to this statement, uniformed men contacting each other out of the corner of their eyes, the two Detectives staring deadpan ahead.

Right, so the friction was somehow

connected with Turley. What had happened to the wretched fellow? Why wasn't he here?

'Shortly before 8.30 this morning,' Yeadings continued imperturbably, 'the body of a man in his middle thirties was discovered partly hidden by a thorn hedge in the parking area of the *Dos Paragueros* pull-in near the eastbound motorway exit. He wore only a singlet and trousers, no underclothes, no footwear, and he had not walked to where he was found. His injuries are consistent with his having been the victim of a violent attack. So far there are no indications that he had made any attempt to defend himself. He carried no identification. Empty pockets. Despite the hot night, the trousers and singlet he wore were quite damp, and judging from their size we can assume them to be his own. There was considerable congealed blood on the head, neck and shoulders. It had been a fine night and the body was dry.

'Dr Littlejohn's preliminary report will be available at next briefing, but for the moment you may consider that he had probably been dead for anything up to ten or eleven hours. That assumption is based solely on the progress of rigor mortis which we all know depends on many external factors and varies according to age, health and so on. It would be safer, at present, to work on the assumption that the unknown man died, probably as a result of his injuries, sometime yesterday—

Sunday—afternoon or evening. Examination of stomach contents may later help us to fix that time more precisely.

'After answering any questions you may have on what I've said so far, Detective-Inspector Mott will give you further details and assign duties.'

A tentative hand went up from the back of the room and the expected query was voiced. 'Sir, in view of the motorway being near, could it have been an RTA death?'

Yeadings nodded to Mott who disposed of that one. 'Bruises to the upper arms indicate the man was gripped tightly from behind and his head bashed against some solid surface. There are also abrasions to the back of his head and neck, with particles found in his hair which resemble brickdust and flaking whitewash. No obvious tyre marks, motor oil, grease or glass fragments yet found on clothes or body. Next?'

'Could he have been dunked in a stream or pond?'

'Because of the wet singlet and trousers? We can't rule that out on present findings, but the water would have been free of obvious mud or slime. Similarly we can't rule out the man having been dumped in a bath while wearing the clothing. On the other hand, as the Superintendent mentioned, the body's surface was quite dry.'

'Could he have drowned?'

'We shall know that after the pathologist's

report comes in. Due to the lapse of time since death, there was no external frothing which might suggest exceptional fluid in the lungs.'

Mott surveyed the room and was met with various expressions of curiosity, fascination, assumed casualness and would-be sagacity.

'Right. Now let's consider this: the man's trousers were black, and braided down the outer seam. Which indicates they belonged with a dinner-jacket. Question one, is this a deliberate red herring to fox us? Question two, where is the upper half? Question three, who would have been wearing such an outfit on a hot Sunday night in August?

'We want that missing jacket. It could have the maker's name in it, or even the dead man's.

'Also, you know your area, you know the people in it. Does the type of clothing provide any suggestions as to our body's identity?'

A stolid sergeant in uniform moved his weight from one leg to the other. He had come in too late for a seat and had to lean his bulk against the wall. 'There's not many hotels hereabouts use waiters,' he commented. 'If you'd said Saturday night ...'

'Go on.'

'Well, there was this special do. The Summer Ball out at Chardleigh Place. A charity thing. All the big nobs round here go. Guests wear black ties. So do the male catering staff.'

'Was there a police presence?'

'Among the guests, the Chief Constable
179

certainly. And we always send a local man on duty. The short straw sort of thing.'

There was an instantly suppressed buzz. Yeadings leaned forward, alerted to the electrically charged atmosphere. He guessed the name just a fraction of a second before the policeman gave it.

'DS Turley was present, sir.'

'Has anyone seen Turley since Saturday night?' Mott asked crisply.

There was total silence, then Lew Duke spoke up, flushed with embarrassment. 'Our stiff wasn't the Skipper, sir. A complete unknown to me.'

There was a ripple of muttered comment, rough-humoured.

Mott gave them three seconds and resumed. 'Well, I suppose that's something to be grateful for. Photographs of the body should be here at any moment. I want them circulated, part of routine house-to-house inquiries. We shall need the Chardleigh Place caterers interviewed. As a priority I want to contact anyone likely to recognize most of the guests present on Saturday night.'

'Charlie Morgan,' said a man in the front row. 'He'd be the one to ask. Their security man on the door. Been doing it for ten years or more, knows all the big nobs. He lives in the village, School Lane, down behind the bus station.'

'That's your job, then. Go and find him.

Report immediately to WDC Zyczynski by phone if you come up with a name. Ah, this looks like the photos now.'

A policewoman came in with a box-file which she dumped where Mott had made room for it on the desk. Z slipped the first photograph out and handed it to the man in the front row, taking a note of his number on a clipboard. Mott turned his attention to tasking the rest.

*   *   *

Mike Yeadings found himself expected to take tea with the uniformed Superintendent in his office. 'Look,' he demanded, 'what's this with Turley? In DI Hadden's absence surely the man knows to report in?'

James Tolliday sucked in his lean cheeks. 'I've had a call from Casualty at the local hospital. He's there receiving treatment for a fall. Not serious, as I understand, but he needed a few stitches in one hand and his cheek.'

'Fall?' Yeadings questioned sardonically. A further suspicion raised its ugly head. '*Is* Turley in fact off duty?'

Tolliday busied himself with pouring. 'No, he was due in at nine this morning. I'm waiting for details.'

'I'll be interested to hear them,' Yeadings said drily.

Tolliday heaved a sigh, holding out cup and saucer. 'Help yourself to milk and sugar.'

'Turley,' Yeadings insisted. 'Has he been in a brawl?'

'If he has, it's his last as a sergeant. Admittedly the man has problems.'

'*Is* a problem, as I understand it.'

'Has a temper. Normally he can cope. Because of his earlier promising performance we've had to—well, felt it better to—turn a blind eye. But he's at the end of his free run now. I had already put in for CID replacements. With Hadden going sick ...'

'That doesn't concern me. I need to know if Turley's usable now.'

Tolliday slumped into his seat, glared at the visitor, then reached for a phone. 'Anything in yet on Turley?' he demanded. 'He ... what? Right. Send him up at once.'

He looked across at Yeadings. 'He's back in the building. Getting notes on your briefing from DC Duke.'

Yeadings put down his tea untasted. 'If you're keeping him on the team he can report to my Inspector. Now perhaps you'll excuse me ...?'

*   *   *

There was an almost immediate reply from the constable sent after Charlie Morgan, and it was negative. According to a neighbour,

182

Charlie had left the previous afternoon to spend a week with his married son at Weston-super-Mare. When his address was available, Rosemary Zyczynski would contact Avon police and fax the photograph through.

Meanwhile, Dr Littlejohn had fixed the post-mortem for that evening at 6.00. 'As an appetizer before dinner,' Mott said darkly. 'And he's offering us open house.'

Yeadings nodded. 'You can count me in. Who are you tasking?'

'I'll be there, Z and young Duke, besides Scenes of Crime and the Coroner's Officer. Littlejohn performs better with a good audience.'

'Give Beaumont a buzz,' Yeadings said. 'I'd feel happier with him across here manning the caravan. He can alternate with Z. D'you need anyone else?'

'Not until things start moving,' Mott said cautiously. 'Then we'll have to play it by ear. Have you got any of your famous vibes on this one?'

The Superintendent grunted. 'It feels quirky. The wet clothes on a dry body. The idea of dress clothes and bare feet. Food for thought there. Has DS Turley reported to you?'

Mott looked up from the notes he'd been making. 'He's fit enough to use. Physically, that is. Hungover mainly. His injuries are consistent with an argument with a dustbin and some concrete steps. Palm and cheek, both

183

on the left side. He's right-handed, but has no bruised knuckles.'

'So we've got us a drunk?'

'In mitigation, Lew Duke told Z the man had domestic troubles.'

'And, what's more, his DCs gossip.' Yeadings sighed.

'It was intended as an excuse for him.'

'What a bloody shambles,' said his chief. 'Let's go and check in at the Robin Hood.'

'Green Man, sir,' Mott reminded him.

'You want to argue, Angus? They'll probably be robbers, anyway.'

*   *   *

Rosemary Zyczynski received the call from Avon police as she was setting off for the post-mortem. She had time to phone the identification through to Mott's hotel room before they were due to meet up at the mortuary.

'A man called Stafford. He was at Chardleigh Place Saturday night. The address is Bentham Lodge, Maze Hill, Fords Green. Morgan thinks he's an architect. It's the wife he knows best. She used to be a nurse at Amersham Hospital.'

'Right. Change of plan, Z. We don't really need you for the PM. Put Turley on, will you? I want you to go with him when he visits the dead man's widow.'

Turley sounded uptight as he made the call. Z hadn't passed the info through him and he hadn't cared for that. 'Stafford?' he queried. 'Yeah, he was there Saturday night. But your girl's got it wrong. Stafford moved out of Bentham Lodge a coupla years back. Lives alone. Has a flat on Southside.'

'Take a look at it sharpish.'

'I'll need a DC. You won't be needing Duke.'

'Take Zyczynski.' Mott made it curt. Turley was out to make trouble. There was a brief silence, then, 'Right. The *girl* it is, then.'

Like many privately-owned police cars, Turley's was a Ford Escort. He walked ahead of Z, climbed in the passenger side and left her to drive. She clipped herself in without comment and prepared to follow his directions. He left them to the last possible moment, so that she had inadequate time for turns and use of indicators. 'You taken your test yet?' he asked, deadpan.

She didn't answer, scanning the nearside for Stafford's block of flats. 'I asked you a question, WDC whatever-your-name-is.'

'Yes, thank you,' she said serenely, adding, 'We seem to be here.'

He gave her a hard stare. 'If you know that much, how come you got his address wrong first time?'

'I looked him up in the telephone directory,' she said tersely, 'while you were speaking to

185

Inspector Mott.'

'Brilliant.' His sarcasm was heavy. 'Now you going to break down the door?'

'After you, Sergeant.'

Turley spoke into the entry phone and they were let in by an elderly woman who lived above Stafford. The prospect of a police visit had her waiting tremulously on the landing as they came up the stairs. 'Is something wrong?' she demanded breathlessly. 'I don't think Mr Stafford has been here for a day or two.'

'Do you know if anyone held a spare key for him?' Z asked.

'I'm afraid not. He didn't have things delivered here.'

'Nothing for it then,' Turley said with some satisfaction. He moved back to the stairs, charged and booted the lock.

'One more good one,' he announced and repeated his effort, shoulders first. The door panel splintered and a second kick got him in.

'They're not very strong, these modern doors,' said the elderly woman, distressed at the violence to property. She began to follow them in, clutching nervously at her double string of pearls.

There didn't appear to have been any earlier break-in. The place was unnaturally tidy. Apart from a single mug and plate left upturned to drain in the kitchen, it could have been a showhouse. Nothing here gave any clue to Stafford's personal habits, nor to why he should have been killed.

Z blocked the woman's way. 'Thank you, Mrs—'

'Mrs Mortimer. Are you sure you need to...? I mean, I don't think Mr Stafford would care for anybody going through his things.'

Turley came back and confronted her. 'How well did you know the dead man?'

She gawked at him, clutching at the door jamb. 'Dead? But he can't be. How...?'

Z took her arm and led her to a chair. 'That's why we're here, Mrs Mortimer. I'm sorry.'

'It—it's a shock,' she said unnecessarily. 'So young. Such a nice man, so respectable.'

'That so?' Turley came and stood over her. 'You wouldn't have seen much of him, living upstairs. People coming and going, that sort of thing.'

'He—there weren't many visitors. He was no trouble, always quiet. Even his son, a nice boy, polite for his age.'

'That so?' Turley turned away impatiently. 'Best leave us to it. Z, empty everything out of the fridge-freezer. I'll take the man's desk.'

Mrs Mortimer rose and backed away. Her heel taps receded uncertainly in the outside corridor as they began their search.

As Z had guessed, there was nothing untoward among the frozen foods. Turley merely meant to keep her out of his way while he looked for anything significant. She took her time removing the jars and packets, then

187

tidily returning them the way they had been. All she had to report was that the late Guy Stafford had a taste for pizzas and lemon sole, with a variety of frozen vegetables. There were no puddings or ice cream in the freezer, a few handy packs of beer together with dairy items in the fridge. To cover her back against Turley she emptied out all the ice cubes, left them in the sink and refilled the containers with water.

When she went into the living-room she found books, papers and tape cassettes spilled over the floor all round the Detective-Sergeant's chair. He had a cheroot clamped between his teeth. 'Find an ashtray,' he commanded over his shoulder.

Apparently Stafford had been a non-smoker. She came up with a saucer. Bringing it from the kitchen she met a tall, sandy-haired man coming through the open doorway from the stairs. He stopped in his tracks, facing her. 'What the blazes . . . ?'

There was the sound of a chair going over as Turley crashed out from the living-room. For a heavy man he could move quickly when he needed to. He squared up to the newcomer, eyes narrowed. 'Who've we got here?' he demanded.

'No. I should ask. Who the devil are you?'

'Thames Valley Police,' snapped Turley. 'Answer my question. What are you doing in this flat?'

The man glanced back quickly at the

splintered door, then returned his icy gaze to the policeman. 'I happen to live here. Guy Stafford. What's happened? Was there a break-in?'

CHAPTER FIFTEEN

TURLEY TURNED INSTANTLY ON Z. 'Where the bloody hell did you get your information?'

While she fought down her embarrassment Stafford demanded of her, 'Are you in charge here?'

'He is,' and she nodded towards the DS.

Wherever the responsibility lay, it was a police gaffe. Someone had to accept it.

'There's been a death,' Z said shortly. 'Identified as a Guy Stafford of this address. Can you prove who you are, sir?'

The big man walked past her and surveyed the mess strewn over the living-room floor. His eyes went to the desktop where he seized a passport Turley had set aside. He waved it under the detective's nose. 'It's got my photograph. Are you blind, man? Unless the dead man's my double!'

Turley gritted his teeth. 'I haven't viewed the body.'

'There are scene-of-crime photos,' said Z faintly.

'So where's my copy?' Turley grated.

'I can't believe this,' said Stafford. 'I come home to find you've broken in—it *was* you two, I suppose? And neither of you seems to have a good excuse for being here. Who's your senior officer? And where are your warrant cards?'

It was galling. They'd lost the initiative entirely, had to endure the man's ringing through for Superintendent Tolliday to confirm the operation, and who was, apparently, an acquaintance. When he was satisfied that it was an official presence, Stafford turned coldly back to Turley. 'While I am waiting for them to make a full explanation, I'd like to hear your version of this farce. Who claimed that the dead man was me?'

As Turley hadn't been in at that stage, Z saw it as her job to shoulder the blame. 'Sir, because the body wore dress trousers, a connection was made with Saturday night's event at Chardleigh Place. Their security man on the door identified your—that is, the dead man's—photograph.'

'So who is this doorman?'

'A Charlie Morgan, sir.'

'I don't know any Charlie Morgan.'

'He claimed to know you, sir.' She stopped, aware there was an anomaly. 'Actually he said it was your wife he knew better. And he provided the wrong address ...'

'I have no wi—what address was that?'

'Bentham Lodge, Maze Hill, Fords Green.'

Stafford's features froze. 'Did you contact Bentham Lodge?'

'No, sir. We understood you had moved here.'

'So you thought you had the address wrong. Whereas you've got the wrong—My God!' He spun round and reached again for the phone, rapidly pressed out a number. While he waited for a reply he snapped, 'The dead man's photograph—show me!'

Z pulled the print from her shoulder-bag and Stafford almost tore it from her hand. He was breathing quickly, scowled at the picture and thrust it on Turley. 'Late in the day, but you might as well take a look at your body. Is that man me? Damn, no answer.' He slammed down the receiver and moved impatiently away to stand with his back to them, staring from the window.

'Your dead man,' he said, when he had mastered his feelings, 'is my *ex*-wife's present husband. Not that that in any way excuses the complete balls-up you've created. His name's Randall, Paul Randall.'

'Not our mistake,' Turley claimed quickly. 'It's that fool doorman's. How does he happen to know your name and not the other man's?'

'Does it matter?'

Z frowned, thinking back to the wording of the report. 'He said your wife had been a nurse at Amersham hospital. Maybe he knew her as Mrs Stafford there?' she ventured.

191

Guy Stafford grunted. 'I'm going over to Bentham Lodge now. Something may have happened to Gillian. There's my son too. God knows where he is.'

'The boy,' Turley suddenly exploded. 'I've met him. We had some trouble with him just a few days back.'

But Stafford was racing away down the stairs and stopped only to shout up, 'See that someone puts the place straight. And have that door mended before I see you again.'

Turley whipped round on Z. 'You heard what he said. Do it. This is what comes of letting women in on the action. No notion what you're getting involved in. Rushing in like a bull at a gate!'

He went out scowling, leaving her to make her own way back.

'Cow,' she said quietly after counting to ten. 'A cow, *waiting* at a gate. A totally different kind of beast.'

* * *

Superintendent Yeadings was called out of the post-mortem and received news of the development with mounting anger. 'I have never,' he told Mott on his return to the bright lights and carnage, 'come across such a shambolic crowd in my life. Get in there, Angus, and sort them out. Bentham Lodge, Maze Hill, and the body's name is now

192

Paul Randall.'

*   *   *

Guy Stafford no longer held a key to his one-time home, but he knew where the spare one was hidden. There was no one to prevent his bursting in and searching through the whole house before any police could get there.

A patrol car was the first to follow him into the driveway, throwing up gravel as it screamed to a halt at the front door. Turley, having parked on the pavement outside, roared in on foot and tore strips off the uniformed men for ruining possible tyre tracks. By the time Mott joined them the air was vibrant with ill-contained spleen. He sent the patrol men outside to radio for a Scenes of Crime team and nodded to Turley to join him with Stafford in the study.

'Now, sir,' he suggested, 'would you tell us when you last saw the dead man, what the circumstances were, and any information you may think relevant to the case.'

*   *   *

Now that the police had already dropped their large feet deeply into Stafford's affairs and occasioned damage to his property, reports were coming in from all sides confirming the identity of the dead man in the photograph as

193

Paul Randall. A certain amount of glee at Thames Valley's discomfiture was observable in some quarters, not least among staff of the local newspaper who'd had reporting freedom curtailed at police insistence in the past.

Mike Yeadings, fresh from observing Dr Littlejohn's dissecting skills, had taken on the mantle of 'a Thames Valley spokesman' and was to give an evening press conference, offering himself as butt to journalists' criticisms. There was little fact to clothe the gaffe of initial failure to name the body correctly, and Superintendent Tolliday was privately threatening dire measures to deal with whoever had been responsible for the premature leak of Stafford's name to the outside world.

While promising further disclosures in the near future, Yeadings sketched the general features of the body's discovery, suppressing only details of the injuries, any precise estimate of the time of death, and the curious fact, phoned in from Bentham Lodge, that Paul Randall's car, a red Sierra, had been discovered in the garage there and was at present being plastic-wrapped for examination by the scientific experts at Aldermaston. He appealed for anyone who had seen the car, and either Randall or his wife, during the early hours of Sunday morning, to ring in with the details.

Guy Stafford himself had refused to speak

194

with the media, being preoccupied with the mystery of his son's and ex-wife's disappearance.

The nursing agency which employed Gillian Randall had recorded three separate messages for her on the answering machine at the house. It appeared that at 9.00 a.m. that morning she had failed to relieve the night nurse on duty with her present client. Nor had she advised the agency of her intended absence.

There were no messages for or from Owen Stafford, and Turley's suggestion that he might be with friends in Alma Terrace had proved incorrect.

At the Incident Caravan parked by the *Dos Paragueros* caff, a stream of callers had offered sightings of Randall in a dozen different places at a score of different times, and these reports were now being followed up. The abstraction of information about cars seen overnight in the vicinity of where the body was found was proving a heavier task. Mott decided to draft a request for help to be broadcast on the late television news.

As he fell wearily into his hotel bed in the early hours of Tuesday, the score stood at one suspected murder and two missing persons. He was wakened at a little before 3.00 a.m. with a message that Owen Stafford had turned up at Bentham Lodge with blistered feet and a tale of a hiking-biking two-day marathon. His father had arranged a room for him overnight at the same hotel where he was staying at present. An appointment had been made for Mott to interview them both that morning at 10.50.

Before the meeting it was necessary to get a formal identification of the body at the mortuary. Owen Stafford who, in his mother's absence, must have known the dead man as well as anybody, was a minor. That left his father. Mott was curious to know what reaction Guy Stafford would show in facing his supposed rival's body. It would certainly be necessary to look into the circumstances of the divorce and the financial background of all parties.

*   *   *

Detective-Sergeant Don Turley was in two minds about continuing to ring around demanding information on Marcia's whereabouts. He had drawn a blank at Nancy Carter's, where her husband was at home minding the toddler and four-year-old. Nancy was at her mother's in Eastbourne, in daily touch with the hospital, following the old lady's stroke. Carter had been emphatic about Marcia not having been in touch. 'Not that I wouldn't have jumped at the chance,' he said gloomily. 'Any help at all with looking after kids would be heaven-sent.'

Apart from Nancy, who had been an early typing-pool acquaintance, Marcia had kept up

196

few contacts. Turley had a vague memory of her mentioning two girls from schooldays, but had no idea of their names or if they still lived in the area. She had worked in an office for only a short time after her marriage and wasn't gregarious. Hadn't many interests at all. However, he felt he had shown more curiosity about her affairs than her recent behaviour merited. So when he was summoned on Tuesday morning to hear from Superintendent Tolliday that Marcia had been reported as a missing person by her mother, he was left with little to offer.

It was hard enough to keep a rein on his language, let alone cast around for reasons for the stupid woman's going off. 'You know how women are,' he complained. 'No kids, nothing to occupy her mind, they get funny ideas.'

The Superintendent, whose rosy little wife was practical rather than imaginative, might have pretended agreement, but for having been briefed on Turley's personal background. He was a thumper. They knew that from his professional record.

Rumour had it that Marcia Turley had twice been seen with a black eye. He knew as well as any the hazards of the job. You built up a case, put heart and soul into nailing the villain and then Crown Prosecution said it wouldn't hold, or some oaf made a premature move and the evidence fell apart. Some of the old school just hadn't the self-discipline to take it and walk away. Drawn from the wrong background, too near in type to the violent men they were dealing with, they had to take it out on someone. Sometimes physically.

He didn't want a scandal just now, especially with Yeadings on his patch. Maybe he should have made a move sooner, got Turley counselled, sent him on a stress-management course, for what such things were worth. He wasn't convinced as yet that they were anything but an encouragement to further quirky behaviour. But if things went badly wrong, if the woman had done something really silly, Tolliday needed to be seen to have taken some action.

'Gone off on her own to think things over,' Turley assured him. 'Her old mum's an invalid, a depressive. She'd have got on Marcia's nerves, I guess. She was going to stay a couple of weeks with her for company,' he lied, 'but it would take someone with a lot more sticking power than Marcia, believe me.'

'But surely she'd have told someone where she was going from there?'

'You'd think so. Anyone sensible would. I guess they had a row. The old girl's probably trying to make trouble all round.'

Tolliday wasn't convinced. He had a feeling he'd been soft-soaped, but he was in a vulnerable position, with Hadden gone and Turley's presence vital to keep the locals' end up with the incoming murder team.

198

'Get over to see your mother-in-law,' he ordered. 'Hertford, isn't it? Make her quieten down if she can't prove there's genuine cause for anxiety. And get straight back. We're short-staffed enough already.'

Driving out there, frustrated by crawling traffic on the choked M25, Turley stewed over how he'd deal with the old woman. Much though she got up his nose, he'd have to put on an act, pretend it had been his own generous notion to come out and cheer the old misery up. He weighed the option of saying he'd heard from Marcia and she was all right. It could keep everyone off his back just a little while longer.

* * *

Mott despatched Rosemary Zyczynski to the Incident Caravan as soon as DS Beaumont arrived. There were women witnesses to be dealt with, waitresses at the *Dos Paragueros*, whereas he was sure the younger Stafford, if not his father, would respond better at an all-male interview.

The architect looked grim, the boy ill at ease. The first matter to be disposed of was the man's relationship with the dead one, and for this stage young Owen was asked to wait in a separate room.

Word was already through from the mortuary that Guy had put a name to the body. It was, as he'd already stated, that of his ex-wife's second husband.

A few obvious questions gave Mott the background. Gillian had left Guy and her son, over three years back, to share Randall's flat over a sports shop which he was then managing at Wycombe. She had met him when he was recommended to her as a golf coach. She had taken up the game to widen her social circle, joining a women's club which met on Tuesday afternoons. She hadn't kept at it for long because it was difficult to get free from nursing duties always on the same day. She had, however, become more closely involved with Randall.

The divorce had been amicable, according to Stafford, although Mott received a strong impression that he had been anything but happy about it. Gillian Stafford had had her way, and subsequently became Gillian Randall.

The surrender of his home and his agreement to allow Owen to live with his mother struck Mott as either feeble-minded, quixotic or something more sinister. It had happened at the point when the sports firm employing Randall had gone bankrupt, so he lost his job, and for extra income Gillian had begun moonlighting in nursing's private sector.

'It's a large house,' Guy excused himself. 'Too big for us when we were there, but I suppose it was always in my mind then that we might have more children.'

'And later that there might be children of your wife's second marriage?'

That, apparently, was too much for Stafford to admit to. He stayed silent a moment. 'I guess I expected them to sell. It was worth quite a bit then, less now perhaps because the market's in recession. It would have set them up and disposed of any further liability on my part. I didn't want to sell it myself and I didn't want Gillian's maintenance forever hanging over my head.'

'Though you would be covering your son's expenses until he was of age.'

'Until he was able to support himself, yes. That's different. I expected—hoped—always to stay in touch with Owen.'

'You didn't dispute your ex-wife's right to custody of him?'

'Custody? He isn't a prisoner. As I saw it, he'd be better off in what he'd always known as his home. More room, stable, not disturbed by my repeated comings and goings.'

'Although you expected them to sell the home.'

'I wanted him to be with—them. To support his mother if—if things didn't turn out as she expected.

'Look, Inspector, I've allowed you to pry and probe this far because I know it's a serious matter and I'm anxious as hell about where

201

Gillian's got off to, but you'll have to draw the line there. I don't properly understand myself what I felt when we split up. The important thing is that I didn't care for Randall but I wouldn't have done anything to harm him, or hurt her. That's what you're really after, isn't it?'

It had to be enough. At any rate for the moment. 'Shall we ask your son to join us now? I need to check on his whereabouts for the past few days.'

'And mine, I imagine?'

'That too, sir. It's routine to ask these questions in the investigation of a serious crime.'

'In a murder case, you mean?'

'If that is what it turns out to be, yes.'

CHAPTER SIXTEEN

Tuesday, 25 August

DETECTIVE-SERGEANT BEAUMONT HAD never worked on a case in Fords Green before and leaned towards his inspector's view of it as a no-account backwater. Not that he imagined the local plods would let him function without making the usual efforts to trip the unwary. He'd been warned that Turley would resent a newcomer of equal rank, and he decided to test the water—even the coffee—at canteen level first. It suited him admirably to be left in charge of the Stafford lad while Mott, with Yeadings sitting in, dealt with the father.

'Fancy a bevvy?' he inquired, looking in on the room where Owen had been left to his own devices.

'Not really.' He was dissociating himself from the whole scene.

Beaumont allowed his Pinocchio features to droop. 'Pity. Rather fancied a cuppa myself. It's more cheerful downstairs.'

He watched the boy consider whether to be obstructive or give in. 'Pepsi, Sprite, coffee?'

'All right then. Maybe a cola. Will there be a long wait?'

'Just until they're through with asking your Dad about Paul Randall.'

Beaumont led the way, unerringly making for the smell of grilling bacon. There were half a dozen uniformed men and a woman at two tables. He went to the hatch for his order before turning and nodding in their direction. The conversation dwindled to silence. Their eyes went curiously over him, then turned on the boy.

'And a Danish,' he told the woman serving them. 'Owen, isn't it? Want a sticky bun?'

He didn't; he was looking pretty sick anyway. Worrying about his father, probably. Brooding, wondering how much bad blood there'd actually been between his mother's two husbands.

When they were seated, Owen tore back the cola ring-pull and took a drink from the can. 'Have you heard—is there any news of my mother?'

'Not yet. Have you any idea where she might have gone?'

'She hasn't *gone* anywhere,' he said with sudden fury. 'Something's happened to her. She can't have had anything to do with—with Randall's death.'

'Maybe not.' Beaumont sugared his coffee. 'That what you called him—Randall? Not his first name?'

'What do you think?'

'Didn't care for the man?'

'He—oh, it doesn't matter. He's dead.'

A relief to the boy, Beaumont decided, but he didn't say it aloud. He had spent twenty minutes on the phone to Z, boning up on the case's outlines. A lot of nasty undercurrents in this family, for all the apparently civilized way things had been managed, settlements made, living arrangements regularized.

Owen raised his eyes from the can of drink as a burst of laughter came from over by the hatch. Something he saw there made him start slightly and his face began flushing. A constable turning away with a loaded tray locked glances with him, hesitated, seemed about to come over, then moved on.

Beaumont followed the man with his eyes:

someone to check up on, but later. The kid had been patently embarrassed.

'Smoke?' He offered a battered packet he kept for such occasions.

'I don't.'

'Nor do I. Carry these to remind myself of mind over matter. Till the next time it beats me,' he added gloomily. He let the boy rest with his thoughts, which weren't good ones. There'd be questions enough for him to answer when they went back upstairs.

A WPC came with a message from Mott. They went up to join Stafford père and the two detectives. The boy's eyes lit at once on the recording equipment. 'Are you taping these interviews?'

'Not at this point,' Mott said easily. 'Take a seat. We're following up as far as we can the movements of your mother and Paul Randall after the charity ball. They were seen together at the end, but there was a whole crowd leaving and some confusion. We believe they may not have left by the main driveway, which would have been the nearest route home.

'Did you happen to see your stepfather's red Sierra before they left to go out Saturday night?'

'No.' He stared noncommittally back, more intent on his negative than on the unexpected question. A thought struck him. 'Wait a minute.'

'Yes?'

'I did. He wanted me to wash it.'

'And did you?'

'No.' How had he replied? Had he actually told Randall to get knotted, or only thought it? Then the scene came back.

'I said I wasn't a boy scout.'

'So he had to wash it himself?'

'Took it to Batt's car-wash, I guess.'

'But at least you saw it in the driveway that afternoon?'

'Yes, it was pretty muddy.'

'Did you have occasion to see it from the front? Would you have noticed anything unusual about it?'

Owen frowned. 'Like balloons or something?'

'Like damage, marks of any kind?'

Owen let it sink home. 'You mean there are dents now? There was a crash? It got back all right. I heard it driven in. Only, quietly.'

'When would this be?'

'Early morning. I didn't look at the time. It woke me up. I sleep that side of the house.'

He was trying to remember. 'There was something about it ...'

'Something unusual?'

'Yes. Quiet, like I said. And then—yes, it was the garage door. He didn't use the zapper. The car stopped and I heard someone get out. Then the door was raised by hand. I wasn't properly awake then, but I remembered it sort of got to me. Randall and my mother have those remote

206

control units. They always use them to get in. I suppose they must both have left them at home.'

Mott made a note to initiate a search. 'So you would have assumed your pare—your mother and her husband had returned home.'

Owen was trying to remember. 'I think I did. But they were very quiet. I didn't actually hear them come in.'

'Nor anyone outside walking away?'

This was a new idea for him. He shook his head. 'I guess I fell asleep again.' Suddenly he looked up at his father and a flash of horror crossed his face, quickly extinguished.

Beaumont, leaning back against the wall, silently watching, thought—ugh, he's just realized his old man could have done the other one in.

Mott turned to Guy Stafford. 'Do you still have a remote control unit for the garage door, sir?'

'No,' the man said shortly. He'd seen that one coming, knew he must be the main suspect.

'Well, back to the car itself,' Mott said, turning to Owen. 'You didn't answer my question about noticing any damage.'

'There wasn't any, I'm almost certain. I looked at it, really saw it, when he said that about me cleaning it. I would have noticed if it had had a bash. Anyway, he was funny about that car. He wouldn't have been seen driving it with anything wrong.' He stared at Mott between the eyes. 'What's happened to it?'

The DI considered him long, then relented. 'Glass of the front driving-side headlight was broken, mostly missing, but the bulb still functions. We've had a minor accident reported in the grounds of Chardleigh Place. No witnesses at the time, but a man was injured early Sunday morning at the rear of the main building. He said he'd gone into the bushes for a call of nature, was dazzled by sudden headlights as he came out, and struck by a car leaving down the back driveway. It failed to stop.

'If it was your stepfather's car, he was heading away from home. We don't know why, unless there was an impossible crush at the front gate.'

Owen kept his face deadpan, furiously thinking. Randall would have been drinking that night, probably taking drugs too. He wouldn't have dared stop and report the accident, because he'd be breathalysed. They'd have run him in and he could have lost his licence. Maybe he panicked and thought it could even be a manslaughter charge.

'Was it Mr Randall's habit to ask your mother to drive after a social outing?' Mott asked quietly.

'No!' The word came out as a croak. But he didn't know, because he had always refused to go out with them. Bad enough to endure the man at home without being seen publicly in

208

his company.

'You have the car,' Guy Stafford put in. 'Aren't there fingerprints on the steering wheel?'

'Oh yes.' Mott was giving no more away. He flicked a glance at Yeadings in case he wished to come in on the questioning. The Boss shook his head, leaning his bulk back with apparent comfort on the inadequate chair.

'So let's go over your movements for the past couple of days,' Mott invited Owen. 'Shall we start with where you were yourself on Saturday night.'

It came across quite clearly to them— accustomed as they were to adding two to two and interpreting the silences between—that Owen's was an uneasy presence at Bentham Lodge. Without claiming as much, he had avoided the other two, communicated little if at all, and either stayed away or in his own room when Gillian and her husband were at home. If he had spent all Sunday out with his bike, it would have been because he expected the couple to be recovering indoors from the previous night's socializing. But why Monday as well? Surely that was a workday? He was the only one of the three on holiday.

He offered them an involved story about a puncture, and leaving his bike in a wood on Sunday to come back to when he'd contacted a repair shop. He'd slept overnight in an abandoned railway station where vandals had

209

conveniently broken in before. Next day, when he had found a garage open, bought materials to fix the bike and trudged back, he couldn't locate the thing for some hours; all the woods looked alike in that part of the county. It was a part he hadn't been to before. When he eventually got home on Monday night the house was in darkness. Rather than risk setting off the burglar alarms and disturbing the others, he had slept on some sacks in the potting shed where a constable had found him, dead to the world, in the early hours of this morning.

All of which might or might not be true. Beaumont would have to go back with him and check on the mended bicycle tyre.

Exasperated as young Stafford was at their persistence, it struck Yeadings, the silent observer, that he was less bothered explaining about his own movements than when conjecturing about others'. And he had two main areas of anxiety: one was the suspicion that his father could be involved in Randall's death, and the other that his mother's absence indicated something even more sinister.

And that, Yeadings thought, rising as the group finally broke up, was precisely how he saw it himself. Their immediate priority was to find the woman, and at present they'd nothing to point them to her but bloodstains: those on the outer roof ledge of the Sierra and faint smears on the inside of the steering wheel

210

where an attempt had been made to wipe it clean.

Fingerprints there were, as Mott had admitted, but all smudged and in need of enhancing. And if Gillian Randall had actually driven the car away from Chardleigh Place, whose were the hands which had later overlaid her prints with the weave- and seam-marks of fabric gloves?

The way he read it was that the Randalls had been waylaid and either never reached home or were taken away immediately the car had been returned. But, for the life of him, he couldn't see why anyone holding the couple, or having stashed their bodies, should return the car to where it belonged. It struck him as unnecessary risk, not to mention waste of a valuable asset.

There had to be a second vehicle involved, since the assailant must have arrived in one, and significantly there were no bloodstains in the rear of the Sierra, which was where you would expect the Randalls to have been confined under threat. Then again, it *was* Paul Randall who'd bled, wasn't it, and not some second casualty of his drunken driving?

So was the car's return meant as a message to someone? They might know more when Aldermaston had finished going over it minutely.

'Sir.' Beaumont was leaning towards him confidentially, keeping his voice low in case the Staffords should overhear.

211

'Well?'

'I'd like to see someone downstairs before I take the lad to Bentham Lodge. Someone I think knows him.'

'Get on with it then.' Yeadings rose and looked inquiringly at Owen. 'Let's go and see what they've given me for an office. I'd like a word with you on our own.'

Owen trailed behind him along the narrow corridor and into a room partitioned with glass above waist level. Beyond it was revealed a similar-sized office with untidy desks and three detectives in shirtsleeves busy with paperwork.

'Take a chair, lad.' Yeadings seated himself at a desk furnished with three phones, eyed them suspiciously, absently took his empty pipe from his jacket pocket and beat once on the desktop with its bowl.

'This is an anxious time for your family. I hope you know that we're putting all our resources on to finding your mother. With a murder case I can call on up to seventy men and use police computer services, so we can turn them all on to the search, but the full operation's on hold until we have information coming in.

'So what can you tell me about her that will give us a lead? Who were her closest friends, was she worried about anything? Had she and Randall any special plans for the near future? Who had called at the house of late?'

As he'd feared, Owen was of little help. He

212

had played the part of outsider too thoroughly, guarded his own privacy, thereby granting his mother and her new husband the same. Now that he needed some familiarity with their comings and goings he felt guilty over his own past indifference.

He suggested the names of two fellow nurses she'd once mentioned. He even knew where she had been working for the last two weeks. And there was her mother, but they didn't seem all that close.

Friends? Well, married people didn't have them exactly. Or that was the way he saw it. Sometimes Randall and she had gone out for a meal together, but he couldn't say where or who with. No, his father never called at the house. He used a solicitor to send any messages.

'Do you have your own friends in sometimes?'

It seemed not. Then Owen hesitated. 'Well, actually, there was someone on Friday, came in for a bite at midday, on the way back from the library.'

'Could you give me his name?'

'A girl,' he blurted. 'Sister of a schoolfriend.'

'Right. So her name?'

Reluctantly he gave it.

'I'll get my woman detective to see her, ask if she noticed anything particular in the house,' said Yeadings easily. 'Females are sticklers for detail, as no doubt you've observed. At times it can be very useful.'

He tried each of the phones in turn, then went back to the middle one. 'Get me WDC Zyczynski on this line,' he demanded. He cocked an eyebrow at Owen. 'Rather a mouthful, so we call her Z.'

He waited a moment, then, 'Z? Pop back and pick up Beaumont, will you? Probably in the canteen. I'd like you to go with him and Owen Stafford to Bentham Lodge, then contact a Miss Suzanne Banks. Owen's here with me in the office.'

Rosemary, familiar with Beaumont's way of working, grinned. When she looked in on the canteen she saw a group of blue shirts in a circle with the Pinocchio face among them. He was in full anecdotal spate as she nodded across.

'So there's this American in Moscow and...' Not a flicker of his features betrayed that he'd received and understood her silent message. Z sauntered across to the hatch and examined the chocolate bars on offer.

'... and the Russki says—wait for it—"Better be a *tova*-rich than have no money at all!"'

Groans all round and the group breaking up, grinning. Z smiled. Beaumont was in, ice broken.

'You wanting me, Z?' he called across, and suddenly the others saw her. She became the centre of interest, with a noticeable straightening of shoulders and tightening of flab.

'The Boss has a job for us.'

Beaumont rose and came across, trailing his jacket. 'See you guys.' He raised a hand and followed her out.

'One of the boys,' she said to him softly over her shoulder.

'Could be quite profitable,' Beaumont claimed smugly. 'I heard a very interesting little story. About young Owen Stafford and a certain Thames Valley sergeant who shall remain nameless ...'

She turned to question him.

'... for fear of embarrassing DS Turley!'

CHAPTER SEVENTEEN

BEAUMONT AND ZYCZYNSKI FOUND PLENTY to interest them in the missing woman's home. 'Well set up, and certainly not chained to the kitchen sink,' the DS remarked sourly, eyeing the lavishly equipped domestic offices when Owen had gone off to his room. 'Would you do a bunk from luxury-living like this?'

Well, would she? Rosemary asked herself. She couldn't imagine herself as a housewife, as an anything-wife. Domesticity didn't attract her and an early acquired disenchantment with men had not been dispelled by experiences in the police force. Although not as extreme as

215

her female colleague on television who regarded men as the enemy and predator of women, she tended to over-caution. Being attractive and intelligent, she received many sexual approaches, but her repeated rebuffs had earned her a reputation for aloofness.

Equally cool towards fellow women officers, and undoubtedly feminine, she was spared the accusation of lesbianism directed against some of her women colleagues in the force. Ignoring sexist remarks made to goad her, Z refused to retaliate. Most times it suited her that within the Yeadings team she was astigmatically regarded as a decent enough chap and an asset in the investigation of serious crimes. Without admitting it, the others closed protectively round her when violence threatened, a factor she appreciated and resented equally.

Ambivalence to the job was a trait she frankly owned to and which she could not define as easily as did Yeadings with his 'tough centre with a soft exterior' appreciation. She wanted above all to be a good jack. And she had never in her life wanted to be a man.

'Very well equipped,' she now gave as her opinion of the kitchen, and overlooked the actual question.

'But you'd expect that in what was an architect's home.'

'Mrs Randall had that outside job too,' Beaumont added. 'Private nursing. We'll have to follow up her recent patients and everyone

216

she's worked with.'

Z noticed the use of the past tense. 'Are you expecting her body to turn up?'

'I don't think she chose to disappear.'

'Unless we discover some association with a new man. We are assuming, aren't we, that the blood on the car was her husband's.'

'Until the pathologist's report says otherwise. It's of his general group, but then it's hers too. We shan't have more details for a while.'

Z helped herself to a studio portrait of Gillian Randall from its silver frame on the bookcase. There was a marked similarity between mother and son, both compact, dark-haired, intense. The woman had what Z thought of as a Welsh face with high slanting cheekbones, deliciously curving from cheek to chin, and a wide, firm, humorous mouth.

'Attractive woman,' Beaumont commented.

'She is.' Or was, perhaps. It seemed ominous that as days went by no news of her came in.

Owen reappeared at the door with a packed hand-grip. 'I've collected some clothes and things. Can I go now?'

'Better wait until your father picks you up. He won't be much longer. I'm taking this if it's all right by you.'

She showed him the photograph and he nodded, tight-lipped. 'Anything if it helps find her.'

'You can wait in the patrol car outside. We

have to re-seal the house until the Scenes of Crime team has finished here.'

Owen sucked his underlip, considering this, decided it had ominous undertones and turned miserably away.

'I hope,' Z said, watching him through the window as he scorned the police car and seated himself on a low stone wall, 'that that young man isn't personally involved in the case.'

'No man is an island,' Beaumont responded portentously. 'But by heck a teenager is.' He spoke with all the fervour of a suffering parent. 'Come on, Z. Let's go and tackle this Banks girl.'

* * *

They found that the entire Banks family was alerted to their arrival. Owen, it seemed, had phoned through from an extension in his bedroom.

Mrs Banks offered them seats together on the living-room sofa and was prepared to give them tea. 'No thanks,' Beaumont refused for them both, and remained standing. 'It's Susie I need to talk to. And maybe you'd stay with her, Mrs Banks.'

'Look,' said the tall young man with fair hair flopping over his eyes, 'if it's about Owen, I'm the one who's his buddy.'

'So maybe we'll talk with you later. For the moment it's your sister we need to question.'

218

'This sounds very serious,' said her mother, semi-jocular, as if that might soften any coming blow.

Beaumont waited until Ned had ushered his little sister out, then turned to her. 'Murder *is* serious, Mrs Banks.'

It shocked her. 'Murder? Are you sure? Owen only mentioned an accident—with the car. His stepfather had been killed and his mother's missing, gone wandering off somewhere. Is that right?'

Z caught the slight nod that indicated she should take over. 'It appears Paul Randall was attacked, Mrs Banks. And his body had been moved to where we found it.'

'How horrible! Murder's not what we're used to here in Fords Green, even in these rough days. But how can Susie help you? As my son said, he's the one who knows Owen the best, though not the family, I'm afraid.'

Z turned to the girl. 'We're rather in the dark about them too. So we're hoping you can help, because you'd been in the house shortly before Mrs Randall disappeared.'

'Had you, Susie? You never told me. When was that?'

'Mrs Banks, would you leave us to ask the questions, please?'

The girl was decidedly uncomfortable. 'It was Friday, Mum. You know Owen and I went to the library together. We called in there on the way back.'

Her mother nodded. 'He offered to go with you, yes. Because of the report of a flasher.'

'Just a minute, that's news to us,' lied Beaumont, eager for confirmation of the patrolmen's version. 'When was this?'

Mrs Banks gave the embellished version of the incident she had had from the baker after Owen's brief mention. 'You police were out in force. I'm surprised you don't know about it.'

'We're not local, and it's hardly our line of business,' Beaumont said, suppressing that he'd winkled out the story in the police canteen. 'Still it's interesting.'

Z had been watching Susie's struggle with herself and her sudden decision to come clean. Not that anything she had to offer was discreditable. She clearly would have preferred her mother not know that she had gone for lunch with Owen and even had a guided tour of Bentham Lodge. But it was over the glimpse of Mrs Randall's evening dress that she seemed to stumble.

'You obviously had a good look at it,' Z suggested. 'Would you describe it for us? This could be important, because no one has told us in detail how she was dressed at the time we think she disappeared.'

'It was the most beautiful dress I've ever seen.' As she spoke Susie's confidence grew. She described colour, cut and fabric in detail. Z was left with a clear picture of the 'mermaid' dress, and the conviction that anyone wearing it could hardly escape being noticed. Since no sightings had been reported, the prospects for Gillian Randall seemed grim indeed. She had gone underground too thoroughly. Perhaps even in a literal sense.

There were other questions, but the replies didn't indicate anything amiss at Bentham Lodge on the day the girl had visited.

'How is Owen?' Susie shyly asked Z as the two detectives were about to leave.

'Pretty shocked, but putting a brave face on it.'

'Yes, he would. It's awful for him, this, coming on top of his exam results.'

'What's that, then?' Beaumont demanded sharply.

Mrs Banks intervened to make light of it. 'He did well really. It's just that he'd wanted a better grade in his special subject. Owen's a sensitive boy, and in the last couple of papers he seemed to have lost his concentration. It happens sometimes, with overstudy and fatigue.'

'Ah.' Beaumont filed the information in his head and turned to observe Ned who was leaning in the living-room doorway. 'Sorry you can't add anything on the Randalls. You never visited Owen at the house?'

'Called once, to pick up some sports equipment for school, but I wasn't asked in. Not considered civilized like Susie.'

His sister ignored the gibe. 'Is he staying on
221

at the house alone?' she asked Z anxiously.

'No, he's going to his father's flat.'

'Oh, I'm so glad. That's just what he wanted.'

Beaumont looked hard at her. 'Is it, then? Right, that's it for the present.' He stretched his rubbery smile, nodded and followed Zyczynski out.

*   *   *

'Next stop, Mrs Randall's mother,' he announced as Z put the car into gear.

They could barely get into the flat for packing cases along one wall of the hallway. Mrs Francis had given up in the middle of the job and was sitting glazed, hands in lap, in the half-stripped lounge. A WPC had made and poured tea for her, but she had left it untasted. A thin skin floated on the surface from the full-cream milk.

'I was going to move house,' she said numbly, excusing the chaos.

'When do you go?' Rosemary sat herself alongside. But Mrs Francis didn't seem to know, might even, in shock, have changed her mind about going.

Z removed the cup and saucer. 'Would you like something a little stronger than this?' she asked.

There was wine in the larder apparently. Beaumont went for it, prepared to unseal it, but it had already been opened, had less than a quarter of the bottle left. He poured some to offer to Mrs Francis, and watched her frozen face dissolve at sight of it. The rather prominent eyes brimmed with tears which ran slowly like glycerine down her quivering cheeks and spilled on clenched hands.

'We—drank it—together,' she said miserably. 'Last time—Gillian was here. Bull's Blood,' and she burst into loud sobbing.

It had been on Saturday morning, they were told, only hours away from her daughter's disappearance. Gillian had been so *understanding*.

It seemed as though her mother had not expected that. And then she explained what it was that had to be understood; her own intended change of lifestyle.

'We've never been really close,' Mrs Francis admitted shamefacedly, 'being so unalike, I suppose. Almost opposites. But on Saturday it was different.

'I had to steel myself to bring the subject up. I thought she'd say I'd gone crazy.'

'We talked about a lot of things, the past, her father, her childhood. Well no, I suppose we didn't exactly talk about them. I mentioned them and then we sat and thought about them, and then—'

'Yes, Mrs Francis?'

'She—she *hugged* me. I keep thinking now— maybe it was the last time I'll ever see her. And there were such a lot of things we left unsaid.'

Missed opportunities, Rosemary accepted: the guilt of the living confronted by a loved one's death.

But maybe the woman's daughter was still alive. 'Tell me,' she begged, 'what she's really like. Nobody could know her as well as you do.'

Mrs Francis closed her eyes a moment. 'She was a wilful little girl, headstrong you could say. But very brave. Liked to go her own way. As she grew up she took things in her stride. And yet—'

They waited, while Mrs Francis frowned over her words. 'She hasn't a lot of confidence. I mean, she blames herself afterwards when things go wrong.'

'What sort of things?'

A silence built up. 'Little things mostly, but she takes them so seriously. She's done well really, with her nursing, and then marrying Guy, having Owen. He's a good son.'

But she wasn't married to Guy any more. They waited for Mrs Francis to catch up with the present. However, no explanation of the break was forthcoming.

'Now this. Paul Randall dead, and my daughter not anywhere to be found. What do you think can have happened?'

Z looked across at Beaumont. He nodded for her to continue.

'We think someone stopped them on the way

home, because it doesn't seem likely they'd have arranged a meeting for that early hour of the morning. They must have been taken away somewhere while the car was returned. Paul Randall—died, as a result of rough treatment, sometime Sunday afternoon or evening.'

'And Gillian?'

'We don't know. Tests on their car may help us follow up her movements.'

'If she isn't dead too, then someone's still holding her. Or she could have been dropped off in some lonely place and can't get in touch. But who would do such a thing? Gillian wasn't one to make enemies. It would be all to do with that man—'

'Paul Randall?' Beaumont suggested.

'I never cared for him, but she—found him exciting. Though I think she'd have stayed married to Guy if he'd made it hard enough for her to leave. He was always too gentle; so he let her have her way. I used to think she went on as she did just to shake him up, make him angry. She was the same way with me when she was little.'

Deliberately perverse, to invite others' disapproval? Z asked herself. And if it didn't come, she disapproved of herself. Was that what Mrs Francis was trying to say?

She leaned forward and laid her hand over the older woman's. 'How do you think she would react to it, if she was being held against her will?'

Mrs Francis sniffed, dabbed at her eyes with a handkerchief and answered with some heat, 'She'd be furious, of course. It would be an awful shock. Scared half to death too but determined not to show it. Poor little scrap, she always thought she wanted a life of spectacular adventure, but you can have too much.

'Lately I've understood her better, because I'd begun myself to think that anything was better than day after day dragging on monotonously with nothing happening. But I was wrong.'

Her face puckered into a pathetic parody of a smile. 'I'd give anything now to go back to being bored.'

*   *   *

'You didn't ask one obvious question,' Beaumont accused Z, when they were again in the car.

'Which one?'

'Whether such a quote-headstrong-unquote daughter was likely to have done her husband in.'

'It occurred to me, but I thought we could spare her mother that for the moment.'

'Softy!' he jeered. 'The freemasonry of women!'

'There was nothing to prevent your asking.'

The Pinocchio face was unmoved. 'We can make up for your omission by having another go at the lad. If Gillian Randall was responsible for killing her husband, however impetuous the final act, there'd have been plenty of spleen leading up to the event. Young Owen was there all the time, living in the house with them. He just had to pick up the vibes. The longer he worries, the more he'll be willing to talk.'

*   *   *

But on rejoining Angus Mott they found that the Detective-Inspector had fresh information, relayed to him through the Boss. 'It may or may not have a connection,' he told them, 'but we're back to the original score of one killing and two missing persons. Fords Green is having a field day. Young Stafford's with us, but a second woman seems to have disappeared on this patch. No less than DS Turley's estranged wife.' He sketched for them what he had learned of the affair.

'Turley's been taken off our case, persuaded to take some leave. It seems his wife left her mother's in Hertford and was seen heading for home last Friday night, just before the thunderstorm. Two officers in a patrol car saw her talking with a man, as yet unidentified, in the car-park of the Green Man. And her mother phoned to say Mrs Turley had received official-looking envelopes from Fords Green. She believed she'd gone across to keep an appointment next day with a solicitor, to arrange for a divorce.'

'Can you see a solicitor giving up his golf to work on a Saturday? Still, it's something we can look into. There can't be many of the species in Fords Green. Could the man in the car-park have been Turley himself?'

'No. The same patrolmen overtook Turley on foot near his house, and informed him she was on her way. They'd assumed the man she was with was offering her a lift home.'

'Is there any known link between the Turleys and the Randalls?' Beaumont demanded.

'Unlikely, it seems, but we're checking. Gossip has it that Mrs T had good reason to leave home, had been gone over a fortnight and was trying to keep it dark that she'd been a battered wife. We haven't been able to contact her doctor who's on holiday, but a neighbour says she was taken to Amersham Casualty with a miscarriage just a few weeks back. Hospital's confirmation isn't in yet.'

'What friends has she locally?' Z asked. 'She must have meant to spend the night somewhere.'

'Again we're waiting. There's a Nancy someone she used to work with, according to the mother. She doesn't know her married name. Mrs Turley seems to have held her cards close to her chest.'

'What kind of work?'

'Shorthand typing, way back, soon after

Mrs Turley left school. She lived here in Clifford Terrace with her mother then. The old lady went back to her family home in Hertford after the Turley marriage. Apparently she's an invalid.'

'Surely she knows *where* her daughter worked?'

'All she remembers is an office in Market Street. Uniform branch are out there now checking for a colleague called Nancy.'

'The miscarriage doesn't concern our present case,' Beaumont claimed. 'Unless she was suffering from depression after losing her baby and either wandered off or did herself in. How about looking for a body in the reeds alongside the Elbourne?'

'We've got men out there now. So far there's nothing. While we're waiting, get your reports up to date on today's interviews. Is there anyone you want to have in for a taped session?'

'Why not?' Beaumont asked Z. 'Let's have another chat with the Staffords. If Owen was so keen to move in with his father, Randall's death and his mother's disappearance seem to have played into his court. And the lad can help over her relations with the dead man. To my mind there could be a whiff of conspiracy in the case: Owen and his father in collusion, though I don't see exactly how. So let's shake everyone up a bit and see what falls out.'

Mott considered this. 'They've only just got

back from the last interview. Give it an hour and then phone for an appointment.'

With that, Beaumont had to be content.

*　　　*　　　*

Owen took the call at the flat, letting the phone ring eight or nine times before he answered cautiously. 'My father's out,' he said. 'I'll tell him when he gets back. No, I can't say where he's gone.'

'But I think he knows, all the same,' Z guessed.

*　　　*　　　*

As Guy Stafford drove the BMW past the site office he leaned forward and waved to the man drinking coffee in the doorway. He had no wish to be delayed, and the chances were that his connection with the local crime was already the subject of gossip and conjecture.

The trailer had been left in position for removal. He backed up, connected and checked on the couplings before turning off the car engine and going to unlock the van's door.

He'd barely had time to notice on Sunday that the place was untidy and stuffy. He found it distasteful to be clearing up another's mess, throwing out half-eaten food, putting away in drawers and cupboards the oddments left about.

Groceries in the fridge must have gone off. He fetched a bin from outside and started to empty the shelves of what was left. And still, despite the open windows and doors, the smell persisted.

He ran fresh water down the sink, disconnected the supply, closed the gas connections and brought in the cylinder from under the floor. Before going out again to knock the chocks away he decided to strip all the linen. He released the catch to let down the folding bed, and suddenly the stench was overpowering.

As he staggered back he heard someone coming up the trailer steps behind. Martinson the site manager caught him by the elbow, thrusting him aside as he went forward to look.

'Oh my God, what have you done?'

'But I didn't, I didn't,' Guy whispered.

The body on the mattress was bloated and stinking. He couldn't look. He dared not see her.

CHAPTER EIGHTEEN

'EVERYONE'S TO KEEP OFF,' YEADINGS ordered, 'until Inspector Mott is on the site. All vehicles to stay on the main road until Scenes of Crime have swept the place.'

He had been at Control when the phone call

came in: a dead woman discovered in Stafford's trailer on a building site out past the place where Randall's body had turned up.

The circumstances of the new discovery seemed confused. Guy Stafford had been present, but it was the site manager who had rung in. Stafford was in shock and being looked after by a workman with first aid experience.

It took some self-control for the Superintendent not to drive out and take over the investigation himself, but he had to give Angus full rein. He busied himself instead with large-scale maps of the locality, listing suitably positioned buildings where unusual comings and goings might have been observed between the early hours when the couple left Chardleigh Place and the probable time Randall was killed on Sunday, at least ten hours later.

While he was plotting positions a call came from Aldermaston. Jeanie Walter, a senior analyst, had just finished her first run of tests on residue in the tyres of Randall's Sierra. 'Woodland,' she told him. 'The car was run on to a peaty surface. Rich mulch with particles of beech mast. Pity there aren't traces of some rarer tree. It's a needle in a haystack, looking for beeches in South Bucks.'

Yes, he thought; the word Bucks being a corruption of Buchen as in Buchenwald, a beech wood. Almost the whole wooded area was covered in the trees. But out where the bodies had turned up there were only conifer plantations.

He thanked Jeanie, wished her luck for the next series of tests and rang off. Sitting over the problem, he couldn't ignore the obvious, which insisted on presenting itself. *Burnham Beeches.* But was that answer too easy?

He measured the route. Twelve minutes' drive from Chardleigh, perhaps fifteen after dark because there was no lighting out there at all. A good place for a spot of skulduggery. Yes, why not? Dozens of suitable spots where a car could pull off the road and—

And what? Not transfer the captives to a building, because the few available would belong to the verderers. They were constantly checking and would know immediately if anyone had forced an entry. But since the Sierra had been returned, there could have been a second car waiting. It would need to be roomy, with dark windows, ideally a van.

'I like it,' he said aloud. The more he thought about it, the more evident it became that this had been a deliberately planned operation. So what was the motivation? Why had these two apparently ordinary people been snatched? Neither of them had any obvious influence in the community; although they lived in a substantial house, it was generally supposed that its upkeep was about all they could manage. So had they run up unmeetable debts with some tough customers? Had they been gambling, involved with drug suppliers, or even tried their hand at blackmail? It seemed unlikely, but the circumstances did suggest a professional operation.

Whatever the Randalls had done to merit the treatment would surely come to light eventually. Meanwhile all traffic must be diverted from Burnham Beeches and the grass verges examined for tyre tracks made since the sudden storm of Friday night. He guessed it would be a mammoth task in such a recognized beauty spot of daily dog-exercising and weekend picnics. The entire area of 600 afforested acres was owned by the Corporation of London; they'd need to be notified about any temporary imposing of restrictions.

He lifted the internal phone and gave orders. The men sent out to Burnham should look for marks where two vehicles had made a rendezvous. Wherever such were found a comparison should be made with tyre patterns from Randall's Sierra, then a fingertip search conducted, and impressions taken of movements between his car and a second vehicle.

Total success unlikely. Even in a more limited area than South Bucks, what Jeanie Walter had said remained true: it was like looking for a needle in a haystack.

* * *

Out at the site of the future pet foods factory, Angus Mott, with Beaumont along, walked cautiously up from the main road, treading on the unmarked grass verge as far as possible. They found Stafford seated in the rear of his BMW, his head in his hands. His face, when he looked up at their approach, was haggard. He seemed to have aged by ten years since their last meeting.

He climbed out and followed dumbly when invited down to the police car. Mott waited until the man had control of himself before starting to question him.

'Mr Stafford, I believe you have something to tell us.'

'My wife,' he said after a pause. 'Gillian, that is. She's up there, in the trailer. Dead. I know nothing about it.'

'When did you last see her, sir?'

But Stafford shook his head. He would say nothing more.

Mott nodded to Beaumont to stay with the man while he went to question Martinson who was sitting apart in another car. From him he got a description of the scene as he entered. He'd gone up to speak with the architect, who had earlier driven past the site hut without stopping.

'He's never done that before,' Martinson told him. 'Always comes in and has something to say. Very pleasant man usually, Mr Stafford. And I know he'd seen me there in the doorway. So I thought something must be wrong, see?

'I followed him up a few minutes later, just in case there was something I should know about. And I walked right in on it. I could see he'd been clearing up all round, and as I came in he was opening the bed up. It's one that folds back into the wall. Well, there she was. No mistaking she was dead. The stench was something awful.'

If the body had been there since the weekend, nothing was to be gained by rushing in and adding to existing traces, Mott considered. The Scenes of Crime team were gathering with their equipment a few cars down, and all they needed now was a police surgeon. Who, on arrival, proved to be a woman.

He tried not to register any reaction but she picked up his disappointment at once. 'Don't worry,' she said. 'You're lucky it's me. I've done that forensic medicine course they give us at the Yard. Our male alternative hasn't.'

He went in behind her, staying back by the doorside wall while she made her examination. She said nothing as she worked, except to throw over her shoulder, 'Do you want me to remove the ligature?'

So the dead woman had been strangled. 'No. The pathologist will do that.'

'Dr Littlejohn's coming out? Good. That's all, then. Except to state officially that the subject's dead. Who is she?'

'A local lady called Gillian Randall, ex-Stafford, apparently.'

The doctor swung round on him. 'Oh no, she isn't. I know Gill. Worked with her often enough. She's a nurse. This woman's nothing like her. Someone I've never seen before.'

At least this time no wrong name had been officially quoted for the body, Mott thought grimly. Not Gillian Randall. Since two local women had been reported missing, the chances were that this was the other, Detective-Sergeant Turley's wife.

Mott had glimpsed Lew Duke's ginger curls down among the uniforms on the main road and he radioed now for him to come up.

'I thought you might care to see the body,' he told the young Detective-Constable when he arrived. 'And put a name to it.'

'If I can.'

And he could. It wasn't easy for him because with strangulation the cyanosed face was so hideously distorted, the tongue obscenely thrust out, like some medieval grotesque in stone. But he had no doubt.

'Gawd,' he said softly. 'It's the Skip's missus. How the hell did she ever get here?'

*   *   *

How? Exactly. Mott thought back wryly to his own reaction on first viewing the corpse of Paul

237

Randall clad in singlet, dress trousers and no shoes. He'd hoped the case might be a weirdo. Well, increasingly it was. Or *they* were—two separate cases—because what connection could there possibly be between this body and what had befallen the Randalls?

Yet there was one. The single link had, of course, to be Guy Stafford: his trailer the woman's body had turned up in, his ex-wife's new husband the first victim.

And oddly enough Stafford had just now spoken of the dead woman as his wife, even named her Gillian. Did that mean that, surprised by Martinson as he opened up the bed, he'd caught only a passing glimpse and *assumed*—? Which must surely mean that he wasn't responsible for that death.

Or else he was a damn good actor and a quick thinker, to create that impression.

But Martinson insisted on Stafford's total amazement at glimpsing the body, and Mott had to admit that the man's state of shock seemed genuine. So was there some other option? Had he genuinely taken the body for his wife's, in the knowledge that he had himself killed her, *but elsewhere*. Did the shock stem from the way it had mysteriously turned up virtually on his doorstep?

A body-shifting operation? But that was pure Whitehall farce. Quite unlikely in the real world of Thames Valley policing. Above all in tranquil Fords Green.

Viewed from the angle of the law of probabilities, since most murders were domestic, Stafford should be the killer of his ex-wife, also (perhaps accidentally?) of the replacement husband. And, being an intelligent man, he was capable of setting up complications fit to confuse the opposition. So, Mott told himself, sort it out, simplify it, take one thing at a time and refuse to be foxed.

The straightforward prime fact was that the body was *not* Gillian Randall's in any case but Mrs Turley's, so there was no obvious reason why Guy Stafford should kill her. They would necessarily be starting by sizing up the Detective-Sergeant in the frame for this, and heaven help what the scandal-loving press would make of the force investigating one of their own!

*　　　*　　　*

Don Turley was at home, balefully occupied with filling two suitcases with the contents of his wife's wardrobe and chest of drawers. When called to answer the doorbell he had dresses and shoes strewn about the floor of the bedroom. Beaumont and Z being already close by, he was spared being brought in for interview by his junior, Lew Duke.

While Beaumont brought the man up to date on the finding of his wife's body—but without any mention of where or under what circumstances—Zyczynski quietly wandered through the house and took in the disorder. In the main upstairs bedroom she sensed an alarming atmosphere of passion, but whether it came from frustrated fury or from a residue of hate already unleashed, she couldn't tell. It was enough that Turley had been taking out his rancour on his wife's possessions. The torn and crumpled garments lay in twisted shapes as if kicked together, pathetic in their inoffensive colours.

The room was painted a matt biscuit shade, the furniture drab, the lined beige-and-white striped curtains machine-sewn but hemmed by hand. The only pictures on the walls were two enlarged black and white framed photographs, one of a dinghy with Turley crouched at the tiller and the other, older, of a country pub with a couple and a young boy standing in the doorway. The child, Z guessed, recognizing the broad forehead and wide-set bovine eyes, had to have been Turley himself.

The view from the window was of a small, neat garden, and slung on a washing line, not pegged out, what looked like a man's dark suit.

Beaumont called from the living-room and Z went down to join the men, taking the wheel of one car while they followed in Turley's. She darted a quick glance at his lowering face as he got in, but was unable to read in it more than bafflement and anger. She wondered how he would respond to questioning once Mott

240

started on him with the Boss alongside.

*   *   *

'Why,' Yeadings demanded of Mott, after being brought up to date on the more recent body, 'just there?'

'It's close to where Randall was found. That seemed logical when we thought the dead woman was his wife Gillian. But there's no connection we have yet discovered between Marcia Turley and the building site or between her and Randall.'

'So we could have two totally independent killings. Even the start of a homicidal epidemic in Fords Green. On the other hand—' and the thick black eyebrows shot up towards his hairline—'we can't overlook that somewhere loosely in the centre between the two events is the person of Guy Stafford. Is it merely coincidence that he was once married to one victim and owns the trailer where the second killing took place? What chance, d'you think, of us finding traces of the Randalls in the same trailer?'

'Evens, I'd say. At the road end there are tyre marks in mud to either side of the concreted service strip, and SOCO are working flat out on that in case we get any more rain. Normally the trucks entering the area wouldn't stop there. The indoor work is put on hold. If there is epidemic killing as you suggest, Kidlington

241

will need to send us reinforcements.'

'Yes?' Yeadings had lifted the buzzing phone. 'Right. We'll give them fifteen minutes, then come down.' He cradled the receiver. 'Beaumont's brought Turley in. Have you got all the information ready on him?'

'So far it's uncorroborated guesswork about his relations with his wife, because she wouldn't make an official complaint. We've yet to trace any near friends who might have received her confidences.'

'Z will be seeing what she can charm out of the hospital about the post-abortion treatment Mrs Turley received in Casualty. They don't like passing on confidential reports but she'll tackle personally whoever actually dealt with the woman.'

'Have you sent Stafford home? I don't want his son left on his own too long.'

'He's gone back to the flat with him. I rang through to check. They'll stay there and wait for any news that comes in about Owen's mother.'

There was a hesitant rap at the door. 'Come in,' shouted Yeadings, and two uniformed officers sidled round the edge of the door. He waited for them to explain their presence.

'PC Norris, sir.'

'And Bailey, sir.'

'Relevant to which case?' Yeadings asked blandly.

The two men looked uncertainly at each

other. The older one took on the role of spokesman. 'Well, either, sir. Or both.'

'Spit it out then.'

'Last Thursday morning, sir, we had a report of a flasher,' and he gave an account of how they'd pulled in a lad who wasn't the right one, but the full description had come through after they'd got him in the car, so they waited for DS Turley to catch up and decide what to do.

'And he gave him a bit of verbal, like.'

'He, him! Use names, man.'

'DS Turley, sir. He took the lad over to his own car and put him through it.'

'As if he was a serious suspect?'

'Yes, sir. The kid was really upset. And he was already, pretty sick about bad exam results.'

'Is this leading anywhere?'

'Well, the lad's name was Stafford, sir. Sergeant Turley sort of lit up when he heard it. Like it made his day. So he gave young Stafford the works.'

'Didn't rough him up physically?'

'No, sir. We'd have seen. Just talked at him, hard. He was—young Stafford, that is—was sure he was going to be charged with indecency. Nearly pissing himself, he was. Only there wasn't anything in it, sir.'

Yeadings stared at the man.

Bailey was moved to put in a word. 'It's only small-time stuff, sir, we know. Only the lad being Guy Stafford's son, and then his mother

243

having gone missing and his stepfather killed ... like Mrs Turley too...'

'Quite,' Yeadings agreed, suddenly amiable. 'Plenty of pieces there, but how many jigsaw puzzles do they come from? Was this Thursday business logged?'

'Yes sir, Duty-Sergeant insisted.'

'Good. Get me a copy, and let's not have any tongue-wagging about it—more than you've done already.' He regarded them sardonically.

'You say it was only when he heard the surname that Turley took such an interest in the boy?'

'Yes sir. They didn't seem to know each other, and young Stafford hadn't any record; we checked.'

'Right.' He nodded to dismiss them.

Mott watched his chief's face darken. 'Owen Stafford is seventeen, still a minor but only just,' he pointed out. 'Are you thinking, sir, that with this incident added to his existing stress, he suffered some kind of brainstorm and turned violent with his stepfather?'

Yeadings sighed. 'That's one possibility. It wouldn't be the first time academic pressures pushed a youngster towards the edge. It's obvious he resented the man's intrusion in the family. And, Angus, we have to bear in mind that for young people with career prospects in jeopardy it's also the season for overdoses: one of the red zones of the year for violence, like the Christmas break. We must accept the

244

possibility that Owen Stafford killed Randall in a frenzied attack. In which case—'

Mott was thinking along the same lines. 'His story of hearing the car come back could have been true, except that he went down to meet them, there was a flare-up (probably over the exam results) and it came to violence, with both adults inflamed by drink. The boy flips his lid, bashes the man's head on the car roof so viciously that he dies later on the same day. Then he would be the one using fabric gloves to put the car away. Passing on the blood smears too.'

'Kills his mother as well?'

'His mother could be lying low to confuse the issue and provide us with an alternative suspect. And his father—'

'Could be innocently suffering the very state of shock you say he's in. Only, what about the death of Mrs Turley? How does that fit the scenario? She's a corpse too many. We don't even know whether Owen knew her, or knew about the trailer.'

Mott was nodding in an almost absent way, his concentration elsewhere. 'Damn,' he said suddenly. 'I knew there was something I forgot to check on. Whether the boy can drive.'

CHAPTER NINETEEN

TURLEY WAS DEFINITELY UNCOMFORTABLE, but he made no effort to present himself as a grieving widower. He had come there straight from visiting the morgue with Beaumont, whose observation of his reactions was yet to be heard.

The identification had been positive: the body was that of Marcia Turley his wife. *Judy* Turley? Mott queried, consulting a statement from the dead woman's mother.

Turley grunted. 'Judith Marcia on her birth certificate. The old lady still used her first name, but round here everyone knew her as Marcia.'

'Ah, *everyone*,' Yeadings slipped in. 'Tell us who this would be, the people who knew her best.'

'Women friends,' Turley said grudgingly. 'I don't know their names. They never came to the house when I was there.'

'Other couples you went around with?' Mott suggested, picking up the thread.

'We didn't socialize.' His face twisted. 'No bridge or golf or barbecues. A working jack doesn't get time—or have the money—for all that.'

The Inspector couldn't miss the lip-curling scorn and the implication that what the Boss and he contributed to Thames Valley didn't merit the name of work.

'So when you went out together, say for drinks or a meal, where did you usually go?'

Turley stared blankly back.

'No?' Yeadings murmured as the silence built up. 'Well, let's look at the past week. She'd been staying with her mother. Did you have any contact with her apart from by telephone?'

Turley treated him to a baffled glare. 'I rang through on Friday lunchtime and the old woman told me Marcia had left. She seemed to think she'd be heading this way.'

'Did she actually say as much?'

'No, but where else would she go?'

'You tell us.'

'I don't know.' Turley appeared to be turning this in his mind. 'Well, she never showed up here, not at the house anyway. I stayed up waiting till Saturday morning and there was no sign of her. Her mother's half-crazy, a vindictive old cow. You can't go by anything she says. She'd be out to make trouble wherever she could.'

'So what do you think happened?'

Turley was holding an internal argument with himself. Eventually he faced up savagely to the Superintendent and said in an accusing voice, 'She must have been having it off with some man.'

Yeadings offered him a little rope. 'She was

seen being offered a lift shortly after the evening bus would have come in at Fords Green. This was Friday, the night of the thunderstorm. Her arrival was mentioned to you by two patrolmen who passed you on the way home. So you might have expected her to follow you in, if only for shelter from the weather.'

'They—were mistaken. If she'd been in Fords Green, of course she would have come home. Where else would she go? So she wasn't there at all.'

'It seems logical,' Yeadings agreed with quiet menace. 'So are you quite sure that she didn't come home that night?'

He could only go on denying it, and they let him go at that. His baffled anger threatened to break out at any moment and they had no need to question who was the object of it. If Mrs Turley had arrived home that Friday night she would have had no uncertain reception. But how had she arrived at Stafford's trailer, which evidence clearly showed was the place where she met her death?

'Is it too fantastic,' Yeadings suggested after Turley had left, 'that for some reason he had such a grudge against Stafford that he dumped the body where suspicion must fall on him?'

'She went there alive,' Mott said shortly. 'Her fingerprints were found on the kettle among other things, although Stafford seemed to have been in a hurry to clear things away and

248

wash up when Martinson caught up with him.'

'So he could know more about it than he's admitting.'

'He's not admitting anything at present. He's relying on us accepting he's in shock.'

*   *   *

Further consideration of this aspect was interrupted by the arrival of Rosemary Zyczynski with a large evidence bag labelled with Turley's name and address and sealed with her own signature and a witness's alongside.

'What's this pretty thing?' Yeadings purred.

'I saw it on the washing line at the Turleys' place. It looked as if he'd been trying to wash a suit, so I came back for the bag and asked a neighbour to witness me taking it.'

'We'd better get it examined sharpish,' the Boss told her. 'There'd have been spatters of blood from Randall's duffing up. How about the Turley strangulation?'

'Yes. The ligature was heavy-duty binding tape,' Mott said. 'Its edges cut into the flesh of her neck. I'm hoping we may find blood from the killer's hands too. The smudges picked up so far are half-wiped dabs, so it's unlikely he wore gloves. I'm having the sink U-bend removed in case he washed afterwards.'

'Had Stafford been running the water when Martinson caught up with him?'

'It looked as if he'd done some washing-up. There were water rings on the draining-board and a tea towel was damp. But any splashed blood from Friday or Saturday might have stayed dried inside the waste pipe, so we still have a chance.'

Yeadings hummed his appreciation and nodded at Z. 'Scenes of Crime must transfer someone from the trailer to Turley's house. If they're nippy on the job we'll not need to seal it.'

*　　　*　　　*

Prompt on the discovery of the still damp dress-suit came more information. First, from the searchers at Bentham Lodge, came the report that Mrs Randall's passport was still in her bureau drawer. There was no sign of her husband's, although several copies of what appeared to be recent photographs of the required size were in the same drawer. Mott phoned Owen and learned that the man had received a new passport about eight months earlier. It was a burgundy-coloured EC one, but the boy didn't know whether his mother's particulars had been included on her husband's passport.

'He would hardly have taken it to the Chardleigh Place do,' Yeadings objected. 'So does it mean they came back to the house to collect it, meaning to do a flit with whatever cash and valuables they had to hand? Or was the passport stashed somewhere else ready to be picked up?'

He gave his imagination free rein. 'Could they have arranged to meet up with some shady characters who for some reason beat Randall up, robbed him, and dumped the body when he pegged out? Maybe it was a link-up with partners who decided they'd get a bigger cut with the Randalls eliminated.'

'Or with Paul Randall eliminated, leaving them to ride off into the sunset with Mrs R?' Mott implemented. 'On the other hand, maybe that scenario's too spectacular, and the passport's not there for the simple reason that young Owen took it, expressly to give the impression Randall was running out on them. The boy had plenty of opportunity in the house alone. Might even have removed it when Beaumont and Z took him back to Bentham Lodge. They couldn't have watched him every minute of the time.'

A phone buzzed and Yeadings delayed his comments to answer it. Duty-Sergeant put through a call from an excited lady claiming to be the vicar's wife in a village two miles upriver from the building site.

This Mrs Radcliff had been pricing items for a jumble sale in the village hall. Following her custom, she'd allowed in one or two known vagrants, who, by the action of a miraculous grapevine, had become aware of the coming

251

event. She had, as ever, put aside for them a few garments considered unsuitable for sale.

'I had a reasonably nice tweed jacket for the Mouse Man,' she complained, 'but would you believe it, he wouldn't take it?'

'Mouse Man?' Mott queried.

'Oh, he's a scruffy old character who's been around here for years. Seasonal though; by autumn he's off somewhere else, turns up again in time for the pre-Easter Bazaar. We call him that because he won't own to a name and carries tame mice around in the pockets of his tattered old overcoat. To amuse the children. Mind, he's very gentle with them—the children, I mean. Well, the mice too, I suppose—'

'Mrs—er, Radcliff,' Yeadings protested, 'is this really a police matter?'

'No, not so far. Oh dear, I'm sorry. I've started at the wrong end, haven't I? To cut a long story short, my dear, he said he already had a nice jacket. Once it had dried out.'

'A nice jacket?'

'My dear, would you believe it? A *dinner-* jacket. Not nearly so warm for winter as the tweed I'd put aside, but he was so taken with it. A bit of a snob under all that wild hair and grime. Isn't it ridiculous?'

'Dinner-jacket,' Mott breathed over his chief's shoulder, instantly alerted.

'And you're looking for one, aren't you? Or so my husband said when I was telling him

252

about the Mouse Man's latest.'

'Mrs Radcliff, did this Mouse Man say how he came to have the jacket?'

'Yes, found it nearby in the Elbourne, just by the edge, caught up in some willows. Of course it was drenched, had been in the water for some time, I expect. He fished it out with a broken branch and spread it out to dry in the sun. Not that I'd care to wear anything un-aired like that. It still felt quite damp to me.'

'This Mouse Man, Mrs Radcliff, is he a big man?'

'Oh, I wouldn't say that. Quite skinny under all his layers of clothes, or so I imagine. About my height, five six.'

So, even after a certain shrinkage, Randall's jacket ought to fit him.

A call went out for patrol cars in the district to bring in the Mouse Man. No description was needed; he was a familiar sight throughout the sub-division. Two hours later he was in the canteen, his hands—mittened even in August—round a mug of heavily sugared peat-black tea, and bemoaning the loss of his smart new jacket: less a surrender than a theft, according to amused onlookers.

*   *   *

Towards four that afternoon, Yeadings' gamble on Burnham Beeches paid off. In answer to a crime notice posted at the entrance

253

from Farnham Royal, a nurseryman from the garden centre in Crown Lane reported a dark blue or black van with two men in the cab having been parked in the Beeches at two different points during the afternoon of Friday 21 August.

He had noticed it particularly because as he passed on the second occasion the men had been standing outside with what looked like a map and were apparently marking their position. He knew there could be no private surveying on London Corporation land and the van bore no forestry insignia. He was suspicious, having been recently burgled by a man seen by neighbours 'casing the joint' (as he described with relish) a few days previously.

He had meant to report the van to the local constable but found the man was on holiday. Fear of being thought fanciful (since there were no houses near) had put him off going higher.

Being long familiar with the complicated layout of the ancient forest, he was able to direct patrolmen to the two areas he'd noted. One showed no fresh vehicle tracks, but impressions on the other, immediately taped off, choreographed the comings and goings of two vehicles and a number of connecting footmarks. The dark blue van could have returned after the storm, perhaps during the night of Saturday to Sunday. Tyre casts were being prepared and photographs would follow.

'If this is the connection we're looking for, it would be only the vehicle exchange point,' Yeadings grunted, 'but let's hope something'll lead from that to where the killing occurred.'

Mott nodded. 'Or back to the men who set it up.'

*   *   *

Z's double trip out to Turley's house had interrupted her scheduled visits. She was due to go off duty, but since the hospital lay almost on her route home she could find no excuse for putting off inquiries there until next day. Particularly since she could not free her mind of Marcia Turley's life story as bandied about the station. Even with due allowance made for prejudice against the Detective-Sergeant, Marcia was now openly accepted as a battered wife, her end seemingly the final act after years of uncomplaining abuse.

Aware how jealously hospital administrators guard details of cases which might invite publicity, Z waited meekly for an interview with the hospital secretary.

'It's just a matter of confirming dates and such,' she explained when at last she was admitted to the administrative heart of the machine. 'About a month back Marcia Turley was admitted to the Casualty Department— miscarriage after a fall on the stairs. I don't know if you've heard yet, but she's just turned up as a murder victim.'

The secretary hadn't heard. He blinked, for a moment looked humanly stirred, then covered up with a show of bland sophistication. 'So now we are obliged to prepare CVs for the departed, eh? Let's see then what we have on the lady.'

He rang for some less elevated person to look up the information, while he made tea in a silver-plated pot and poured it out, after consulting his watch, into a pair of floral Worcester cups.

On arrival the file was not handed to the policewoman, but she was sufficiently practised at reading upside down. She copied the details in her notebook as he dictated, simpering with apparent gratitude to cover her sudden excitement at a detail he had failed to offer. The signature of the senior nurse on duty referring the admission was Stafford.

Not such a very common name. Perhaps, if Gillian had worked here for some time, she had kept it unchanged after her second marriage. Many women even preferred to use their maiden names professionally.

It was simple enough to check on. She stopped at the porters' rest room on the way out. 'Looking for a nurse called Gillian Randall,' she said wistfully. 'No one seems able to help me.'

'Oh, you won't find her here, duck,' a little jockey-sized man offered. 'She went private, full-time. Used to work in Casualty till a few weeks back. We all knew her as Stafford.'

CHAPTER TWENTY

SUPERINTENDENT MIKE YEADINGS HAD never been one to scorn computers, but he acknowledged that before it ever got to the stage of pulling the plums out, the important area of his work was finding and clarifying every last detail that had to go in. So, having sought the seclusion of his hotel bedroom, and checked that at home it would be quarter of an hour short of the children's bathtime, he rang Nan, ascertained that all was well there, and settled to his paperwork with a bottle of Macon and some rare beef sandwiches on the side.

Randall's body was the first to be found, death having occurred loosely during the afternoon or evening of Sunday. The woman's body, recovered from the trailer only that day, pre-dated the other—according to a phone call from Dr Littlejohn—by twenty-four to forty-eight hours. So if there was a link—*proper hoc* rather than merely *post hoc*— hcrs was the case to be considered first.

Not that there was much yet to collate on the lady. She appeared to have led a dull enough existence both before and since her unhappy marriage. Opinions expressed by her mother and husband had to be assessed minus a deal of prejudice and counter-accusation. Gossip at divisional level was based mainly on guesswork in the domestic area, and soured experience in police matters. Because Yeadings found Turley personally distasteful, he was determined to start by taking a good look at the man's possible innocence.

He reached for a block of lined paper and headed it: *Means, Motive, Opportunity*. The murder probe trinity. He began to write down his impressions.

Means lay to hand for whoever chose to look round the site. Binding tape of the kind used as a ligature was commonly used in baling sealed plastic-sheeted quantities of building materials. But none would necessarily be found inside the trailer. So had the killer to interrupt the attempted rape, go outside to obtain a suitable length and then return to complete his attack? Or had he brought the binding tape in with him—a pointer to premeditation, in fact?

Nothing in this pointed to Turley more than to any other person. The killer could equally well have been a chance prowler or someone who came intentionally to see her.

So consider *Motive*: in Turley's case this appeared inescapable. The majority of murders arose from domestic discord, so Turley had to be in the forefront of any suspects. But only because so far there was no recognizable alternative.

Judith Marcia Turley might, like Fords Green itself, have an innocent public face that covered dark secrets. Far more delving into her private life was needed before one could assume she was simply what she had seemed. Just because Turley hadn't been sufficiently interested to know what friends she had, it didn't mean she had none.

Another point: Littlejohn had spoken of attempted rape. The blunt words he had used on the phone were 'a botched job. He never got it up'. There was a chance that the scientific experts would find some trace to prove the opposite, but the pathologist seldom chanced his luck on a positive statement on first view of a body. So were they to suppose that for some reason the killer had been rendered impotent? Or been interrupted? Or the woman's death intervening had scared him off?

None of this sounded like the bullish Turley. But appearances could be deceptive. Had he indeed been the cause of Marcia's pregnancy? If, in fact, there had been another man in the background, it made some sense of the wife-beating, though it couldn't excuse it.

Yeadings sighed and started a new section.

Opportunity: if Turley had killed his wife he had to have known where she was and be able to get to her.

He claimed to have stayed at home all
259

Friday evening. At this point there were a lot of ifs. If the patrolmen had seen the right woman; if she had been on her way home; if she had accepted the lift they thought she might have been offered: if all that, then she might have walked in on the expectant Turley, and the scenario from that point on was anybody's guess. Turley just could have driven her to where she was killed, but equally there was no apparent reason why he should.

So had he stayed at home all night, as he'd claimed? It was too late now to find any traces of building site materials on his car, but he might have left traces of himself up there, either in the trailer or outside. If lack of them didn't positively clear him, at least it would serve the defence in any case built up against him.

One thing certainly stood in his favour—the sloppily smudged fingerprints, unidentifiable but present. With all his experience as a jack, he would have known how hard it is to remove dabs completely. Surely he'd have had the sense to cover his hands or make a better job of erasure? Even when panicking?

The phone's ringing broke his line of thought. Yeadings bent down for it, dumped by his feet to accommodate his supper on the inadequate table. 'Yes?' he said, confident that only those familiar with his voice would have access to the number.

'Ah, Z, are you still on the trail?'

He listened, nodding. 'So there is a Randall-

Turley link, through the womenfolk. Of course, this corner of South Bucks is a small, tight world. Any woman working in Amersham hospital must eventually have a number of Fords Green locals through her hands. The point to follow up is this: did the association go further? I'd like you to work on that tomorrow. And don't overlook the Chardleigh Place do. Mrs Turley could have been dead some hours by then, but all the other parties we're interested in seem to have been present. Somebody may have observed meetings between them.

'I take it you've reported it to Inspector Mott? Good. Did he? Well, I expect he'll be joining me soon. Thank you, Z. Good girl.'

He looked around for somewhere to dump the phone and opted for tossing it on to the bed, then considered the remains of his meal. If he took the tray down to the kitchen himself, all matey like, there might be somebody around ready for a casual gossip. Might as well make use of sitting on one of the action bases in the case. Friday night's storm would have fixed things in people's minds. Maybe some of the regulars would remember who was down in the bar then.

He'd give a lot to know whether anyone else claimed to have seen Marcia Turley in the car-park talking with a man.

*   *   *

261

It was over an hour later that Mott turned up hungry and weary from mainly fruitless inquiries. Yeadings left him to work through a microwaved steak pie and a pint of real ale before allowing business to intervene. Beaumont, Mott said between mouthfuls, had wanted to put up in the village. He hadn't sanctioned it on account of restricted expenses. But the man obviously wasn't keen to go home and he'd said he'd cover the Bed and Breakfast himself at least for a couple of nights. Z had driven back to her digs in their shared car.

When he judged Mott had finished eating, Yeadings stretched his legs, yawned and said mildly, 'Ever wondered how and when Turley got his car back from the pub yard?'

'He mentioned in his statement that he went home on foot, knowing it could cost him his job if uniformed men picked him up for breathalysing. The patrolmen confirm this. But the pub manager swears the Escort had gone when he let out his incontinent dog at three the next morning. He always takes note of which customers leave vehicles in the car-park.'

'So it's not true he stayed in all night, unless he's got kindly friends we haven't heard of. What else did you pick up downstairs that the locals missed?'

Yeadings smiled. 'Like to make a guess who, besides the Detective-Sergeant, dropped in here for a drink last Friday at the crucial time for Marcia Turley?'

Mott looked thoughtful. 'Inquiries didn't come up with any interesting names.'

'Because the man wasn't known here. He usually drinks elsewhere. But old Sally Crocker, the door-to-door tinker, knew him, having been chased off with threats of violence when she called once. She hadn't been in since, till we shared a jar together tonight.'

'Tell me, then.'

'Paul Randall. "Tanking himself up", she said. Left in a hurry a few minutes before the first clap of thunder. That sent her scuttling because she hadn't transport and she didn't want to get wet. As she left the forecourt a red car swerved past and she had to jump for it. She saw Randall in the driver's seat with someone else alongside.'

'He was killed at least a day after the Turley woman,' Mott said sombrely. 'So he could have taken her to the trailer, set about the rape, and been interrupted.'

'Then what?'

'Panicked, finished her off quickly, managed to slip away but was observed by someone who'd followed him there.'

'Go on.'

'Eventually the witness catches up and overdoes duffing him up.'

'A day or two later?'

'It would take time to plan, with the Chardleigh kidnap business. In any case it involves a third, possibly fourth party.'

'And what would they do with Randall's wife, these avengers? Are they protectors of females in general, or do they see her as a further means of getting at him?'

'She could be wandering in shock still.'

'Dressed the way she was? No, we'd have heard by now. Suppose they hung on to her. What then?'

'Depends on whether she could identify them. They might not have set out to kill, but once they realized Randall was dead they're facing a life sentence. I wouldn't give much for an eye-witness's chances.'

Yeadings nodded slowly. 'And who are we putting in the frame for all this?'

Mott grunted. 'If the two crimes are actually connected, who else have we but Turley? With associates; God knows he must have criminal contacts enough. He could even have interrupted a scene of passion at the trailer, and been obliged to let Randall escape temporarily while he garrotted his wife ...'

'Out of jealous anger? Did she matter so much to him?'

'He's never been slow to go berserk. And his property, after all. A blow to male pride.'

'Maybe. So what did you find back at his house?'

'A drunken mess. Nothing conclusive. Except Z picked up his dress-suit which appeared to have been washed. Which

264

shouldn't have happened, because it was an old-fashioned one, all wool. It's gone for examination. He'd casually slung it on a line in the garden: hardly the action of a guilty man, but he must have been pissed as a handcart over the weekend. The house was a wreck, stank to high heaven.'

*　　*　　*

Don Turley let himself in by his back door and gazed around. The place was a bloody shambles. No, just a shambles. No blood here, thank God.

The stench of burnt toast and stale booze made him want to throw up. And he hadn't yet cleaned up in the bathroom.

He leaned on the sink before reaching over to open the casement. And saw the clothes-line swinging gently in the breeze, empty. So the perishing neighbourhood kids had made off with his dress-suit. Just as well, perhaps. He'd not want it again, even if it hadn't shrunk out of recognition.

He pushed aside the stack of dishes and put his head under the cold tap, pulled the roller towel from its rail and rubbed at his face and hair. When he looked at himself in Marcia's little wall mirror: a wild, redfaced, unshaven man glared back from bloodshot eyes. He hated himself.

It came to him then that he had always hated

265

himself. More than anyone ever.

The bedroom appeared as he'd left it, with Marcia's things lying about, some crammed into suitcases. They could all be taken away now, leave him more space. Leave him—what?

Like an automaton he moved across to the wall where the photographs hung, and stared at them, went back through the years into the person he'd once been. A boy again, secure with a home and parents. This shot had been taken just three months before it all broke up, his mother killed in the car crash, his father dying of injuries eight days later, his home eventually sold. A few months with a bachelor uncle who didn't want him, and then the Children's Home.

All that was over. He reached out, took the frame from its hook and let it drop to the ground. He heard the tinkle of glass shattering.

Dully he passed on to the second picture. Which left him older—about twenty-eight—on a choppy lake, handling the dinghy that had been his pride and joy.

He'd reached his peak then, but thought the future would still lead upwards. The little boat had been a symbol of achievement, proof that he had his life and all around him well under control. He'd painted it with yacht enamel, bright red: *Dolphin*. Don's *Dolphin* the chaps at the sailing club used to call it. Sold to raise the cash to get married. Marcia—she was Judy then—claiming, mistakenly, she was pregnant.

Gone. Everything in ruins. The past, his marriage, almost certainly his job. Nothing left. Except anger and the need to make somebody suffer for it.

A wild, painful sound burst from his throat as he threw himself on the bed and hurled blankets, pillows, mattress against the farther wall. On his knees, he beat with his fists on the coiled springs exposed, tore at them with his fingers but they failed to give way. He sucked the blood away from his nails, lifted the bedstead bodily and flung it from him. He stumbled blindly downstairs.

They had taken his car for tests. *They*: he wasn't one of them any more. But it was nothing new; he'd been an outsider a long time.

So he'd walk. He went out into the moonless dark, down through Bardells Wood, over the Green and the hump-backed bridge, up the hill on the other side where the incomers lived, the yuppies, the commuters, the stinking rich. He marched like an automaton, blind and mindless, but he knew where he was headed, knew who he was going for, and why he had to fix him.

CHAPTER TWENTY-ONE

GUY STAFFORD STARTED UP FROM his chair. He had fallen asleep in front of the TV screen

267

with the sound turned off in case the telephone should ring. Was that what had disturbed him? Could he have slept through and missed it?

He listened. From the second bedroom came music turned low, which seemed to indicate that Owen was still awake. He got up stiffly, about to check, when there came a dull thud from outside, as though something heavy had fallen against the new door just fitted since the police break-in. He moved out into the hall and switched on the central light.

Through the fish-eye lens he could see only darkness. Cautiously he turned the lock and began to open up.

The door swung rapidly inwards and a violent blow caught him between the eyes. Staggering back he tried to make out the silhouette of the man standing over him, but a punch to the belly doubled him up. He put out a hand as he slithered down the wall, rocking the telephone table, and it made contact with something hard and smooth: the antique ship's bell that he left his mail under until he found time to deal with it.

His fingers closed round it as a savage kick landed on his ribs. With his free hand he caught on to the man's trousers, tugged, raising his body to topple him. The man lashed out with the other leg but it missed him. Caught off balance, the intruder felt a cracking blow on the kneecap and went down. Stafford was on top of him, raised the heavy bell and heard

Owen behind him shouting. In that split second of hesitation, the man twisted his head and the blow was deflected to the side of his jaw.

Then Owen was beside Stafford, pulling on his arm. 'Dad, no! You can't!'

Stafford shook his head to dispel the giddiness that had overcome him. He felt the man roll away, heard the door slam and stumbling footfalls on the stairs outside. Stafford wrenched himself free from his son's hands. 'He broke in! I've got to get him!'

'No! Didn't you see who it was? He's police! He must have been watching the place.'

'Police?' Stafford put a hand up to the back of his head where it had struck against the wall. His fingers came away red and tacky. He let Owen push him into a chair.

'Look, I just don't believe this. He was trying to fiddle the lock. It woke me up. When I opened the door he went for me. Is that police procedure?'

'He's a Detective-Sergeant. His name's Turley. I—I've seen him about.'

'*That*'s Turley? Oh, my God!'

Stafford groaned, leaning his face into his hands. His voice came out hushed. 'He must have guessed.'

Guessed what? But Owen kept the words unspoken. It was at Dad's trailer that Turley's wife had been killed. He'd heard it on the late news and it hadn't made sense. He'd been lying

269

on his bed ever since trying to work it out. It had been Thursday night he'd spent at the trailer himself and everything seemed all right then. Dad had been away a lot in the next few days and it was only today he'd decided to move the thing on to the next site.

He was gone for hours, and when he came back he was withdrawn and shaky. Owen had felt it wiser to leave him alone.

So if Turley had *guessed* something— something that would send him here crazy for blood—who was he after? Owen, or his father this time?

*   *   *

DS Beaumont leaned over his arms on the edge of the bridge. He had a lot on his mind. The calm of the starlit summer night with the lazy chuckle of the stream flowing below him was conducive to conciliatory thoughts.

Mott had been right in thinking he was loth to go home. Ever since Cathy had reversed her decision to leave him, it had been an impossible situation. For young Stuart's sake he'd kept off open warfare, just chugged along with his head down, taking her as part of the furniture; separate rooms, separate existence, minimum communication. But you couldn't call it family life.

Even if the job had been an easy one, coming home of an evening you needed to be at peace

270

with yourself. He couldn't be, so he used every excuse to stay away. But it didn't resolve the problem. He knew that sometime there would have to be a definite break or else a reconciliation.

To be fair, it wasn't all Cathy's fault. She'd grown tired of unrewarding domestic ties and gone off to do her own thing. An adolescent fancy in a mid-life crisis. And he hadn't been there much to help.

He couldn't dismiss the notion that there was a parallel here with Turley's situation. Not that he was anything like a wife-beater himself. He'd never gone so far, but he'd a sharp tongue and he'd sometimes thought it would relieve tension to lash out around him.

It was the job, for one thing. The constant hitting your head against a wall of restrictions; the inadmissibility of hard-won evidence; the Crown Prosecution's refusal to take on anything but a surefire case, and even then losing out; the hobbling of the bloody Police and Criminal Evidence Act.

No one outside the job could possibly understand, and you got so shit-weary that you gave up expecting them to. You wanted to bury yourself in something warm and comforting—well, some*body* warm and comforting—and you went home to complaints and more hassle, and your blood began to boil. Then the rows began. All the same, he wasn't in the same league as Turley.

It was as though by thinking of the man he'd conjured him up. Beaumont raised his eyes from the softly swirling pattern of dark water and there was Turley quite close, coming across the Green, hunched and solid, bowed arms swinging clenched fists, a bully-boy out to make trouble.

So Beaumont lowered his head in the shadows and let him go by, stood back and watched him stomp up the road on the other side of the valley, turn off halfway into Maze Hill. Which could eventually take him to Bentham Lodge at the top. So it might be worth someone's while to follow, and see what the man had in mind.

But Turley wasn't making for the top. He turned off again quite soon, heading towards an unassuming block of flats, where he stood a while in the shadowed doorway, possibly fiddling with a key. And then there was no movement in the pool of darkness, so he must have gone in. Beaumont crossed the street, came close and shone his pencil-light on the name-plates. The third-floor occupant's name was Stafford.

The self-locking outer door had its snib pushed up. For a rapid departure? Beaumont eased himself past, regretting that he'd left his radio back in his room. Suddenly an almighty row broke out somewhere upstairs, with thuds, banging and shouting. The boy Owen was yelling, 'No, Dad! No!'

Then scrabbling sounds and the pounding of feet coming closer. The light-timer gave out overhead and the stairway was plunged in darkness. Beaumont flattened himself against the wall, and when he judged the moment right he stuck out one leg. The fleeing man went plunging head over heels down the last few stairs, pulling Beaumont on top of him.

There was no call for heroics and Beaumont was glad, because weightwise they weren't in the same class. Turley had struck his head on the base of the newel post and was out cold.

*   *   *

Mott was notified of the incident by divisional Control, who had received a call from Beaumont at Guy Stafford's flat. Two patrol cars were diverted to bring in all involved. He decided against disturbing the Boss, but, before he had flung his clothes on, Yeadings was there at his door demanding what was up.

'Let them stew a bit, Angus,' he advised. 'You're not going out of here without a hot drink in you. I've got a kettle on the boil in my room.'

Just as well, Mott agreed, sipping his coffee black and scalding; this new development needed a little pondering before he rushed in on it. He appreciated that the Boss was prepared to leave it to him and get a report decently after daybreak.

He found Turley sitting up and surly, being ministered to by the same woman police surgeon who had examined the second body.

'He'll need an X-ray as soon as you've done with him,' she said briskly, 'but in my opinion he's as strong as an ox, a splendidly thick-skulled specimen. Only unconscious a matter of seconds. But his jaw's madly dislocated and mentally he's under considerable strain. I think he has something to get off his chest.'

*   *   *

There was a lot of anger in the man, but he was enough of a jack himself to insist on making a statement before being packed off to hospital. Talking with obvious pain, he started by admitting he'd lied in his previous statement. On hearing this, Mott ordered the interview to be taped, and Turley repeated the admission.

'I said I never went out Friday night because it wasn't relevant then,' he argued. 'I never knew where my wife's body had been found until the late news tonight. Then it all fitted together. Killed sometime Friday or Saturday out at a trailer on the pet foods factory site.'

Mott looked grim. He'd given orders for that last item to be kept from the media, but somehow it had leaked. The official press conference was to be later this morning at twelve o'clock.

'So what made the difference?'

'In the early hours of Saturday I followed her killer out there.' He managed a grim smile at the effect it had.

'I'd walked out to the Green Man to pick up the car, and on the way back I saw this kid, Stafford's son, sneak out of the house.'

Mott stared hard at him. 'But he lives on the opposite side of Fords Green. Maze Hill is nowhere near the route from the Green Man to your home.'

'He was staying the night with friends in Alma Villas. I saw him go in with his girl earlier.'

'Which house is this? Do you know the names of these people?'

Turley shook his head, then put a hand up to the bandage. 'Shouldna done that.'

He frowned, thinking back. 'Seen them around, but don't know them from Adam. No, I wasn't bothered with them, just him.'

Beaumont straightened from where he leaned against the window. 'Yes, we know you're gunning for Owen Stafford. There was that flasher business, just the day before. Didn't you do enough to him then?'

Turley looked thunderous. 'He was there in Bardells Wood. He had to be checked on. He'd changed his clothes by the time we picked him up. It's likely he had other shoes and things out at this other house. He was using it like a second home. I saw him in the trainers and baseball cap later. He was wearing them the

275

night he went after my wife. It was him all right, both times.'

A teenage flasher from a broken home? Mott wondered. And Littlejohn had described Marcia Turley's attack as a botched rape. The two sometimes went together. He'd never been quite comfortable with the idea of Turley doing half a job sexually. And Owen Stafford had taken a bad knock about losing his university place. That could be enough to send a precarious mind over the edge.

But it didn't smell quite right even now. He wished he had the Boss's incomparable nose for a fiction.

'You were in your car,' he reminded Turley. 'And the boy was on foot.'

'I never said he was. He went for a car in a lockup near the house, and I followed it. Right to the turning for the building site. He turned off and I missed him, went past and had to go back. But he was in there, took the car right up to what I thought was a bungalow or hut. Must have been the trailer. It had lights on behind the curtains. I saw the door open and she stood there calling out, then he went in. That's when I left. I was too far away to see who the woman was.

'If I'd known . . .' He broke off and glared at Mott. 'Those Stafford bastards!'

Mott formally closed the interview and removed the tape from the machine.

'We'll leave it there,' he said, 'and get you to

276

Casualty for an X-ray.' He needed to question Owen and his father before he heard more from Turley.

*　　*　　*

And Owen Stafford denied everything, the flashing incident of Thursday, the sneaking out in the early hours of Saturday, taking a car— though yes, he could drive—and the journey out to the building site.

'Right, best get back to bed now. We'll continue this later,' Mott allowed. 'I want you both to come in at 11.00 a.m. and see Superintendent Yeadings.'

He could do with snatching some sleep himself. He left instructions for young Stafford to be fingerprinted when he next turned up. They had the father's dabs already.

Driving back to the Green Man, he rehearsed his précis for the Boss. And his conclusion? It was that one, if not both, of the contradictory statements was a load of codswallop.

But in any case, Turley had it in for the boy, and it had certainly been Owen he was after when he'd used skeleton keys to gain entry to the father's apartment block.

But he had said 'those Stafford bastards'— plural. So what had Guy Stafford done to upset him?

Mott and Yeadings arrived at Division together later that morning, to find that Guy Stafford was there before them, alone, insisting on seeing them.

'I should have spoken up yesterday,' he told them when they were in an interview room and the tape was running, 'but I'd had a double shock. I saw a body and I thought it must be Gill. I couldn't take a second look. Then, after I'd heard who it actually was, I realized that somehow Turley must have found out. So really it was my fault.'

He faced Yeadings, his mouth a grim line. 'It was Turley who killed her, wasn't it? Not some passing tramp?'

'We have no proof one way or the other. But I'd like to get this in chronological order. You said "so it was my fault." What did you mean by that, Mr Stafford?'

'I took her there. It seemed the best thing at the time. She'd meant to stay with a friend, Nancy Carter, but—'

'We'll return to that. For the moment let's go back a little further. How long had you known the dead woman? And how did you happen to meet?'

'She did some work for me several years back. I was using the typing agency in Market Street at the time. Later I opened a small office locally and Nancy Carter ran it until her first baby came. Then I closed it, but I still kept in touch with her and she does freelance work at home when there's a rush on at my Amersham office.

'I had wanted Marcia to take over the office from her, but Turley made her give up working altogether. She said he didn't like her not being there when he got home. And the noise of the typewriter prevented him resting.'

'Did that strike you as unreasonable?'

'Selfish, certainly. But as far as I was concerned it was her life, her choice. She said he was an intensely jealous man, not that he ever had cause. Marcia was always very correct, even puritanical.'

'When did you know she intended leaving her husband?'

'Not until she'd gone already. Nancy mentioned it to me. Then I had a call from Marcia, wanting to know if I could recommend a solicitor to deal with her divorce. I gave her a name and heard no more until Nancy came in with some contracts and mentioned Marcia was coming across from Hertford for a consultation. I didn't know exactly when, but I wrote and said I'd be happy to take her for a meal when she did come. It was by chance I happened on her Friday as she was slipping home from the bus station. She was scared of running into her husband, and I offered to go with her.'

'You said she'd been going to stay with this

Nancy Carter.'

'They'd arranged that some time back, an open invitation. Marcia came Friday night because the solicitor made a last-minute offer to come in early on the Saturday, fitting her in specially, and the first bus would have arrived too late. Meanwhile Nancy Carter had a panic call that her mother was taken ill. She rang to turn down some work I had offered, which was how I knew. But her arrangement with Marcia must have gone out of her mind. She left without getting in touch. Marcia rang through, didn't get an answer, but assumed the invitation still stood.'

'So Mrs Turley was stranded with nowhere to stay.'

'I suggested alternatives, but obviously she hadn't much money, and she'd have been too proud to let me pay. The trailer was available, had gas laid on and enough supplies for a makeshift breakfast. She did let me take her out for dinner before I left her there, because she'd accepted earlier.'

'I have to ask this, Mr Stafford—'

'There was no question of a romantic attachment, Superintendent.'

'I wasn't thinking of romance, sir. Something more earthy.'

'We never had sex. It didn't come into it. I felt sorry for a thoroughly nice woman who'd been having a rough time.'

'Did she ever say how rough?'

280

'She never complained of bad treatment, but I heard in a roundabout way. I had actually seen her once with a split lip and a badly swollen cheek, though she tried to cover them up.'

'And at what time on Friday night or Saturday morning did you take your leave of Mrs Turley at the trailer, sir?'

'I'm not sure of it exactly, but I was home for the tail end of the ITV weather forecast. About 10.30 p.m.'

'Friday night?'

'Yes.'

'Thank you, sir. It would have helped if you'd come forward as soon as you knew she was missing.'

'But I didn't know. I'd been away on business over the weekend. I came back to hear that Randall was dead and no one knew where Gill was. That's why ...'

'... you assumed the dead woman was your ex-wife. Yes, I see.'

Stafford had a question of his own. 'So when did you actually know Mrs Turley was missing?'

Yeadings eyed him steadily. 'When Mr Etheridge the solicitor rang through to report she hadn't turned up on Saturday. That call was only made yesterday, after he'd tried to contact her at her mother's in Hertford and Turley himself was asking around. Mr Etheridge was able to confirm his client's standing arrangements with himself and Nancy Carter. What he wasn't aware of was any link she had with you.'

*　　*　　*

'So how does it stand?' Mott demanded when Stafford had departed.

'According to Stafford, Turley killed her, having somehow traced her out to the trailer, maddened by her trying to get free. According to Turley, it was the boy Owen in a frustrated sex attack. Old Ma Crocker thinks it was Randall because he's a bastard anyway. And there's nothing to back up Guy Stafford's story of getting home for the sign-off of the late ITV news and going straight to his solitary bed. Since it has been solitary for so long, was he overstepping the Samaritan role and pressing unwanted attentions which Marcia Turley rebuffed? It could equally well have been any of them.

'Four suspects. Yer pays yer money and yer takes yer choice. So, Angus, have you any other names you'd like to add in for good measure?'

CHAPTER TWENTY-TWO

Wednesday, 26 August

AFTER SUCH A DISTURBED NIGHT Guy Stafford had been determined to bypass Inspector Mott if necessary and seek out Superintendent Yeadings. For this reason he had left the flat early, before the post arrived. The school-teacher who lived on the ground floor collected it as usual from the mat and distributed it to the appropriate wire cages in the hall. Except for one item.

Among the envelopes had been a home-made one constructed from a lined page from an exercise book, folded and secured with sticky tape. It was addressed by hand in block capitals to G. Stafford and had never been franked. So unless the Post Office had been unusually forgiving, it must have been delivered by hand during the half hour between Guy's departure and her lifting of the mail.

Since little went on in the flats without this sharp-eyed lady's knowledge, she was aware of Guy's comings and goings with the police. Chancing that it was to them he had dashed off this morning and that the communication could be an urgent demand from kidnappers, she rang through to the station to ask for him.

The message arrived as he was leaving the

building and a WPC ran out to call him back. Switchboard meanwhile had passed the call through to Yeadings' number. Under the circumstances Stafford had little choice but to let the Superintendent send a car to pick the envelope up.

The enclosed note, folded round a hank of Gillian's near-black hair, was in her handwriting and demanded £30,000 for her safe return. Instructions for the transfer would shortly come by telephone. The amount, in figures, was scribbled in a looser hand above a heavy deletion, and suggested someone's second thoughts on the sum, added after the woman had been forced to write the note.

'But so amateur,' Stafford marvelled, his fingers gingerly turning the envelope inside its protective plastic cover. 'It's as though children have done it. This paper has come from an exercise book.'

'An old one,' Yeadings agreed. 'Look at the yellowing edges, and there was a smell of mould. But we're not dealing with children here. The mud impressions at Burnham Beeches were of large men's shoes.'

'So could this letter just be a hoax?'

'We have to assume it's genuine until proved otherwise. It's a large sum to put your hand on at short notice, so demand more time, keep the caller talking long enough for us to get a fix on him. We'll get a listening van in the neighbourhood as soon as we can. And refuse to cooperate until you've proof your—Mrs Randall's safe. Insist she speaks to you. They could try to use a recording, which guarantees nothing. So go home and wait by the telephone. Make your plans for raising the money from there. I'll see you're given one of our tape-recorders. Tape everything that comes through, no matter who it is.'

* * *

Yeadings rang through to make the necessary arrangements then went with Mott to open the morning's briefing to a crowded room.

'It'll be no surprise to any of you,' he said tersely, 'that the press are baying for results: two bodies in two days; we're forty-eight hours on from discovery of the first, and no sign of a coming arrest.

'Questioning continues, and so far we have no positive link between the two cases. A lot of data is still coming in. Inspector Mott will fill you in on that.'

Angus rose to take over. 'We've pointers in several directions, which means spreading the spadework widely. The experts at Aldermaston have been going flat out and I'll briefly give you the more interesting results.

'First, the apparent abduction leading to the death of Paul Randall. Glass fragments picked up at Chardleigh Place after a guest was struck by a car beside the shrubbery early on Sunday

285

morning certainly came from the shattered driver's-side headlight on his red Sierra. It's of the right type, and we have matching fragments.

'The same car left tyre tracks in Burnham Beeches sometime after Friday's storm, probably during a rendezvous with a heavier vehicle, which we believe was a dark blue van. And an emerald ear-stud found during the fingertip search there was definitely Mrs Randall's.

'Every other material clue we have so far ranks as "probable". The same goes for some link between the two deaths but, as Superintendent Yeadings mentioned, there is no substantial evidence to suggest a common killer.

'A number of vans have been checked on locally. We still haven't found the right one. Go on asking, and poking into any places it might be concealed. Sketches from an eye-witness will be handed out. You may well think it looks like a Bedford.

'Medical evidence: general as yet, but Randall died several hours after the original attack, though almost certainly from injuries received then. We have to consider that the intention may not have been to kill. Nevertheless, the two or more men we are looking for must be regarded as dangerous, and no heroics are expected. Their footwear comes in sizes eleven and twelve, so they'll be pretty big guys, and we know they're dangerous. So report in and get back-up whenever and wherever.

'Our second body hits close to home, a fellow-officer's wife. Asphyxiation by ligature. Evidence from torn clothing and bruising suggests a sexual attack interrupted short of rape; no semen was found. Small quantities of two types of blood were present on the ligature, which was heavy duty binding tape, sharp-edged, so that it tore both the neck and some part of the killer's hands. Specimens of the unidentified blood are reserved for DNA comparison once we have someone firmly in the frame.'

A hand went up at the back of the room. 'Yes?'

'Soft hands and no semen. Did it have to be a man?'

'We're considering this. Try out some garrotting movements yourself with heavy duty binding tape. See how you get on and decide for yourself. Right?'

There was an undercurrent of muttering. Mott picked up the threads again.

'Fingerprints: not surprisingly, Guy Stafford's were found everywhere in the trailer, a number overprinting the woman's. According to his statement, he drove Mrs Turley there for her to spend Friday night, showed her how the retracting bed worked, how to turn on the gas and what provisions

287

were in the fridge. He left her filling a kettle for tea, refused to stay himself for any, reached home about 10.30 p.m. and claims he never went out again.

'Still quoting his statement: he visited the trailer on Sunday to pick up some papers, was in a hurry and took little notice of the inside. Yesterday afternoon he needed to move it to another site, was surprised that the woman hadn't tidied up better after her stay, so started in on it himself. Intended stripping off the sheets to be laundered, opened the wall-bed, and the dead woman was in it. The face was covered by her torn nightdress, and the body naked. As the site manager entered, Stafford had merely glimpsed the woman and assumed her to be his missing ex-wife.'

He looked around. 'Any questions so far?'

'Why didn't Stafford go back next day and pick the Turley woman up if she hadn't any transport?'

'There's a telephone laid on. He said she had intended ringing for a taxi when she was ready to leave. Next?'

'Were hers and Stafford's the only fingerprints found?'

'No. Theirs and the site manager's are the only ones so far identified. There were several other prints. The binding tape didn't pick up anything useful, being of a heavy basket-weave texture. We found smears in several places, including the door-latch, where an attempt had been made to remove prints.

'Next, clothing: dress-suits. Randall's missing jacket, vouched for by the gents' outfitter who sold it to him two years back, was fished from the Elbourne about here.' He turned and tapped a point on the wall map.

'You'll notice it's upriver of where we found Randall's body, and also of the building site where the trailer stands, so the search for Mrs Randall is to be concentrated above where the jacket was found. This allows for it having floated downstream after being flung in *en route* between where Paul Randall died and where he was dumped.

'The dampness of Randall's clothing when found—singlet and dress trousers—was due to them having been roughly and liberally sponged, using something like washing-up liquid. As the injuries were head wounds, the jacket is where greatest staining is likely to have occurred, but due to immersion in flowing water, no obvious blood remains.

'So it appears that an attempt was made to clean Randall up, his clothes were removed for washing and some put back on him, the jacket disposed of as beyond saving. Threads removed from the areas of congealed blood in the head wounds came from a cotton-polyester cloth such as shirting, possibly blue and white striped. Any makeshift bandaging or swabs used were removed before the dumping of the body, presumably from fear of providing a clue

289

to their source. The shoes and socks were probably removed to prevent any indication of where Randall walked while held captive.'

Mott paused to make sure he was receiving total concentration. 'A second dress-suit, also damp and sent for scientific examination, has led to unsubstantiated rumours. These garments, worn at Chardleigh Place by a local police officer and later rinsed under a shower, have now shown nothing more sinister than residual stains from vomit. They are no longer considered exhibits in either case.'

'So Turley's eliminated?' demanded a low, anonymous voice.

Mott looked sharply at the massed faces to find its source but they were all suddenly deadpan.

He chose his next words carefully. 'The dress-suit would have been relevant only to the night of Saturday to Sunday, which could cover one incident but not that of the previous twenty-four hours.'

He watched the significance sink in: after the Charity Ball Turley was presumed in no condition to help with the Randalls' kidnap, but could remain in the frame for his wife's killing of the night before. There were barely perceptible nods among his colleagues.

Mott watched as a WPC slid into the room with a note for the Superintendent, who read it and shook his head.

'That's it, then. You all know what you're

tasked for. We need urgently to see anyone owning or using a dark blue van who hasn't already been pulled in. We still want a complete record of the Randalls' movements for the two days leading up to their disappearance, and we need a lot more on Mrs Turley's contacts in Fords Green. So get to it.'

Mott left with Yeadings who was now wearing a sour expression. On reaching their borrowed office, he flipped the note towards his junior.

'Owen Stafford came in as arranged for his dabs to be taken. They turn out to be one of the sets found inside the trailer. So maybe Turley's story was true after all and the young man did drive out to the building site on Friday night, when he was supposed to be staying with friends. It's reasonable to suppose he knew his father's trailer was set up there and he could have had a means of access.

'In view of the latest move in the Randall case—the letter demanding ransom—it's a bad time to add to Stafford's troubles, but we have to follow this up. Send Lew Duke out to look through all the lad's clothes. Turley's description was quite clear. He saw him in daylight as well as after dark. We want a baseball cap, jeans and a pair of blue and white trainers—which could match up with tracks in mud at the building site.'

When Mott had left, Yeadings sat on, slumped at the desk, and took from his folder a photocopy of the ransom letter supposedly from Gillian Randall. He still didn't know how to take it. But he was sure it was the right thing to keep its arrival under his hat. Never more so than at the coming press conference.

*   *   *

Confounding his suspicions that the letter might be a hoax, the promised call came less than two hours after Stafford's return to the flat. It was no child's voice, but deep and muffled, with a countrified southern accent. The man knew enough to keep his message short. He read it out in a wooden voice.

'Stafford? Thirty thousand in old tenners. In a hundred packs of thirty wrapped in newspaper inside four plastic carrier bags from Tesco. Have them ready, and be ready to move when I ring at 5.00. And stay shut or she gets carved up for good.'

'You have to give me time. It's a lot of money. Listen, let me talk to . . .'

'Raise it. Do it now. That's all.'

'How do I know she . . . ?'

'Do it. Or else.' And the call was cut.

It struck Yeadings that Stafford had left the flat before Lew Duke's arrival to pick up Owen's clothes, because it was only the kidnapper's message he passed on when he rang from a public phone box.

'Can you raise that much?' Yeadings asked

when the call was put through.

'Some of it. I'm getting on to that now. I believe I can borrow the rest on trust, maybe using Gill's house as collateral. I've a friend who'd take that risk, and Gill would want me to. It's the price of her life.'

'They're rushing him. I don't like it. There's barely time to set anything up,' Mott said grimly, listening in.

'For God's sake don't let them know I'm in touch with you,' Stafford pleaded. 'It could leak back.'

'It won't,' Yeadings promised. 'I shall use officers from another district. The kidnappers will be expecting you to leave at once. Cooperate. Go without locking your door. Have your car ready at the kerb. They're definitely out for speed.'

'It's a weirdo right enough,' Mott muttered when Stafford had rung off. 'It doesn't fit any recognized pattern. We don't actually know this man's got her. Or that she's still alive. She was when she wrote the letter, but then that change of the amount ... Did they finish her off, chicken out, cut the ransom and settle for a quick getaway?'

'It smells panicky,' Yeadings agreed. 'And odd, as you said. Whoever saw bundles of notes made up in thirties? They'd all have to be repacked after leaving the bank.'

'But that way it would be simpler to check thirty thousand, if your arithmetic's not much good.'

'*Simple*, yes. Maybe that's the sort of people we're dealing with. A home-made envelope and a school notebook, because there's nothing else to hand. Ill-formed figures, and there are some funny phrases in the letter you wouldn't expect an educated woman to use.'

'Four plastic carrier bags,' Mott considered. 'From a Tesco store. How could they be sure Stafford could lay his hands on them?'

'Tesco have a supermarket in Amersham, and another in Slough,' Yeadings remembered. 'It's quite likely he's used one or other in the past, and most people keep a few carrier bags by them.'

'His ex-wife could have told them where he shops.'

Yeadings looked thoughtful. 'So how far is she cooperating with her captors? Is it just to save her own skin, or ...?'

The two detectives treated each other to a hard stare. Mott was the first to take it all the way. 'Or running the whole show? The Randalls were known to be short of cash to keep that big place going. And they weren't getting on together.'

The Superintendent nodded, his black eyebrows rising. 'How shattered would she be, d'you think, if her present husband was killed in the process of milking her ex of what she needed? Let's not forget that her mother called her "impetuous".'

'And we thought of Fords Green as an innocent little backwater,' Mott marvelled. 'God, when you start turning over the stones, there are some slimy creatures wriggle out.'

CHAPTER TWENTY-THREE

YEADINGS WENT THROUGH TO DEAL with the noon press conference, feeding in enough information to give an assurance that the police were beavering away and still needing help from the general public. But as ever the mikes were pushed aggressively forward with questions slanted to provoke him into saying more than he had intended.

'Until the present moment,' one whippet-like reporter insisted, 'have you been holding anyone "to help the police with their inquiries"?'

Yeadings let a little silence build, then amiably answered, 'Yes. And if any progress is to be made I must get back to the interviews now. Thank you for your cooperation, gentlemen.'

He left them baffled and debating the significance of 'interviews' in the plural. Two murders, so had they separate suspects for each? Or were the police so stymied that they were pulling in any number of likely persons and fishing in the dark? It provided plenty of scope for editorial interpretation and innuendo.

The last media man was firmly ushered out, precautions having been taken to prevent sneak interviews with civilian staff and lesser police entering or leaving the building.

*   *   *

Since Stafford's call about raising the ransom, the Superintendent had taken over the questioning of Mott's two suspects, both in respect of the murder of Marcia Turley.

Turley, back in custody at the station after his X-rays showed no fractures, seemed to regard his attack on Stafford in the early hours as a perfectly logical and permissible follow-up on his suspicions. He continued to rant on about Owen Stafford as a twisted and sexually frustrated adolescent, the unstable child of a broken marriage—if not of an unnatural marital trio. He harped on the crash of the boy's career prospects, his role as a flasher, his night trip out to the building site and his brainstorm attack on Marcia when he came on her at the trailer.

Pressed to say whether he thought they met by chance or by arrangement, he broke suddenly into raucous sobbing which turned into an attack of breathlessness like asthma. The man seemed demented, and Yeadings put through an emergency call for the Duty Police

Surgeon to examine him.

The other detainee had been Owen himself, brought in by Lew Duke with the clothes the boy had been wearing on Friday. The baseball cap, jeans and trainers were as Turley had described. While the doctor was still present, Yeadings asked him to perform a blood test on the boy.

Since Owen was a minor and his father involved elsewhere, Yeadings had Duke take him to the canteen for his lunch. At a little after two o'clock Guy Stafford came storming in to demand why they were holding him. He had the money business sorted apart from the repacking, he said, but what the hell did the police think they were playing at, pulling in his son?

It wasn't an ideal arrangement to have Stafford sitting in to watch over Owen's interests, because if Owen could prove his innocence, it might well be Guy who would end in the hot seat after him. On the other hand, Yeadings found it interesting to observe their interreactions.

There was little physical resemblance between the two, the young man being compact and dark like his mother. Guy had a large Nordic frame, an open, weathered face with sun-bleached hair, and he moved with an assurance his son lacked. But there was a similarity of manner in the way they gave their information, with an almost wearied

297

conciseness, as though not expecting belief, but doggedly pursuing the line they had taken.

Owen again made a statement about his movements on Thursday morning. He denied any involvement in the flasher incident, making no complaint about his treatment by Turley, although his efforts to control his voice at that point of the story spoke volumes. His version matched up with the reports from PCs Bailey and Norris.

Questioned about the trailer, he agreed he had known about it, and was able to account for the presence of his fingerprints. On Thursday he had spent the night there (licking his wounds, Yeadings appreciated). He had walked out to the site and back, dropping in early on Friday for breakfast at Paco's Caff.

A phone call to Martinez, passed on to Delia, confirmed this. She remembered him well. Nice boy, she said.

Owen kept his fingers crossed as questioning bypassed his method of entry to the trailer, both his father and the Superintendent seeming to assume that he'd picked up the keys from Guy's flat.

Yeadings might have dismissed all his movements of that day as innocent, but for the inclusion of a photograph with Turley's report on the flasher incident, a close-up of a shoe impression in woodland grit. The logo of a dolphin enclosed in a circle also appeared in photographs taken by Scenes of Crime experts

298

near the trailer and had clearly been made after Friday's torrential rain. Owen's blue and white trainers had just such a sole, yet he continued to deny having made the prints.

His clothes taken from the flat were now sealed in bags marked with an exhibit number ready for microscopic examination. The decision to charge Owen Stafford as Thursday's flasher and the frustrated rapist of Marcia Turley hung in the balance. If his blood was found to be of the same group as the unidentified type on the ligature, there would be no reason to hold back even the charge of murder.

But Yeadings went on probing, not satisfied that he had a full picture of the young man. 'You'd received your examination results that Thursday morning, and you were disappointed, feared you would lose your university place?'

'Yes. I was depressed, but not—'

'Not what?'

'Not angry. I didn't go berserk. I was just down, and there was nobody to talk to about it. There must have been hundreds of guys feeling the same way then.'

'Mmm. You'd wanted an A in History. It came out a C. How do you think that happened? I believe there's been some criticism of uneven marking.'

'No, it wasn't that. I knew I'd done badly. I couldn't even remember what I'd written in

299

those two papers on the last day.'

'Overtired?'

'I guess.'

But there had been something a little odd about his hesitation then, darting an almost guilty sideways look in his father's direction.

'That would have been back in June,' Yeadings mused, watching him. 'So what put you off your stroke?'

'Not much sleep the night before, is all.'

'Why, Owen?' His father was pressing him now.

'Aw shit! Still, what does it matter now? If you have to know, they were going at it hammer and tongs all evening. I went out for a walk until about two in the morning. They were rowing again when I got back.'

'What about?'

'Basically money. It was always money. Only they couldn't leave it there. There were— personal things.'

'I'm sorry. I didn't realize it was that bad.'

'Ma got hysterical and locked him out of their room. I thought he was going to break the door down. He'd been taking some stuff; speed, I guess. But suddenly he rushed downstairs and started dialling. So I went and listened.'

'On an extension?'

'Yes. I thought it would be to some woman, but it wasn't.'

'Who, then?'

300

'A guy called Eddie. It was about some deal they were setting up, only Randall said they'd have to go for more. It wasn't enough, and he was being kept short. I guessed it was something to do with drugs.'

'You should have come and told me,' his father said grimly.

'I thought about it. I couldn't decide one way or the other. It kept me awake all night. I couldn't think straight. I was almost sure Ma was using too. Little signs, you know. I didn't want to give her away. I thought maybe she'd realize and stop before it really got a hold on her. Being a nurse and all. And I think since then she's been more careful.'

'This Eddie,' Yeadings prompted, 'have you come across him in any other connection?'

Owen was silent, then, 'Maybe. At end of term we went over to St Albans with the school. It was a juniors' history outing— Roman Verulamium. It's not my period; I'm a modernist. But I went as a prefect, to help. And I saw him in the car park; Randall, I mean, as we were getting out of the coach.

'He was sitting in another man's car, a big beige Toyota, last year's registration. They had their heads together, talking. Suddenly Randall laughed and slapped this guy's hand, as if they'd made some bargain. He got out and went across to his own car about twenty yards away. He was unlocking it when the other man drove past and I heard Randall call out, 'So long, Eddie, keep your nose clean!'

'Could you describe this man?'

Owen looked at him wearily. 'Does it matter? Randall's dead. So what, if he's been buying or dealing? This is all in the past.'

'*Can* you describe him?' Stafford was leaning forward now, insistent. 'Any little detail may help the police find your mother. Some clue to who he was linked with.'

'A man called Eddie, with a big beige Toyota, frequents St Albans car-parks,' Yeadings mused. 'That's not a lot for me to pass to the Hertfordshire force. Try to give me a little more.'

Owen shook his head. 'I never saw him outside his car, but he looked big. About Dad's size, wide shoulders, darkish. Not much hair, sort of razor-cut. Fortyish. A flat, brown monkey-face. It had wrinkles all over when he grinned.'

'And his voice on the phone?'

'Deep. A bit rough.'

'Any accent?'

'He wasn't a northerner. Not quite a cockney.'

'Good,' Yeadings said, rising. And to their surprise, 'You can both get off home now.'

The Staffords returned to the flat to repack the bank-notes and wait for the 5.00 p.m. call. On Mott's side everything became action stations, while Yeadings went thoughtfully off to brood on the information.

Turley had been sedated and was awaiting transport to hospital. It would mean tying down a uniformed man at his bedside until he was ready for further interview. And, even if they ever got him to court, he might be found not responsible for his actions. The breakdown he'd been working towards for some time, Yeadings thought bitterly, had overwhelmed him at last. How much of this personal disaster could have been avoided if his mental state had been acknowledged earlier and he'd been sent on a stress-management course?

Not that shrinks could do much about an unsuitable marriage or sheer overwork. If they sorted you out temporarily, you were still left afterwards to face the choice of continuing in the same way or making a complete break and a new start in a suspicious and alien outside world. The man seemed friendless. From what he'd gathered, talking with Turley's colleagues, he hadn't enjoyed much camaraderie in the job.

* * *

Guy Stafford sat by the telephone, his head plunged in his hands. He was grateful to Owen for keeping to his room. There was no sound of music coming from it now. Maybe the boy was plagued by regrets as painful as his own.

Gillian dominated his mind. Gillian as he'd first seen her: quick-moving, quiet, responsible, a pretty young nurse setting about the bloody job of shearing clothes off the car crash victim he'd brought in. Closing the cubicle curtain on him with a grave smile. 'Sorry, Mr Stafford.'

God! Gillian sorry? Never as much as he was now. Surely he could have done more, done something to prevent all this? He should have given the man a hiding when he first found him hanging round Gill. He should at least have found out if she was all that keen on having a divorce. He'd just assumed ... Not that it was the first time she'd looked elsewhere for what he apparently hadn't given her.

It was his fault that they hadn't been open enough with each other. He'd let his work preoccupy him, or at least he'd made that his excuse. But the trouble lay within himself, that he kept his feelings too close, preferring to give the surface appearance that everything was all right, while knowing that underneath things had been going wrong for a long, long time. Which they shouldn't have done, because he understood how she was, just did nothing about it.

Gillian had never been one of those boring women who say and do things because it's expected of them. She would react openly; she would compliment, enthuse, storm, briefly sulk, because that was how she felt all the way

304

through. You never had to ask yourself, now what did she mean by that? And because the one thing she didn't do was criticize, he had the feeling that basically she'd approved of him.

But he had failed her by not expanding into all the many sorts of persons she seemed to need. He lacked variety, which was what she craved. He was a dull dog, and so he'd lost her, he'd let her go, for Randall to destroy her.

He forced himself back to the present, to imagine what sort of hell she might even now be going through, how she'd cope and how, please God, she'd come out of it. If ever she did. Because they might already have done with her as they did with Randall. She could be hidden away somewhere like he was, not yet discovered.

But not *she*. Her body.

He tightened his fists, and his nails bit into the flesh. He thought of her body, alive, vivacious, gentle, responsive, enjoying his own.

And the phone rang. It was two minutes to five.

*   *   *

Mott breathed into the hand-held mike, 'He's leaving the house. No one's to follow.'

It was essential that no sudden movement was seen at Stafford's departure. There was more than one man involved in the kidnap.

305

While one picked up the ransom, another could be keeping watch.

Mott had taken a risk, reading significance into the instruction about using Tesco plastic bags to contain the money. At this time of day the supermarkets would be thronged with people leaving work and picking up supplies. Going there Stafford would be only one in a crowd. Was that really what the kidnappers intended?

If so, it was most likely to happen in the car-park, a jostling and a snatch, maybe a second person there to hold a gun on Stafford while the other made off. If there was too great a chance of onlookers seeing him slugged, he'd be forced to drive off in another direction with the gun still trained on him. To some quiet place. Where he might end up like Randall.

However, the mini-transmitter affixed to Stafford's car should quickly tell them what direction he was taking. There were unmarked police vehicles already in the car-parks at both supermarkets, with one prepared to draw out and leave a space as soon as the BMW was sighted.

And still he might have put his money on the wrong horse. The rendezvous could be somewhere else completely. In which case Mott would be picking up the trail himself.

*   *   *

Superintendent Yeadings had meanwhile received the results of Owen's blood test. He sat for a few minutes immersed in unpleasant thoughts, staring at the photographs before him on the desk. He had already spoken with the manager of the local shop retailing the trainers with the dolphin logo.

Suddenly heaving himself upright, he went into the corridor and hollered for Beaumont whose head popped out of a nearby door like a rabbit's from its hole.

'Get Z along here. I want you both to go and make an arrest.'

He glowered, issuing his instructions. He was a father himself and serious crime involving youngsters plunged him in an almost superstitious unease. They could seem to be bowling along so nicely, everything in the garden not necessarily lovely but holding up. Then comes the crash. Below the surface a foul rot has been invading, and all the good things are at risk along with the evil. The misery from it would spread to destroy the innocent.

There were times when he bitterly regretted the requirements of his job.

*   *   *

It looked to Mott as if his hunch was paying off. The listening van in touch with directional bug on Stafford's car reported him turning off the A40 for Amersham. The intercepted phone message had been passed on.

'He's to drive alone to the public phone box at Chalfont St Peter precinct for 5.15 p.m. That's all,' the operator told Mott.

So the Amersham supermarket was the one for the exchange to be made—or, more likely, the money bags snatched. Mott ordered the listening van to bypass St Peter and continue to the Pheasant Inn at St Giles, park there and follow the BMW when it reappeared, keeping out of sight. The order was passed to the unmarked cars at Amersham to stay alerted. As well as Stafford's BMW, a special lookout was to be kept for a large beige Toyota.

Mott was about to take off in the Amersham direction himself when a call came through from the Boss. 'I've had something promising from St Albans,' he said. 'A strong possible on Eddie, Randall's connection. He fits the description given by Owen Stafford and he has an interesting record. Two charges for affray, one of aggravated burglary, one of obtaining money with menaces. Nothing so far for GBH. Been out of Parkhurst five months. Could be into small-time drugs, they think. Pop across and see them, Angus, will you? They're holding him for us at Central.'

'Holding him? So what about this ransom rendezvous?'

'Well, we know there were two of them. You've got it set up. Leave it to your team.

Could still be a hoax, or some outsider trying it on. Whereas this Eddie Goble—I like the sound of him. He's been "trading in second-hand goods" in the Herts area pretty widely, using an old Bedford van, at present in his garage for a respray. No prizes for guessing the colour.'

Mott whistled low.

'Two more details. Eddie Goble has a younger brother Stevie works with him, bit of an oddball. Periodically under treatment for unspecified mental problems. They haven't been able to locate him. The brothers live together, but according to neighbours Stevie's been gone several days.

'Oh, and the other thing is we're charging someone for Mrs Turley's death. Beaumont's gone for the lad now.'

*   *   *

Mott gave only a fleeting thought to the Turley case, regretting that he'd felt some sympathy for Owen Stafford. Like Yeadings he despaired of minors' increasing involvement in serious crime but, being closer in age himself, had rather less patience with young offenders. It was the double kidnap and fatal beating-up of Paul Randall which held centre stage for him just then.

So what had actually happened? he asked himself as he drove towards the M25. Had

Randall been in some dodgy business with Eddie Goble and reneged, holding back cash payment?

No, that didn't fit in with the reported phone conversation overheard by the boy. Randall had insisted he needed more; which meant he was the supplier asking a higher price. Or was it a drug quantity he needed increased because he'd found more customers?

If Eddie Goble was the man they were after, it looked as though all the answers might lie at the end of this journey.

CHAPTER TWENTY-FOUR

NOT EVERYONE AT THE STATION was sobered by the prospect of a minor standing trial for murder. The heavy cloud of suspicion hanging over one of their own number having suddenly dispersed, canteen society was rumbustious. Led by the outsider Beaumont, they voiced their ambivalence over the exonerated Detective-Sergeant Turley in a roar of abusive song.

Z, returning from her depressing part in writing up the arrest, caught the tail end of Beaumont's solo:

'—a four-letter friend, a four-letter friend,
He'll always let you down.

He's fitful and shitful right up to the end—'

swallowed by a raucous western-style male voice chorus:

'A wonderful, one two three,
Four-letter friend!'

'All the same,' she reminded them as they made room for her in their midst, 'Turley's in a bad way. I can't see him ever coming back. How about the ransom chase—is it over?'

'Got clean away,' a uniformed man told her. 'Stevie Goble may be a marble or two short of a whole game, but he used what he has.' He explained how they'd got the man's name but not managed to collar him.

The police had been concentrated in the car-park, only one man inside the store entrance. He'd been astounded when Stafford, with his carrier bags, shouldered his way through the revolving door and made straight for the corridor leading to the toilets.

He had contacted the men outside on his handset. Two of them had rushed in to join him and they'd charged into the men's room. The elderly man vulnerably occupied at the stalls had wet himself in terror. There was no one in the cubicles. Nor in the ladies' room which they next burst into.

In the baby-changing area, which had a window, they found Stafford sprawled breathless on the floor, raising himself on an unsteady arm and pointing to where the metal frame struts had been wrenched away and a gap yawned, large enough to allow a man through.

Outside was the pick-up area with a minibus loading elderly folk. And a Yamaha motorbike with saddle-bags speeding from the exit.

They'd given chase up Station Hill but the man was going full out by then. They'd lost sight of the bike beyond the railway arch, and six cars deployed widely to search through the lanes of Chesham Bois had found no trace. A police helicopter was circling the area but any motor-cycle traffic appeared innocent.

'What about Gillian Randall?' Z demanded. 'Did the man say where she could be picked up?'

'No joy.'

The others jostled to get their word in. 'Inspector Mott hared off to St Albans to question Eddie Goble, the ransom one's brother. They've held him for us.'

'I was on switchboard when DI Mott phoned back. Goble hasn't spilled much yet, but it sounds like he's the one that held a gun on Randall and smashed his head on the car roof. He's trying to protect brother Stevie, said he just drove the van while Eddie returned the Sierra to Randall's place.'

'Which never made sense,' Z said. 'Why didn't they hang on to the car—small-time

312

crooks like that?'

'He hasn't given anything yet about where the woman's being held or any ransom deal. But the brothers must have planned to meet up. DI Mott shouldn't take long getting him to spill where and when. We're all on hold here, ready to scramble when a shout comes through.'

*   *   *

'Listen,' Eddie Goble pleaded. 'Stevie just did what I told him. He can drive and he can shove a meal together, but he's not up to much more. Can't you leave him out of it? And what happened to Paul; God, I'd never intended that! It was an accident. He told me to hit him and hit him good, so's the marks'd last until he got back to ask for the money.'

'When did you set all this up?'

'Over a coupla months back. I've known him for years, knew he had more use for money than what he could get, like. He useda let me know when some property was coming on the market and I'd go round picking stuff up cheap.'

'You're a knocker.'

'Antiques specialist. I watch the local papers and see who's just died, then call on the bereaved. They don't wanna be bothered most times with cleaning silver and all that junk, especially when it's the woman that's snuffed it. Then I offer a fair price and ...'

'And take advantage of the situation. Yes. So, as Paul Randall was an assistant in an estate agency, he was able to put you on to likely customers selling up?'

'Thass what I said. I'd give him a bitta commission when a fancy job turned up. Only then he said we could do each other a lotta good, because he had a plan to make real money. He was gonna pretend to be kidnapped along with his wife, and her ex would pay anything to get the girl back.'

'So what would your part in it be?'

'Take care of them, like.'

'How were you to do this?'

'There was this old schoolhouse, a bit tumbledown and no one in their right mind was ever going to view it, let alone offer cash. He gave us the keys and we gave it a onceover, got some food in and that. Then when he was ready we lifted them, after some society do out at Chardleigh.'

'What was your part in that?'

'I had to wait outside in the bushes. Paul came out and tipped me the wink they were just going to leave and I got in the back of the car. With his keys. No break-in, mind.

'Then when they came out he shoved his wife in to drive. I let her get a few yards on and I stuck a gun against her ear—only a replica, I swear. I've still got it at home. I can show you.'

'Don't worry. It will have been found by

314

now. Your flat is being taken to pieces. So, you threatened the woman and forced her to drive where?'

'Out to Burnham, the woods there.'

'Burnham Beeches.'

'Thass right. Then Paul got hurt a bit, like he said I had to, and Stevie loaded them in the van and drove off. I had to take Paul's car back. He didn't want that written off, see? I told him people'd think that was funny, but he was mean over little things.'

'So then you rejoined your brother in the van, drove to the old schoolhouse and locked your prisoners in?'

'Yeah. Only it went off the rails, didden it? Paul really seemed sick and said he couldn't go to Stafford with the ransom note. So we got the girl to write one and I was going to deliver it by hand. And then Paul went and croaked. Well, it was all down the drain then. There wasn't no joy in sharing three hundred grand, even two ways, if someone was going to make out there was a murder rap in it.'

'How much did you say?'

'Three hundred thousand. That's what Paul said the man would be able to raise. He wanted real hard to take him to the fair, because his wife was still keen on the bloke. That meant a hundred grand each and was worth taking a risk for. But not with Paul snuffing it. So we just gave up.'

'Gave up?'

'Let her go and called it a day.'

'You just went home? But not your brother.'

'Thass right. Stevie and me, we'd arranged to go to Ibiza when the money was shared out, and Stevie said he still wanted to go. I let him have some cash, enough to get by, and his ticket and passport. It seemed best to split up then for a while.'

'Did you see your brother on to the plane?' Mott made no attempt to disguise the sarcasm in his voice.

'Course not. He's a big boy. Why?'

'Because he never flew out, and Gillian Randall never reached home. As well you'd know if you ever read a paper or listened to the news. Your Stevie cut the ransom to a tenth and he's just taken delivery all on his own.'

'Gawd, I told him to let her go, dump her down by the M25. I can't help it if something's happened to her since, can I?'

Mott suppressed his anger, broke off the interview, removed the tape, sealed and signed the envelope it went into. He telephoned through to the Boss with the address of the schoolhouse and particulars of Stevie's flight. Then he went to arrange transport for taking Goble back to Fords Green.

*   *   *

As soon as they had the address, the waiting detail made off to the old schoolhouse. They

316

found the place apparently deserted and unlocked. In the kitchen were empty milk cartons with a sour white deposit inside, wrappings from take-away food and the end of a sliced loaf. A fireproof door in the scullery was locked, with the key removed.

The Sergeant in charge banged on the door and called through but there was no sound from inside. Grimly he returned to his car and radioed in for a locksmith. Armed back-up was standing by, so as a last resort they could always shoot the lock out.

He returned to the mill entrance, to be confronted by Guy Stafford with a whippet-like man hanging on alongside. 'Is she here?' Guy demanded.

'I'm sorry, sir. I'll have to ask you to wait in your car. You too, sir, whoever you are.'

The little man exposed a gleaming denture and gave the name of a London tabloid. The Sergeant glared back and detailed a constable to stay with the reporter.

'Mr Stafford,' he said, more gently, 'it's possible your ex-wife is still in the building but we can't get through to her yet. It's a question of waiting.'

'Can't I wait inside here? When you reach her, she'll need someone she knows. For God's sake, man ...'

The Sergeant relented. 'You can wait in the kitchen, sir. But you must understand we have to go in first. Then I'll call you.'

Because they didn't know what they'd find, Guy thought chillingly. He had to be prepared for the worst. If so they might not call him at all.

The locksmith took half an hour to get there, shook his head at the door and started sorting rings of keys in his case. Even then it was over twelve minutes before the steel door swung open.

And then the terrible sounds began, a terrified gurgling deep in the throat, while the woman's mouth stayed clamped shut and her eyes were starting from her head.

Guy hadn't waited to be called but pushed through, was down the cellar steps and in the front row of police.

Gillian sat in the far corner, knees under chin, her arms wound tightly about her legs. The muscles in her neck and jaw stood out like bunched twigs and the sounds didn't stop until Guy knelt beside her and covered her from sight of the others. Even then she was frozen in shock, unable to loosen hold on herself. One of the constables carried her up the cellar steps. Guy was forced to follow helplessly after and watch as they made for one of the unmarked cars.

'You too, sir. Mr Yeadings wants you to sit in the back with her. I'll see your car gets home all right, if you'll give me the keys, sir.'

Guy recognized the Superintendent in the driving seat, grim-faced but forcing a

318

reassuring smile for the woman.

'Soon have you more comfortable, m'dear,' he said.

She moaned quietly in Guy's arms. As they drove, he could feel the warmth coming back into her body, the rigidity subsiding. Only four days since he'd spoken with her at Chardleigh Place, but she was another person, haggard and dirty, her eye sockets shadowed like bruising. He slipped his jacket over the rags of her finery. She stank of sweat and urine. But she was back, and safe.

CHAPTER TWENTY-FIVE

BEFORE EVER SHE COULD WASH or change they gave Gillian tea and made her talk. It was left to Guy to break the news that her husband was dead and how he'd been found two days before.

She was silent a while, then said wearily, 'I know.' She appeared to be torn by some inner struggle, shaking her head, her fingers kneading at the rug that lay over her knees. Eventually she made up her mind, her eyes focused distantly. She spoke as if thinking aloud.

'You could say he killed himself. He'd made up this clever, clever plan. Like a parcel, with himself in the middle. Me too, but I didn't

319

count. I was just a part of the packaging. And he drew it all together, pulled the drawstrings tight—and choked himself to death.'

Yeadings leaned forward, searching her eyes, gently persuasive. 'But your husband wasn't strangled, Mrs Randall.'

His voice changed, became less personal, factual in tone. 'He was beaten with a brick gouged loose from a wall of the cellar you were kept in. It's been found by my men. We need you to tell us how it happened.'

He thought she hadn't heard, her eyes were so vacant. Then she started to speak again, in a low, monotonous voice. 'There were two of them. They tried to fool me, changing their masks, but there were only two. One had— wild eyes. Jeering, or—threatening.' She shuddered and closed her eyes.

'He was the one that came back and raped me.'

Z tensed on her chair beside the woman. This was new. They must get that doctor to her at once.

'Rape,' Yeadings said softly, almost in an encouraging tone.

'Rape. Except that I—eventually I said I'd go with it if only he'd let me out after. Just leave the door open when he left, and I'd wait half an hour. For him to get clear.

'But he cheated on me. In the end everyone does. At the top of the steps he turned round and laughed. Said how could I tell half an hour,

320

when they'd taken my watch away.'

'So he went off, and left you still shut in.'

She looked up hopelessly. 'To starve, yes. He said he'd take the key with him—as a souvenir. Well, he had to. I could have identified him. I knew as soon as he took off his mask. I knew then I was dead.'

Yeadings touched her cold hand. 'You aren't dead, Mrs Randall. We'll get him. He'll find a special reception for him at Gatwick when he checks in for his flight. You *can* identify him. Then we'll make it stick, I promise.'

She seemed to be considering this, then drew an agonized breath. 'No, I *am* dead. I killed myself with Paul. When I killed him.'

'It *was* you, then.' Yeadings' voice was level, unsurprised.

'He betrayed me. He sold me. He didn't care what happened to me so long as he got the money.'

'To pay off the two who were holding you?'

'Them too. But most was for himself.'

'He *told* you this?'

She frowned, concentrating. 'When they first took us they tried to make it look real. He pretended to defend me. So they roughed him up. They—were too rough. He must have had a thin skull. I told them he was concussed, but they wouldn't listen. He was unconscious, then sick all over himself. He should have gone to hospital.'

321

'You say they were actually working for him?'

'But it had to look convincing. To me at first, and then when he would go to Guy for the ransom. It was crazy. They liked roughing us up, you could tell.'

The intelligence faded in her eyes. The monotonous voice came back. 'So they cracked his skull. Pressure built up in the brain. He started rambling. He took me for one of the men, called me Eddie.'

She turned cavernous eyes on Yeadings. 'Then I knew. All along he'd meant to sell me. He'd made out he loved me; there was no one could do for him what I did. And really he was using me. How could he ever do that to me? I did—'

A silence began to build. 'Yes?'

'I did what any woman would. I'd have shot him—like a mad dog—but I'd no gun. Just a brick.

'I pushed his false face into the mattress and I bashed at him real hard. Later I turned him back face up, so that it didn't show so much. And when they came to fetch him I said he'd just died.'

The flow stopped suddenly.

'What did they do then?'

'Panicked.' A little smile tugged briefly at her mouth. 'They put a black plastic sack over his head and shoulders, to take him away.'

'They decided to run for it?'

'And leave me behind.'

'But taking your husband's body along?'

'To dump it. In case anyone found it there and connected it with them. Trying to save their own skins.'

'But they left you still shut up. To die slowly—of hunger.'

'Maybe they half-meant to come back. They hadn't worked anything out. It was Paul who'd done all their thinking. They went, anyway. I tried telling them they could still get the money for me, they'd got the note I'd written. But they were too scared. Murder, you see. They knew they'd get life.'

Getting life for taking life, yes. The irony of the words always came fresh to Yeadings each time. And—greater irony, this—it was their prisoner who'd done the killing. Or hastened death on. There could be a clash of expert witnesses when it came to court. Hadn't the two captors done enough to ensure the man's death in any case?

'Z,' Yeadings said, leading her aside, 'take Mrs Randall now to the rape clinic. Make sure she knows how important it is for her defence that she should cooperate fully there. I'll have a car sent round.'

'You're not charging her?'

'Time to consider that later. Just see to her, will you?'

*   *   *

323

Yeadings went back to his borrowed office and found Mott there, having handed over his prisoner from St Albans.

'I saw young Stafford outside, with his father,' Angus said. 'I thought he'd been charged with the Turley killing.'

'No. It was just like the patrolmen found over the flasher business: wrong shoes. But all the kids have to conform with modern fashions. Half the seniors of the Crane School must have the same kind of trainers, jeans, baseball caps.

'It was Ned Banks Turley followed out to the building site, using his mother's car. His feet are one size larger than Owen's, or we might have made a bad mistake.'

'But Owen Stafford's dabs were all over the trailer.'

'From the previous night. And Banks was the flasher in Bardells Wood. He'd bounced off to tell Owen about his good results, saw the girl and had a sudden urge to show off something more.'

Mott shook his head in disbelief. 'Banks? The successful kid with the loving family background? I don't get it. The pervert profile fitted Owen Stafford like a glove. He had all the right features.'

'The right disadvantages, yes, but enough guts to surmount them. No, it's complicated, but then Ned is ... complex and arrogant, and full of resentment for the way he considers fate has unfairly stacked things up against him. Bitterly jealous of the lad supposed to be his best friend.

'Ned has managed to explain it all himself. He is, after all, quite a bright lad. Too bright, it seems, for his own good. I've got a copy here of a taped interview, with his mother and Zyczynski present. There, this is the bit you'll find most interesting.'

The young voice came over loud and piercing as if he were high on something. Probably was, Mott thought: fear and self-justification.

'D'you think I care a damn about my bloody exam results? They're just another shackle. It's set the bloody horse at one more effing fence after another. There's no let-up. It's shove, shove, shove, look what my wonderful son can do. Haven't I made a success of him?

'D'you think I wouldn't swop it all for Owen's middle grades? He doesn't need to set records. God, he's got everything laid on, born with a silver spoon. And now he's broken free. He can take all the time off in the world before he has to get back in the rat race. If he ever does. Live for himself!

'What bloody right has he to come patronizing us, slumming it, having it off with my dumb sister who doesn't even know what day it is? So damn superior with his money and his fancy quotations and his big house and his smooth way of talking! And that little fool

Susie falling for it all, letting him up her skirt while he's slagging off God knows how many other rutty little tramps out at that trailer.

'Well, one night I knew right enough where he was because he was in my home, up in my room. So it was my turn. When everyone had gone to bed I rang Delia, yeah, Delia who lives out at Paco's place. She's a waitress. We got pretty het up together one night round the back only she wouldn't have it off there. She said if I put on a party, somewhere cosy, she might feel different. I'd only to ring and we'd make beautiful music together. God, does she talk undiluted drivel! So I rang through and said just when I'd pick her up in the car-park, but if I got held up to start walking out towards the new factory site. And I told her where the trailer was.'

'And did she—walk on ahead?'

Yeadings remembered the short silence then when the boy stared wild-eyed around, fists balled, beating his knuckles rhythmically together.

'I thought she must've hurried. I thought it was her there at first. She'd got a light on behind the curtains. It was dark outside and I knocked up against something—a dustbin or an oil drum—and she opened the door to see what the row was. She called out, and I said, "It's me," and I followed her in.'

'But it was somebody else?'

'And she was only half dressed, sort of

326

teasing me with a towel round her top, and no skirt. She was quite pretty, a bit like Susie only older. And I thought again of Owen having it off with my sister, and I got angry.

'She'd got the bed all opened out ready and I thought it doesn't matter. Delia's sent this other girl. It's just the same. But she kept dragging at my hands, sticking her nails in and sort of squealing in the back of her throat.'

'And the plastic tape?'

'I was going to tie her hands but when I got on top she started screaming. I had to keep her quiet ...'

* * *

'Yes,' Yeadings said, when the tape was played through. 'That's how it often is, an attempted rape gone wrong. And it ends in strangulation. The sharp plastic tape cut into his finger ends and it's his blood we found as well as Mrs Turley's. We're lucky we have DNA analysis. He tried to implicate young Stafford, but they're of different blood groups. By the time his case comes up we'll have incontrovertible proof of his guilt from the lab.'

'And the plastic tape?'

'Was the piece Owen Stafford had used originally to get the window open. When he told us about being there the previous night he kept quiet about that. He'd kept it in his canvas satchel, thinking he might use it again. It was with the things he'd taken to the Banks' house. He'd told Ned how he got in. So Ned helped himself to it when he decided to entertain the waitress Delia out there. He'd no idea the door would be opened to him and he'd be able to walk straight in. He'd had the tape ready in his pocket, so it was close to hand when he needed to keep the girl quiet.'

Mott nodded. 'But it wasn't Delia or one of her friends. It was Turley's estranged wife,' he marvelled, 'taken there Friday night— ironically enough, for safety—so that she'd be close enough to keep her solicitor's appointment next day.

'I had a feeling from the start that Fords Green was going to produce a weirdo. At one point we had four reasonable suspects for this killing, and then it isn't any of them!'

Yeadings got up and stretched stiffly, knocking the empty bowl of his pipe in one palm. 'It's grim for the Banks family. Ned had them all fooled about himself; the cool exterior, and all that anger pent up inside. Nice people, I doubt if they'll ever understand what went wrong. But I'm damn glad it wasn't young Stafford. I'll admit I quite got to like the boy.'

Owen Stafford, huddled on the hall window-sill, saw a car draw up and watched his father let in Hamley the solicitor, come to discuss his mother's defence.

It turned his stomach. He didn't want to

think how there must be law courts and shrieking publicity, a jury empowered to examine minutely every detail of his mother's private life. However simple or corrupted, these twelve people selected by chance would consider themselves fit to condemn her.

At best she'd remain tainted. At worst— from a great height a judge would hand down a sentence. She would be locked away. All things which happened to others, not to people like his family.

He sat on, his mind a tortured blank. From beyond the study door came the constant rise and fall of voices.

I should be in there, he told himself. I stood by and watched it all happening. Paul and Mother, destroying each other. I'm the only one who really knew what a hell their life was together, the repeated cycles of lust and fury, her bouts of desperation.

Slowly he got up and crossed the hall to the study, steeled to meet the two grim-faced men who looked up as he came in. 'I want to help,' he said. 'We must do all we can to support her. She told the police he sort of killed himself, didn't she? And she was right.'

They waited for what else he had to say, Guy distressed by the need to inform him yet keep him free of involvement. He was still a minor, but over the last few days his face had shown lines that he'd grow into as an old man.

Owen faced up to Hamley. 'I want to testify.

Even if they prove Paul died by her hand, not those men's, I know I can convince the court she isn't guilty. Because it had to happen.'

He saw clearly now his own vital part of spectator, of unwilling recorder: why he needed to have missed out at university. To devote this extra year to work that was infinitely more important. And bring to it a passion equal to his mother's.

It was the only logical end, he thought. I understand now the inevitable way that history builds, only you don't see just how it is at the time. Finally she would have had to kill him, or he to kill her. And you can't sentence history.

'It had to happen,' he repeated aloud. 'We have to make them see it was the natural outcome. In a way, a natural death.'

We hope you have enjoyed this Large Print book. Other Chivers Press or Thorndike Press Large Print books are available at your library or directly from the publishers. For more information about current and forthcoming titles, please call or write, without obligation, to:

Chivers Press Limited
Windsor Bridge Road
Bath BA2 3AX
England
Tel. (01225) 335336

OR
Thorndike Press
P.O. Box 159
Thorndike, ME 04986
USA
Tel. (800) 223–6121
(207) 948–2962
(in Maine and Canada, call collect)

All our Large Print titles are designed for easy reading, and all our books are made to last.

Thomastown Branch 12